By Lynn Schnurnberger and Janice Kaplan

The Botox Diaries
Mine Are Spectacular!
The Men I Didn't Marry

The
Best Laid
Plans

The Best Laid Plans

A NOVEL

Lynn Schnurnberger

BALLANTINE BOOKS

NEW YORK

The Best Laid Plans is a work of fiction. Names, characters, places,
and incidents are the products of the author's imagination or are used
fictitiously. Any resemblance to actual events, locales,
or persons, living or dead, is entirely coincidental.

Copyright © 2011 by Lynn Schnurnberger

All rights reserved.

Published in the United States by Ballantine Books,
an imprint of The Random House Publishing Group,
a division of Random House, Inc., New York.

BALLANTINE and colophon are registered trademarks of
Random House, Inc.

ISBN 978-0-345-49119-0

Printed in the United States of America on acid-free paper

www.ballantinebooks.com

2 4 6 8 9 7 5 3 1

FIRST EDITION

Book design by Mary A. Wirth

To Martin and Alliana

The smartest decision I ever made
was to go on that blind date.
You are both awesome and amazing
and I wake up every morning
thankful for my good luck.

The
Best Laid
Plans

One

❦

The Party to End
All Parties

"Are the marzipan mummies too much?"

Anxiously I look around the Temple of Dendur—the two-thousand-year-old ancient Egyptian pantheon reconstructed brick-by-brick in the Metropolitan Museum of Art, which we're turning into a party room tonight for New York's rich and famous. The setting seems appropriate. Diane von Fürstenberg, Mayor Bloomberg, Jay-Z, and all of my darling investment-banker husband Peter's well-heeled clients should feel right at home among the statues of Cleopatra, King Tut, and the powerful sun god Ra—although I'm hoping they don't read too much meaning into the temple's wall paintings of vultures. Tea candles flicker and the faux topiary letters spelling out the reason for tonight's fund-raiser, RACE AGAINST GLOBAL WARMING, are flawlessly clipped and placed. My nightmares about them being lined up in the wrong order and reading CAR ANGST GLOB WAR—or, in the worst of my delusional anagrams, WARM LABIA GIRL—were nothing more than the product of a too fertile imagination. Or Ambien.

A platoon of black-clad junior volunteers swirls around the ballroom with impeccably calligraphed place cards. I've spent months agonizing over the seating arrangements, but Rosie O'Donnell's last-minute RSVP is throwing everyone into a tizzy. I knew that Hulk Hogan didn't like her, but now that the readers of *Parade* magazine have voted Rosie "America's Most Annoying Celebrity," I have to worry about not seating her next to any of them, and the magazine has more than thirty million readers.

And then there's the marzipan. Each of the eighty intimate tables for six has been swathed in gold cloth—600-thread-count Egyptian cotton, of course—and festooned with center-pieces of chocolate papyrus leaves and towering marzipan mummies that the guests can snack on for dessert. But although I haven't so much as tasted them, the sugary sar-cophaguses are giving me heartburn. Are they just a little too Hollywood-on-the-Nile? Why oh why didn't I pick some-thing safer, like simple glass bowls filled with peonies or the green orchids everyone's raving about?

"There's time," I say, eyeing the trees in Central Park, just outside the museum's pitched glass wall, as a quick check of my watch tells me that we still have twenty-six minutes until the first guest arrives. "We could chop down some branches and scatter the leaves in the middle of the tables."

"Cut down trees? Not exactly in keeping with the global warming theme of the evening," my friend Sienna Post laughs, a tinkling sound that bounces around the room like a ray of sunshine. It still surprises me when I turn on the six o'clock news each night and see Sienna sitting at the local anchor desk, although after all this time it shouldn't. She's smart and tena-cious, a born newscaster. Plus, Sienna's gorgeous. She has glowing porcelain skin, eyes as intensely blue as the night sky in an El Greco painting, and enough well-placed curves to stop traffic. I was named for Truman Capote, a short pudgy writer who ended up friendless. But Sienna's mother named her after an Italian city known for its soft round hills and glorious light—and she lives up to the description. "Don't worry," Sienna says, looking around the room with a satisfied grin. "The mummies are inspired. You've done a great job, everything's perfect!"

"Oh no, don't say that!" I reach under one of the cheetah-covered couches that we've brought in for the party, searching for the sofa frame—which is likely to be unvarnished and the closest thing to real bark—to knock on wood. "Never say 'perfect'!"

"I swear, Tru, you're the most superstitious person I know. If you spent as much time pitching baseballs as you do throwing salt over your shoulder you could be the next Derek Jeter."

"Well, I have to have something to believe in. Being raised by the beauty queen Naomi Finklestein didn't exactly nurture a sense of self-esteem."

"Does Miss Subways May 1959 still pinch your cheeks when she sees you?" Sienna giggles, fussing with a napkin.

"Of course. 'Tru, your color, you look like a dead salmon!' she shrieks. And remember the story about the day I was born?"

"How could I forget?" Sienna laughs.

It was Easter morning and the nurse had fashioned the fuzzy pink corners of my swaddling blanket into bunny ears. Naomi took one horrified look and handed me right back.

"That's not my baby!" she cried, refusing to set eyes on me again for another three whole days. "My husband and I are good-looking!"

Still, I guess some good came out of the whole thing because it was telling Sienna that story in the junior high school cafeteria that bonded us for life. "I'm sure you were adorable back

then and you'll be adorable now!" she'd declared, giving me a
dab of Dep hair gel to sweep my badly cut bangs off my forehead. It was Sienna who taught me the importance of using
conditioner, sweet-talked her own mother into paying for my
braces, and who, as we got older, introduced me, literally, to
the international world of beauty: Brazilian waxing, Thai massages, and Japanese hair straightening. With Sienna's help I
eventually got over Naomi constantly calling me an ugly duck-
ling. I can even laugh about it now. Most of the time. The same
way Sienna made me laugh about how my mother named me
Truman. Not because she loved *Breakfast at Tiffany's,* but because Truman Capote hosted the world's most exclusive party,
the famous Black and White Ball.

"That was some shindig. Everyone who was anyone in the
world was there," Naomi would say dreamily, as though, if she
hadn't been so inconveniently detained in Queens making
dinner for my father, she would have been sipping mimosas at
the Plaza Hotel with Frank Sinatra—or at least George Hamil-
ton.

Watching Naomi has been an up-close cautionary lesson in
the folly of chasing rainbows, of being resentful about what
you don't have and not appreciating what you do. Surely being
Miss Subways and having your photo plastered in every New
York City subway car for one whole month would lead to a life-
changing call—from a casting agent, a modeling agency, or at
the very least a rich suitor. But when that call didn't come
Naomi married my blue-collar dad—and until the day he died
four years ago she never let him forget that he was nothing
more than a consolation prize, a plastic ring plucked from a
Cracker Jack box that Naomi reluctantly accepted when the
sparkly-diamond-life she was hoping for never materialized.

Not me. If nothing else, I learned from Naomi's mistakes.
When my sexy, funny, wonderful, loyal, loving college sweet-

heart Peter Newman asked me to marry him I knew I'd struck gold. Even if Sienna did have some misgivings about his name.

"I know he's smart, ambitious, and all you can think about is jumping him. But do you realize that if you two get married you'll be 'Truman Newman'?" Sienna had teased. "Think you can live with that?"

Two months later I had the answer. Peter and I were walking through Washington Square Park back to our dorms at NYU to cram for senior finals when he bent down on one knee to propose.

"Yes!" I squealed, nearly knocking over my husband-to-be as I tumbled onto the sun-scorched grass to give him a big, long kiss.

I let out a sigh.

"Earth to Tru," Sienna says, waving a hand in front of my face. "Where did you go?"

"Sorry, I was thinking about how I became Truman Newman." I smile, fingering the tiny diamond chip ring that Peter had saved up for months to buy and that now—even though we can afford something more extravagant—I'd never replace. Then I nervously turn my attention back to the party and see a million things that still need to be fixed. I grab a napkin off one of the tables and start vigorously rubbing the crevices of an ancient sculpture.

"Hey, lady, get your hand out of Cleopatra's butt!" a security guard bellows from across the room. Sienna snatches the makeshift cleaning rag out of my hand and brandishes it like a white flag.

"Stop worrying, will you?" she says.

"I can't, there are too many things that can go wrong. Will people notice that the linen is folded to look like pyramids? Will they like the music, the lighting, the food? Oh lord, you should have heard the fights the benefit committee members had over the food! I had to deal with locavores, who won't eat anything grown out of their zip code. Then there was the raw foodist who insisted that nothing we serve be heated above one hundred sixty degrees."

Sienna walks over to the bar and asks for a gin and tonic. "Did you run into any of the calorie reduction people? My producer swears that eating as little as possible will help you get to be a hundred." Sienna tosses the lime wedge out of her drink and takes a sip. "Frankly, I'm not sure that a life without alcohol is worth living."

"Well, don't get me started on the serving pieces. One woman insisted that we couldn't use paper because it gets dumped in landfills. Another, that we'd waste a ton of energy running the dishwasher if we had glasses. We finally settled on disposable cups made from biodegradable cornstarch and sugarcane plates. I'm just praying that none of the guests is diabetic."

Sienna laughs. "You know it's just a party."

"It's not, it's a party to do something about global warming," I snap defensively. "Aren't you worried that our country pumps more carbon dioxide into the air than any other country in the world? I know I am! I've switched all of our lightbulbs to LEDs. I make Peter and the girls turn off their computers at night. And I'm lobbying for our co-op to do something about clean energy, although I'm meeting strong resistance from the president of the board—he keeps insisting that 'Putting solar panels on our beautiful Beaux Arts building would be like wrapping the *Pietà* in tinfoil.' But I'm trying. This is not 'just a party'!"

"Okay, okay, don't get so excited. I did a thirty-second satellite interview with George Clooney about glob . . ." Sienna says, and then she pauses. "This isn't about me having a job and your not, is it?"

"No, of course not. I never had a job worth liking and Molly and Paige are the best thing that ever happened to me. I love being a stay-at-home mom. I know it's a luxury and I'm grateful for Peter's generous paycheck. And if that makes me an M&M, I'm proud to wear the badge."

"A what?"

"An M&M, a woman who's into Mothering and Maintenance. Growing up, I never could have imagined that I'd know an Eames chair from an IKEA knockoff or an alpha-beta peel from the alphabet. Or that I'd care about myself enough to care. Besides," I say lightly, "not all of us can be big deal TV anchors."

"I'm a local TV anchor and there's enough competition out there already. Do you know how many twentysomethings with Katie Couric haircuts are yapping at my heels, trying to push me out of that anchor chair?" Defiantly, Sienna tosses back her thick auburn mane of shoulder-length waves.

"I think Katie Couric's hair is *dreadful*," I tell her loyally.

"Thanks. And I'm glad that you're married. Can you imagine me hosting Thanksgiving? Besides, as an old married lady you're still enthralled by my dating stories." She pulls out a gold compact to reapply her lip gloss.

"Well, who wouldn't be? The Russian billionaire. The accidental real estate mogul—although explain that to me again. How do you 'accidentally' end up owning eighty buildings and a small Greek island?"

"Poker. A five-card flush."

"Anyway, my favorite was Alonzo, the assistant nursery school teacher."

"Mine too. We made wild, passionate love and then he'd read me a bedtime story until I fell asleep. No, marriage isn't for me," Sienna says decisively, snapping shut the compact. "But it seems to agree with you. You and Peter, the marriage,

it's per—really good," she says, remembering not to use the
P word. "But I'm between boyfriends at the moment so don't
dare tell me how you two still have the hots for each other,
okay?"

Not lately, I think, scratching my head trying to remember
the last time my good-looking husband and I made love. I've
been busy with the benefit and Peter has seemed a little distracted lately. Still, on the plus side, he has been around a lot
more. Peter used to barely make it through the door in time to
kiss the girls goodnight, but these days he's home every night
before six, sitting right next to us on the couch as we watch Sienna on the news. Good for him. Maybe my alpha-male
hubby is finally learning to delegate some of those details that
used to keep him chained to his desk 24/7 to the firm's junior
brokers. As for sex, right after I get this benefit out of the way
I'll have to make it my next priority. Maybe I'll buy some luscious new nighties or pick up some of those erotic massage oils
my manicurist is so wild about (as soon as I check whether jas-
mine and rose are the aphrodisiacs—or the diuretics). I'm sure
I can turn up the heat in the bedroom. Besides, I muse, as a big
smile crosses my face just picturing them, I love Peter and our
fourteen-year-old twins, Paige and Molly. And then, before I
have a chance to think about it, the words come tumbling out
of me.

"I like my life. I'm happy."

Talk about tempting fate! Someone says, "What a beautiful
vase," and next thing you know, it breaks. A compliment on
your new outfit? Just means you're going to be spilling coffee
all over it. Say your life is going well and . . . "Pooh, pooh," I
cry, quickly adding the Yiddish *"kineahora"* to ward off the
evil eye. "Garlic, we need some garlic," I say to a passing
waiter, "and maybe some raw chicken eggs . . ."

"Oh sweetie, relax, it's okay, you've earned it. You deserve to be happy," Sienna says firmly. She pauses, and I hear an un-characteristic catch in her mellifluous TV-newscaster voice. "We all do."

"Something wrong?"

"No, nothing we need to talk about now," Sienna recovers. Then she walks over to the coatroom and retrieves a small blue velvet pouch. Opening it, I pull out a beautiful turquoise neck-lace with a pendant in the shape of a scarab.

"How did you know?"

"That the Egyptians believe the beetle is a good omen? Please, do you think I don't know the real reason why your first car was a Volkswagen?" she teases.

"It's gorgeous."

"For luck," Sienna says, stepping behind me to fasten the chain around my neck.

"For luck." I close my eyes and clasp the amulet's cool in-scribed stone in my hand. For the first time all day I feel almost calm. There's a small commotion in the hallway as a handful of guests arrive. I take a deep breath, tilt my head back, and stride confidently toward the front of the museum. Then as I take my place on the receiving line I hear a light *ping*. I look down just in time to see the stone scarab fall off the delicate gold chain and hit the ground.

THE OVERHEAD LIGHTS dim to a face-flattering level and a laser show bounces off the Egyptian statues. In the glow of the blue and yellow strobes the boy pharaoh Tut and the goddess Isis are the true king and queen of the gala. Although, in their party coverage, *The New York Times* (which is struggling for a younger demographic) is sure to anoint the honor to a cou-ple in the room who are several thousand years younger. The eighteen-piece orchestra swings into a medley of Sondheim tunes and our attractive waitstaff, dressed in crisp navy uniforms designed by season three's *Project Runway* winner, spread out across the cavernous room carrying papyrus-lined trays—the chef has prepared avocado wasabi wraps, salmon carpaccio, and chicken tarragon over artichoke bottom canapés that, I'm assured, are to die for.

For a blessed seventeen minutes everything goes smoothly. But then, as if on cue, the sky turns an ominous black and blue and a bolt of thunder crashes against the skylights. Within seconds, buckets of rain are pounding against the temple's fragile-looking glass wall and I envision leaks of biblical proportions. I try reminding myself that rain can be lucky, but that's at a wedding and besides, what the hell else are you going to say to the bride? *You've just spent a hundred thousand dollars on "the most magical day of your life" and you're going to look like you shared a hairstylist with Art Garfunkel.* And speaking of Art Garfunkel, where is Paul Simon's less famous former partner, anyway? This benefit was a hot ticket, sold out months ago, but now there's not even a B-list celebrity in sight. None of Peter's fat cat clients who promised to stop by are here, and neither, except for a couple of secretaries he gave free tickets to, is anyone from Peter's office. Or Peter, for that matter. Not to mention that, judging by the homespun look of the guests' outfits, only the environmentalists were tough enough to brave the storm.

I point to a woman in black pants and a turquoise T-shirt with the slogan THIS IS ORGANIC! emblazoned across her boobs.

"I ask you"—Sienna sighs dramatically—"when-oh-when will Carolina Herrera make sustainable cocktail dresses? Is Karl Lagerfeld never going to come out with a line of socially conscious ballroom gowns? It's commendable that these gals are into saving the planet—but couldn't they reduce the carbon footprint in a pair of Jimmy Choos?"

"I'm wearing Louboutins, isn't that even better?" my friend Olivia says gaily. She's one of the group of neighborhood M&Ms I meet every morning for lattes and I'm grateful to see she's with the whole gang.

"I'm so glad you came!" I say, exuberantly embracing the four women.

Melissa, a class mother at Paige and Molly's school, reaches out for my hand.

"We're here for you, Tru," she says meaningfully.

"That's right," says Pamela, the PTA president and unofficial group leader. "Whatever you need." Then she grabs Melissa's elbow and steers my neighborhood friends off in the opposite direction.

What was that all about? I think. I'm glad they're all here, but what is with all the emotional sighing? I take out my cellphone to call Joan Rivers—a tornado wouldn't keep *her* away from the opening of an envelope—when a woman leans in and fingers my wispy Escada gown.

"Pity," she says, tugging at the fabric with the glint in her eye of a mama bear about to eat her young. "That dress you're wearing is so very pretty. Too bad blue's such a terrible color for you."

The woman herself is wearing a too-tight gold lamé gown with a jeweled collar and a banged, bobbed black wig. Her eyes are rimmed in smoky black kohl, Cleopatra-style.

"Hi, Mom," I say nervously, as Naomi reaches around my back and digs her nails into my vertebrae.

"Truman, shoulders up!" My mother, as usual, is standing ramrod straight and she turns toward the center of the room like a heat-seeking missile. "I'm so very, very glad to be here tonight," she says, gazing past me to address a small group of startled onlookers. "Anything to support my daughter, the chairperson of this wonderful event. And of course, anything, anything at all I can do to help the global warming."

Like turn on her air conditioner? Naomi thinks climate change is what happens when you fly from New York to Miami. I'm just scanning the room for a volunteer to take Naomi off my hands when I'm distracted by a low growl. I swivel around to see Avery Peyton Chandler, the pouffed-haired trophy wife of a Texas oil tycoon. She campaigned hard to be the chair of the global warming fund-raiser and when the committee picked me instead, Avery Peyton Chandler was fit to be tied.

Avery Peyton (who's never referred to by less than at least two of her names), is decked out in a low-cut hot pink satin gown that's almost as attention grabbing as my mother's, al-though her dress comes from Donatella Versace, not the local Halloween store. Much to my horror Avery Peyton Chandler and Naomi exchange the instant recognition of kindred, if competitive, spirits and I smell axis-of-evil potential in their budding alliance. Then, damn, I hear that low, snarling hiss again. Even if she's grinning like a Cheshire, the growl isn't coming from Avery Peyton.

"For you, Tru," Avery Peyton drawls, as she reaches into an oversized bag to give me a small token of appreciation. A cat— a very, very black cat—that she's somehow smuggled into the museum.

The ancient Egyptians liked black cats, the ancient Egyptians liked black cats, the ancient Egyptians liked black cats, I chant silently—although I'm a modern American and I'm scared out of my wits. Plus my throat is starting to close up. Avery Peyton Chandler tries to foist the feline on me and I jump about fifty feet.

"What's the matter, Tru?" asks Avery Peyton in a voice so treacly Rachael Ray could whip it into a meringue.

"Uh, uh, huh!" I gasp."Can't talk. Cat's got my, *u-huh,* lung."

"Nonsense, he's nonallergenic. An Egyptian hairless, isn't that just too priceless? I simply had to bring him!"

I've read about these cats. I don't know if they live up to their no-wheeze, no-sneeze promise. Though if you ask me, their price—$4,000—is enough to take anyone's breath away.

"Oh don't be so dramatic," Naomi, the queen of drama, chirps. "How delightful of Avery Peyton Chandler to bring you such a thoughtful present."

"You're not afraid he'll jinx your little sphinx party, are you?" Avery Peyton purrs.

"Of course not," says Naomi, reaching for the cat and enfolding him in her arms with an affection she only reserves for occasional small animals—and herself. "What a cute little kitty!"

I move two steps back and take a gulp of air. Avery Peyton's out to spook me but I'm not going to let her have the satisfaction.

"He's ador-able," I say, still standing as far away as possible and stretching out my hand in the petting equivalent of an air kiss. "I only wish more people had thought to bring their pets."

Avery Peyton Chandler looks around and lets out a whoop. "Well, a few more cats and dogs would make the place more lively," she says. "Where is everybody tonight, Tru? I thought the party would be absolutely *packed* with Peter's high-profile clients. Wasn't that P. *Diddly*-ish fellow supposed to be here? Isn't that how you bamboozled the committee into putting you in charge? I guess things don't always turn out as planned, do they now, dear?"

Sienna's across the room, dealing with the petulant florist.

(The one who'd tried to sell me the green orchids. When I'd left them, Monsieur René was clutching Sienna's arm, teetering between outrage and tears. *"Zee* Mrs. Newman, she makes *zee* huge *mistook."*) Seeing my distress she ditches the overwrought posy arranger to rush to my side. Since I'm allergic to alcohol, she brings me a stiff cup of ginger ale. Then a waitress proffering a large tray comes over, beseeching us all to try the house specialty. My stomach's tied up in knots, I can't eat a thing, but at least Avery Peyton Chandler's sidetracked for the moment from torturing me.

"You really must try the chicken tarragon," the waitress says.

"Is the chicken free range? Are the artichoke bottoms grown in Manhattan?" demands Avery Peyton, our committee's obstreperous locavore, interrogating the waitress with the vigor of the carnivore I know her to be.

"Of course," the waitress answers efficiently. "No foods have crossed state lines."

Avery Peyton Chandler pops an artichoke canapé in her mouth and in a rush of enthusiasm declares them delicious. "I mean they're adequate," she says, and scarfs down two more. Naomi nabs three for herself and feeds one to the feline, who's still cradled in her arms.

Up until now Naomi's been preoccupied with stroking the cat. But suddenly, like a giant black bear stoked with energy after a long hibernation, she's roused.

Her eyes are bright, her head twitches searchingly from side to side, and everything about my mother's body is hyper-alert. I see the train wreck coming—I just don't know how to get my party off the tracks.

"It *is* a little quiet in here," Naomi says, eyeing the crowd. "Time to shake things up." Quicker than you can say, *Stop that crazy woman before she embarrasses the hell out of me,*

Naomi props the cat up on his hind legs and stretches out his front paws, positioning the unwitting feline to be her Fred Astaire. Then my sixty-eight-year-old, gold-lamé-clad, party-loving mother sashays onto the middle of the dance floor. "Okay," she booms, motioning to the ambushed bandleader. "We're in the friggin' Temple of Dendur! Everybody 'Walk Like an Egyptian'!"

I don't know what's most alarming: Naomi's ten-inch-high dance partner or the sight of her wriggling her hips and dancing with her arms and head pointed—à la Egyptian wall paintings—in different directions. I don't imagine Cleopatra would have gotten very far with Mark Antony if this had been her best shot, but Naomi's attracted at least one admirer—Dr. Barasch, *P-H-D.*, as he likes to call himself, the headmaster of my children's private school.

"Walk like, walk like an Egyptian," Naomi croons as she pulls the usually uptight Dr. Barasch, P-H-D onto center stage. She closes her eyes and grinds her pelvis at the Harvard-educated headmaster who's became putty—or should I say nutty?—in my mother's diabolical hands. Dr. Barasch isn't much of a dancer, but he is a wiggler. I watch aghast as the man to whom I've entrusted my children's education, the man I'd hoped would write their recommendations to Princeton, bumps his hips suggestively against my mother's. The cat—who's been stuck like a monkey in the middle—makes a break for it and jumps to the ground, allowing Naomi to drape her arms around Dr. Barasch's neck and shimmy closer.

"You go, girl," someone in the crowd calls out, egging Naomi on—not that she needs any encouragement.

"Ay, oh, whey, oh," Naomi warbles the song's refrain, reminding me of the poetry of the lyrics.

"Ay, oh, whey, oh," Dr. Barasch echoes Naomi's mating call.

"Ay, oh, whey, oh—ooh!" Naomi says. *"Ooh, ooh, ooh."*

"Ooh, ooh, ooh," Dr. Barasch mimics, still lost in the moment and unaware that Naomi has dropped her arms to her sides and is clutching her stomach.

"Sick," Naomi mumbles. The color drains from her face, her shoulders slump, and she cups her hand over her mouth. "Food poisoning," she croaks, lurching toward the bathroom. Followed, in quick succession, by Muffy, Dr. Barasch, the cat, and at least thirty other guests, all the victims of tainted canapés. While everyone was worrying about the provenance of the chicken, no one bothered to think about how long the mayonnaise had been left unrefrigerated. The band, having watched *Titanic* too many times, keeps playing.

Naomi finally stumbles out of the restroom with black kohl streaking down her cheeks and her Cleopatra wig askew. She's a mess but so is my party—and to her, both are all my fault. "You've sullied my good looks and our good name," she says, tugging at her bangs. "This sure as hell was no Black and White Ball."

Guests in various states of illness and disarray continue to enter and exit the bathroom. On their way in, they clutch their bellies and moan for a doctor. On the way out, they grab their coats and mutter about lawyers. Melissa, one of my four M&Ms, makes her way across the room to offer her condolences. But it isn't the sympathy call I'm expecting.

"I'm so sorry about Peter," Melissa says quietly. "I'm not exactly sure what to say."

"Oh, Peter's the least of my worries," I reassure her. "He was probably tied up with a client. It's just as well he wasn't part of this fiasco."

"That's not what Melissa means, now is it, dear?" says Avery Peyton Chandler, who's come over to gloat.

Melissa shifts uncomfortably from side to side on her spindly heels as Sienna and I exchange puzzled looks.

"His j-job," Melissa finally stutters as she backs up, heading toward the door. "I mean I'm sorry that Peter lost his job."

"Didn't you *know*, Tru?" squeals Avery Peyton Chandler. "I ran into him at Starbucks at least three weeks ago in the middle of the afternoon playing some game on his computer and drinking a mochachino. A tall, not a grande—that was the tip-off. I guessed that you two had already started economizing."

Peter lost his job? His job lost Peter? Lost, Peter, his job? I rearrange the words in my head, trying to make sense of them. I freeze in place, squinting into the blinding strobe lights, panicked and unable to move. Then my hand flails against a table and my body crashes in a dead faint to the floor, taking down one of the marzipan mummies. The melting gooey paste ends up stuck all over my dress and hair, and the bitter almond smell is overwhelming.

Somewhere in the distance I see Rosie O'Donnell and the florist, Monsieur René, standing over me. "We're here for you," says Rosie, bending down to swipe a dollop of marzipan off my forehead. She sucks the congealed confection off her fingertip and shrugs. "Not bad, not bad at all. But Tru, honey, you shoulda gone with the orchids."

Two

The House of
the Rising Sum

Sienna takes me home in a cab but I insist on going up to the apartment alone. Terrance, our doorman, walks a couple of steps ahead of me through the lobby to push open the heavy ornamental elevator gate. He reaches a white-gloved hand inside the cab to punch the "penthouse" button. "Tough night, Mrs. N?"

"You could say that, I guess." Absentmindedly, I finger one of the elevator's two alabaster sconces, imported from Spain and rumored to cost over five figures apiece.

"Everyone has their rough patches. This, too, will pass," says Terrance—who's been studying meditation with Madonna's kabbalah teacher's ex-assistant.

"Quickly, will it pass quickly? Like a breeze on the Sahara? Or Amy Winehouse's attempts at rehab?" I ask, willing to grab onto any shred of hope.

"Not quickly," says Terrance, as the elevator door slams shut. "But by the end of the journey you will be in a different place from the one you started out in."

I fumble for my keys and open the thick mahogany door to our spacious apartment. How many times have I carelessly tossed the mail onto the Georgian table in the front hall and not even noticed the sumptuous bouquet of calla lilies that are delivered fresh like clockwork each week? I tiptoe down the wide front hall lined with family photos: the girls on their first day of preschool clutching my hands and their matching Pocahontas lunchboxes, the four of us splashing around in the waves at Easthampton, and—the one that gives me pause—a photo from the year Paige and Molly wore big feathery white wings and halos to go trick-or-treating and Peter dressed as the devil.

I call out for my husband but there's no answer. I've been trying to reach him on his cellphone for over an hour, but he hasn't picked up. Not that I'd know what to say. "Why the hell didn't you tell me?" "Are we going to be okay?" "I'm mad," "Angry," "Worried" are all possibilities, as are "It's just a job. You'll get another one" and "What possessed you to buy me those wildly expensive antique gold filigree earrings just last week?"

At the end of the hall I stop outside the girls' bedroom and glance at my watch. I don't want to wake them, but I have to see for myself that they're all right. Gingerly I open the bedroom door and circle past the mound of half-written-in notebooks, art supplies, DVD holders, backpacks, sneakers, sweatshirts, outfits worn (and outfits discarded because they weren't good enough to wear that never made it back into the closet), and a copy of *Catcher in the Rye*—untouched since its purchase—that Paige, my messy, more tempestuous daughter, has amassed on her side of the room. I bend down to kick off my sling-backs. My bare feet sink into the plush hot pink flokati rug but I lose my footing in the darkened bedroom and noisily bang my knee against a swivel chair that rolls into the girls' double-sized desk.

"You okay, Mom?" Molly asks, turning toward me dreamily and propping herself up on an elbow.

"Yes, honey." I crouch down to kiss her forehead. "Sorry to wake you, go back to sleep."

"No problem," she says, nestling her lithe body back under the covers.

Paige, in the bed just across from her, typically doesn't stir—like her father, she could sleep through an earthquake. It still amazes me how two girls nurtured for nine months in the same uterus could be so different. Paige is blond, fun-loving, and game for anything, while Molly, two minutes older, is a studious curly-haired brunette. I exhale and kiss them each one more time on the top of their heads before picking up my shoes and closing the door behind me. Stopping in the kitchen for a glass of water, I let the cool clear liquid wash over my wrists and splash some onto my face. Then, unable to avoid the inevitable for any longer, I steel myself to walk into Peter's study.

Maybe Peter forgot about the party. Maybe he's engrossed in a Mets game or tied up on an overseas call. Or maybe he's sitting in his leather armchair with a stack of papers on his lap, exhausted and happy from having figured out a plan to save our financial future. But all of the possible explanations as to why he was a no-show at the party are dashed as I enter the teak-paneled room and snap on the light. Cellphones, text messages, a solid trusting marriage—none of the things I depend on to keep track of my husband are any help now. Peter normally keeps me abreast of his every move. I still tease him about the detailed message he left on my voicemail before our second date: "I'm having a ham and cheese sandwich for lunch, returning the Samuelson textbook to the library, and going to buy a typewriter ribbon. Pick you up at three." For the first time since college, I realize with a start, Peter—

my loving, considerate, never-makes-me-worry-about-him husband—is nowhere to be found.

Despite my commitment to saving energy, Peter just can't get used to turning off the computer screen and its flickering light beckons me toward his wide cherrywood desk. Stacks of colored folders are fanned out like cards in a game of solitaire, waiting to be shuffled and reorganized into a winning hand. I've always left everything to do with money up to Peter—how much we have, what we can afford to spend. But now as I flip through the monthly bills I see that they're staggering. Cable, Con Edison, cars, cellphones, Chapman (the girls' private school), clothes, cello lessons, a particularly thick folder for credit cards—and that's just the C's.

I sink into the black desk chair, my head in my hands. My expenses come out of our general house account that Peter just refills, whenever I ask him to, the way you would a tank of gas. I have no idea what he knows, or doesn't, about the actual cost of the things I buy. And when he finds out, what he's going to want me to cut down. "Does Peter have any idea what I spend on Botox? Or that milk is four dollars a gallon?" I say despondently.

"I've read that it's the price of toilet paper that's truly shocking," says Peter softly as he walks toward me. The top button of his tuxedo shirt is undone and his silk black bow tie hangs like a Rat Packer's around his neck. "Tru, honey, I'm sorry," he says, bending down beside me and pushing aside the folders. His jacket, which was slung over his shoulder, falls in a puddle to the floor and he interlaces his hand with mine, squeezing my fingers tightly, the same way the girls used to when they were getting a booster shot. "I didn't want you to worry, I was sure I'd find something else. The market, the subprime loans, business has been terrible, everyone's downsizing. They let five hundred people go, I never expected, it's been three months . . . Can you ever forgive me?" Peter asks, as his run-on sentences wind down and his voice starts to crack.

I could tell him that I'm furious that he kept me in the dark. I could cry or scream or make him sleep in the guest room. But all I want to do is hold him.

"Come here," I say, taking Peter's hand and leading him toward the sofa. I sit down and as he stands in front of me, I unbuckle his belt and tug at his zipper. Admiringly, I run my hand across Peter's smooth, muscular midsection and cast my gaze below. "Funny," I say, as I reach for my husband and entreat him to come inside me. "No downsizing that I can see going on here, mister."

❧❧❧

In the morning, I get the girls off to school by pretending it's just another day, and after they've left, I try to assess the damage.

"It can't be that bad, right?" I ask hopefully as Peter plugs in the coffeemaker. "I mean we can still afford the Splenda?" I set out the creamer and sugar bowl—which more accurately should be renamed the 1% milk and artificial sweetener holders.

"It's not good," says Peter, as he pushes two pieces of whole wheat bread into the toaster. He turns to face me and I realize from the helpless look in his eyes just how not good things are. "Our savings, my pension—everything tanked along with the company stock. I borrowed money against the apartment hoping to turn things around, but that didn't happen. We're going to be in default to the mortgage company and the co-op board in sixty days. Sixty days! Our home, the earrings I bought you because I didn't want you to think anything was wrong, all of it, our whole damned lifestyle, everything is built on a house of cards."

"A house of cards?" I gasp, thinking that wood—or even straw—sounds sturdier.

"Visa and American Express. And they're totally maxed out."

"Peter, how—how could you ?" I stutter. "How could you gamble with our futures like that and not even say a word?"

Peter bangs his hand in frustration against the polished black granite counter we had installed just last year. "That's what investment bankers do: We gamble. You didn't seem to mind when we were winning."

My eyes well up with tears and I grab my purse from the counter.

"Tru, I'm sorry, I was just trying to protect you," Peter says as I brush past him to head for the door.

"I know. I know you didn't mean to hurt us. I just have to get out of here and get some air to clear my head."

❧᯽❧

I WALK UP and down Fifth Avenue for what seems like hours, looking into store windows that for once don't seem the least bit tempting, past the flower-filled sunken plaza at Rockefeller Plaza. The towering Art Deco buildings cast a gilded shadow and I stop to look down at the skating rink, remembering all the good times we've had there and that we'll probably never be able to afford again. At one end of the plaza is a gleaming gold sculpture of Prometheus, who stole fire from Zeus to give it to mortals. At the other, a hulking statue of Atlas, who's carrying the weight of the world on his shoulders.

"I know how you feel, big boy," I say, reaching out to pat one of the overworked Greek god's well-toned bronze calves.

At the corner of Sixth Avenue and Fiftieth Street, across the street from Radio City Music Hall, a well-dressed man is standing on top of a makeshift stage with a bullhorn. Beside him, a comely woman presides over a card table stacked high with books and motivational tapes featuring a grinning picture of the speaker.

"Eliminate the word 'failure' from your vocabulary. Think positive thoughts, have positive energy in every day, every way," the man says to a growing crowd that seems to be hanging on his every word. "Repeat after me, 'I am money.' "

"I am money!" the crowd says as the man with the bullhorn entreats them to say it again with more conviction.

"I am money," I try chanting with them. As if a simple verb switch—from "I *spend* money" to "I *am* money" is all I need to change my ways.

"Again!"

"I AM MONEY," we roar back in unison, as the man tells us, "Close your eyes and picture prosperity."

Images of hundred-dollar bills float through my mind, huge stacks of them, piled high to the ceiling. I visualize myself picking one up, and like Narcissus looking into the water, I see my face, instead of Ben Franklin's. If I remember right, the Founding Father believed that success was the result of hard work. But that was so three hundred years ago! I was raised on Tinker Bell, *Field of Dreams,* and Joel Osteen—wish it, build it, or tithe to a televangelist to pray for it, and your every request will be granted.

"I-am-money, I-am-money." I'm practically humming now. The man with the bullhorn tells us, "My books and tapes will teach each and every one of you how to be a magnet, attracting people, places, and opportunities that will increase your fortunes." Judging by the people jockeying to buy his products, at the very least the program is working for him.

I'm just starting to slap down a twenty-dollar bill of my own for his words of wisdom, when the speaker issues one more instruction.

"Picture your life five years from today. . . ." he says as a gush of steam rises out of the sewer grate next to the sidewalk where I'm standing.

I imagine myself wearing a babushka and a long soiled skirt. I'm clutching a paper cup containing a few coins. "Oh no, oh no, oh no!" I wail. "In five years I'll be a bag lady!"

⋯⋯

I'M STILL SHAKEN when I arrive back to the apartment, but I pull myself together for the sake of the girls. Paige and Molly are sitting at the dining room table with yogurts, granola bars, and their textbooks spread out before them. Molly's on Facebook, one of the *Twilight* movies is streaming through Paige's computer, and it's anyone's guess what's swelling through the iPods each of them is connected to.

"How do you girls ever manage to get any work done?" I say, gently tugging on their earphones so they can say a proper hello.

"Mom, you ask us that same question every day," Paige says, with just the right tone of teenage condescension that lets me know I am *so* out of it. Molly smiles and reaches across the table to offer me a snack. "Strawberry or chocolate chewy?"

"Chocolate," I say without, for once, glancing at the nutritional label. They may sell these energy bars at the health food store, but some of them have more artery-clogging fats than a Milky Way. When the girls were little I wouldn't let them eat sugar or processed foods and until they went to school, the only McDonald they'd ever heard of was the farmer. But now that the twins are teenagers I'm just glad they're not doing crack.

Rosie, the perky housekeeper we hired two months ago after the girls' nanny finally retired, comes in. She's carrying a bamboo tray loaded down with fresh-baked cookies and cans of cola. "For the workmen," she explains, bustling toward the back of the apartment.

"What workmen?" I ask, flustered, as I hurry after Rosie wondering what in the world I could ever have imagined was bad about anything that smelled as delicious as those oatmeal raisin cookies she'd just baked. And who the heck she'd made them for.

The girls traipse single file behind us, trusting baby mallards. We march through my bedroom past the four-poster bed that Peter and I bought at a garage sale when we were first married. An old straw hat with blue ribbons, a souvenir of my chorus role in our college production of *The Music Man*, sits gaily atop the broken spindle that we never bothered to replace, just as it did in the old days. As we cross into the bathroom I see two workmen in overalls leisurely kicking around stray tiles. Wrenches, rags, crowbars, copper piping, army-sized tubs of caulk and putty are strewn about everywhere. My claw-foot tub has been uprooted from its spot in the middle of the room and rudely pushed up against the mirrored vanity. Our beautiful nickel-plated faucets sit like orphans ten feet away from the tub and a trio of cut pipes spring through the debris like weeds. One of the workmen reaches for a cookie. "Thanks," he says.

"Oh shit, I mean *damn*, I forgot you were coming. That's right, you're installing the new tub today," I say, realizing that the eighteen-hundred-pound Carrara marble model we'd ordered is nowhere in sight.

"We were," says the other workman, reaching for a cola. "Our boss just called. Says we can't install the new tub until you pay the eleven thousand dollars you owe us. The check Mr. Newman gave him bounced."

The girls look at me quizzically. Rosie sighs deeply and

shakes her head. "Not again," she says, her brow knit in frustration. "This is why I had to leave my last job."

"No, Rosie, no problem," I say, trying to reassure us both that we won't have to let her go. I take the plate from her hand and urge everyone to have another cookie, playing hostess to my worried housekeeper, confused daughters, and bathtub installers in the unlikeliest room in the house for entertaining.

"I'm sure it was just a mistake?" Molly says, sounding confident until the last syllable, when she can't help turning her statement into a high-pitched question. "Right, Mom?"

"Absolutely. Daddy is no longer affiliated with the bank and we're just having a little cash flow problem," I say carefully.

"Daddy lost his job?" Paige shrieks.

"He's going to be working for a new company any day now. We'll talk about it later," I say as calmly as I can. And then turning toward the workers I add, "This is all just a silly misunderstanding. Why don't I just write you a postdated check and you can finish up here."

"No can do. Cash or nothing, otherwise we have to leave."

I search for a compromise. "How about this: Why don't you just put the old one back? We don't even want a new bathtub, I can't imagine why I ever thought we did. I mean, all we need is something that holds water." I wedge myself between the vanity and the claw-foot tub. I grip my fingers around the lip of the tub and try to push. Hard. Nothing happens. Hold your breath, count to ten and push, I can still hear my Lamaze teacher's voice in my head. But nothing, unless you count my quickening pulse, bulging eyes, and the vein that's starting to pop out of my neck. The girls and Rosie line up behind me, but still the stubborn tub—more difficult to move across the room than a pair of five-pound twins through a three-millimeter birth canal—doesn't give, not an inch.

And neither do the workmen.

"Sorry, lady, it's out of our hands." The cola drinker shrugs as they both collect their tools and the rest of the cookies and leave. Rosie and the girls and I plop onto the cold torn-up floor and lean against the back of the tub. The girls start to pepper me with questions and I promise I'll explain everything later, after Rosie's gone and Peter and I can talk to them together. Peter comes into the bathroom, drops his briefcase, and slumps down beside us. He takes off his shoes, loosens his tie, and starts pitching broken tiles.

"'We don't have any openings.' 'You're overqualified, Mr. Newman.' 'Wow, you were earning how much?'" Peter says, recounting what amounted to another fruitless day of job hunting, as with each shot he tries to land a tile in the toilet and misses. "Guess it's not my day," he says, shrugging and giving up.

"That's okay, Daddy," says Paige, who despite her occasional outbursts these days is still a sweet girl at heart. She picks up a handful of tile and leans over to give Peter a kiss. "How about ten out of twenty?"

My eyes well up with tears at the sight of Peter and the girls playing toilet tiddlywinks, though I hope they keep missing their mark—the last thing we can afford is to call a plumber.

"Who needs money?" I say jauntily. "There are two other bathrooms in the house that work just fine. And you know what?" I say, turning around and running my hand along the inside of the cracked porcelain tub. "I've always thought this baby would make a great planter."

Of course, eventually we have to leave the cosseted, fairy-tale world of the master bathroom, and when we do, my Pollyannaish attitude fades more quickly than my blond highlights. I retreat to the library, where I have a small desk and a computer to keep track of my charity work and appointments.

I pull out a legal-sized yellow pad and with a black Sharpie left over from labeling the girls' summer camp clothes, I start making a list of "How to Save Money." *Turn down the thermostat (better for the environment!!!!!)* I write in big, loopy letters. I pause, stumped. I go back and write a big number 1 next to my one and only brainstorm. As I sit puzzling over number 2, Paige and Molly come in, full of anxious questions about the future.

"How bad is it, Mom?" Molly, my practical daughter, wants to know. "Will we be able to stay in school?" Paige is worried that we'll have to cancel HBO and her extra Verizon minutes. Both of them ask if we're going to have to move—according to Peter, a very real possibility.

"Daddy and I are very resourceful," I say, trying to allay their insecurities without actually lying. "We'll figure something out. We love you, we love each other, we're a great family. Everything that we need we have right here." I give them each a kiss. Pleading that they need to finish their homework, the girls head back to their room.

"I told you," says Paige poutily, when she thinks she's out of earshot. "We're not going to be able to go on the class trip to The Hague."

"Oh my God, you are such a retard," Molly says, as the bedroom door slams behind them. "Didn't you hear what Mom was really saying? We might not even have a place to live."

Three
❦

Sha Na Na Na,
Sha Na Na Na Na

PETER'S IN THE DINING room early the next morning stuffing a last piece of bacon into his mouth. My husband seems to think the Lipitor he takes is a condom providing impunity for him to eat whatever the heck he wants. But it's not worth making a federal case, today of all days, about his cholesterol.

"What's all this?" I ask, pointing to the table, which is set with our best serving pieces filled with an array of our favorite foods.

Peter swipes a napkin across his fingers and shows me a handwritten note. "It's Rosie's last meal. She took a job with our neighbors, the Mortons. She says she's sorry she has to leave but she has to think about making a living."

"And so do we," says Molly, coming up behind her father just as he's about to serve himself some eggs. She snatches a silver ladle out of his hand and replaces it with a plastic spoon. "I'm selling all the good stuff on eBay."

I follow Molly into the living room where she's amassed a pile of chairs, tables, lamps, picture frames, and a sweater I bought at a celebrity auction "knit by Julia Roberts"—although I've always suspected it's the work of Brooke Shields. I rummage through the mound and clutch a small pink and white cloisonné box to my chest. "You can't have it, it was from our anniversary trip to Hong Kong!"

Molly extricates the box from my grip and tosses it back on the pile. "Mom, get a life. We're fighting to keep this family afloat."

On the other side of the room, Paige is sitting on a folding chair with her computer balanced on her knees. I look over her shoulder and let out a yelp.

"Paige Newman, how can you be shopping at a time like this?" I ask, startled to see her clicking on a picture of a cashmere cardigan and adding it to her virtual shopping cart, which is already overflowing. "Don't you understand that we need to save money, not spend it?"

"Chillax, Mom, I *am* saving money. Everything is on sale."

Molly moans. "Type in 'thrifty dinners.' With Rosie gone we'll have to do our own cooking."

"Ugh! Couldn't we just get the take-out menu from Sarabeth's?" But a few minutes later Paige reads off a recipe. "Barbecue Rice Night, yum! A dollar's worth of chicken, two slices of processed American cheese, white rice, and twenty-four cents' worth of barbecue sauce . . ."

"How do you *measure* twenty-four cents' worth of barbecue sauce?" Peter asks plaintively. He comes up behind me and rests his head on my shoulder.

"I don't know, honey, maybe with a thimble?" I turn around and give him a kiss. Then I put on my jacket and tell the girls not to be late to school. "Don't sell the crystal," I say, with as much confidence as I can muster. "Fingers crossed, I might have a way out of this mess."

THIRTY MINUTES LATER, wearing a white T-shirt and my best
Chanel suit, I'm sitting across a table from Suze Orman.
We've served on a PBS fund-raising committee together and
when I called, Suze suggested meeting in her favorite diner, a
dive with worn checkered linoleum floors and beat-up black
leather booths held together with silver duct tape. Not the sort
of place most wildly successful authors and TV show hosts frequent, but then again, maybe that's why Suze has the money to
pay for a perpetual spray tan, and I don't, at least not anymore.
A waitress named Vy takes our order and returns with two
cups of watery Sanka and a pair of bran muffins. Suze just has
to be able to help us, she's a financial genius, isn't she? When I
finish telling her our troubles, she shakes her head and runs
her hand through her trademark wedged bob. Just like she
does on TV.

"Tru, sweetheart, girlfriend, how can you expect to be flush
with a broken bathroom? Fix it!" She leans in to tap a perfectly
French-manicured nail on my handbag, which is propped in
front of the jukebox. "And what's with the *red* bag? Do you see
what's going on here? Do you know what I'm saying?"

"It was on sale," I lie, quickly snatching the strap of the
purse and taking it off the table.

"It was not! And it's not just about the price, it's about the
color. *Red,* girlfriend, *red!* This bag is sending the wrong message. You want your finances to be in the *black!*"

I take a gulp of coffee and pick at the top of the muffin. I love
the bag but if that's all it takes, I guess it's worth the sacrifice. I
dump my wallet, makeup, keys, and credit cards onto the table
and I call over our waitress.

"Here, would you like this?" I say, resigned to relinquishing
the fire-truck-red Birkin I waited six months to get. Vy looks
suspicious, but before she has a moment to consider, Suze
seizes the pocketbook and tosses it into a nearby wastebasket.

"What's up with that, sister? You want our friend Vy here to go bankrupt, too?"

"A twenty-percent tip would be fine," Vy says, warily.

"You see, our girlfriend here's got her head on straight," says Suze, motioning for Vy to sit down and join us.

"You want to hold cash and bonds but stay away from domestic and foreign stocks and for heaven's sake, *burn those credit cards!*" Suze rat-tat-tats. Lacking access to a book of matches, she reaches for my Visa and American Express cards and determinedly starts to saw through them with a butter knife.

"But . . ." I say.

"No buts," says Suze. "You have to bite the bullet. No credit, credit is bad. I own seven homes and I don't have a mortgage on any of them."

"I just put down all cash for a one-bedroom condo," Vy says.

"That's what you should have done, Tru," Suze says, as I slink down a little farther on my side of the booth. "So your husband's out of work and you're racking up debt. Boo-hoo! Snap out of it, sweetheart! My father sold chickens. When his business failed he took in boarders. When one of the boarders fell down a flight of stairs and sued us my mother became an Avon lady."

"I love their Skin So Soft!" Vy says.

"Did you know that it's not only a moisturizer, but it works as a bug repellant? Mom kept a roof over our head selling those products door-to-door, one sale at a time. Though she never told anyone she was working—she was embarrassed about being the family breadwinner."

"You do what you gotta do," says Vy, the philosopher of the Four Brothers Coffee Shop.

"After college I became a waitress, just like you!" Suze says clapping her hand over Vy's. "One of my clients gave me fifty thousand dollars to start my own business and I invested the money with a stockbroker, but the son of a bitch stole every last dime. Did I crawl under the covers and cry? Not a chance!" Suze says, turning toward me and, although I didn't think it was possible, opening her wide eyes even wider, so that she looks like one of those unnaturally bug-eyed children in a Keane painting who are supposed to evoke pathos but frankly give me the willies. "I became a stockbroker myself and made a ton of money. Then I made a ton more money teaching other women how to make money!"

Suze's story reminds me of Scarlett O'Hara's I'll-never-be-hungry-again speech. I wouldn't be surprised to learn that at one time in her life, Suze had made a ball gown out of curtains, too. I lean in, waiting eagerly for Suze's words of wisdom.

"Do you understand what I'm saying, do you know what you have to do?" she asks urgently.

"Kill chickens, learn to sling hash, stay away from bad stockbrokers? Please, Suze, tell me!"

"Get a job!"

"Get a job?" I sputter. "That's it? Don't you have something like . . . like an insider trading tip?"

"If that's what you wanted you should have called Martha Stewart. Of course then you'd wind up in jail. Get a job!"

"But I haven't worked in twenty years. Who would hire me? What would I do?"

"Start by checking with your last employer, maybe they'll have something or can give you some leads." Suze pulls a copy of her latest book out of her handbag—her *green*, color-of-money handbag—writes an inscription and hands it to Vy. Then she stands to leave and gives me a go-get-'em thumbs-up. "Remember, sister, today is the beginning of the rest of your life!"

"The rest of my life," I repeat numbly. But first, I have a more pressing problem. Now that I'm bagless, I have to stuff my lipstick, keys, and limited cash into the pockets of my beautiful Chanel suit jacket. And then there's the matter of the check. It takes me a moment before I realize—thank goodness!—that Suze already paid it on her way out.

⚭⚭⚭

I ZIGZAG ACROSS Fifty-fourth Street and walk up Madison Avenue at a glacial pace, even an eighty-year-old woman with a walker races past me. If I knew how to play Tetris on my cellphone I could probably delay the inevitable a little longer, but finally, I find myself standing in front of the Addison Gallery, the site of my one—gulp—and only job.

"Suze said get a job," I plead with my feet, imploring them to move just another five steps to the left so I can open the gallery door. But no luck, my Tod-shod tootsies refuse to budge. "Fine, we'll just wait till you're ready," I say in the same reassuring tone I used with the girls when they needed a few minutes before jumping into the pool. I press my nose to the gallery's glass-fronted window and look inside.

When I first started working at the gallery after college I was passionate about being in the art world. It seemed exciting and glamorous and I looked forward to the same sorts of heady debates I'd had as an art history major—one time we stayed up half the night just arguing about whether it had been a disservice to clean the windows at the cathedral in Chartres. (Without eight hundred years of grime, now they're as brightly colored as a handful of Skittles.) But at the Addison all we ever talked about were auction prices and stealing other gallery's artists. My title was "gallery assistant." Ha! "Underpaid Kreskin" was more like it. I was expected to magically Windex fingerprints off the glass before they even appeared, beat the

meter maid to a client's car even though the clients never remembered exactly where or at what time they'd parked, and
deal with artists' egos, which are as delicate—and inflated—as
soufflés. When I wanted to quit after only eighteen months,
Peter was all for it. By then he'd landed a promising position in
one of the city's largest investment banks and we agreed that
we'd both be happier if I took charge of making a comfortable
home.

"It was a lousy fit. They'd never give me a job again anyway.
The director of the gallery always graded my Windexing abil-
ities as 'below par.' You were right, feet," I concede, deciding
that what I really need is to go home and start looking through
the want ads. I'm just turning around to find a subway when I
see Georgina Wright, (the very same director of the gallery
who gave me that C-minus in window cleaning all those many
years ago), bounding out the door in my direction.

"I thought that was you!" Georgina says, throwing her arms
around me and practically pulling my shoulder out of the
socket to haul me inside. Georgina's hair is gathered in a chic
knot at the nape of her neck and her tiny body is overwhelmed
by a crinkly black dress that looks two sizes too big, but actually fits as its Japanese designer meant it to be worn. When I
was her employee, the best I ever got from Georgina was a
vague nod in my direction. But today she's practically giddy.

"It's really you!" she gushes.

"And it's really you!" I echo, having learned from the Dis-
covery Channel that if you don't want to be eaten by a wild animal, you should model its behavior.

After the usual opening pleasantries about how I haven't
aged a day, she loves my Chanel, and what a clever girl I am to
actually *use* the suit pockets ("So few people do," Georgina
coos, although we both know that Coco must be rolling over in
her grave), the reason for Georgina's thaw becomes transpar-

ent. "Isn't it wonderful that you've come back to us! I hear that you're married to a very rich investment banker."

"I was, I am, well yes." Now that Georgina's got me here, I guess I might as well try to ask about that job. Still the one thing I know about human nature is that people only want to give you something if they think you don't need it. Why else did Converse airlift crystal-studded sneakers to both Brangelina twins? With the fourteen million dollars *People* paid for their baby pictures those kids could have bought shoes for the entire planet Earth—with some money left over for the Republic of Pluto. So no, I can't possibly say something simple, like *I need work.* "I've been *missing* you," I say sweetly. "The art world, the gallery, all of it. Now that my girls are getting a little older, I was thinking I might like to dip my toe back in the water, maybe . . ."

"Start buying art! We have just what you need!" says Georgina, taking my elbow and leading me through the exhibition: slick Technicolor pictures of pole dancers. Different from the pole dancers you see in *Playboy,* of course, because the artist, according to the foot-high letters after his name, is a Rhodes Scholar. Georgina stops in front of the brashest, most lurid picture in the group.

"This one's a little large," I say, diverting my eyes from the young lady's fifteen-foot-high triple-D breasts and her X-rated pose. "I still have teenagers in the house. And what I really was thinking . . ."

". . . was that you wanted something a little more subtle, right? You always were a sly girl!" Georgina says, buttering me up like a Thanksgiving turkey. "You know we keep the best work in the back room for our very favorite people. Come with me right now!"

Just as in the old days, when Georgina speaks, I listen. I have no choice but to trail behind her, past those arty-farty photos of pole dancers. And past a half dozen weary-bleary-eyed gallery assistants—all doing the job I used to do, and not one of them over the age of twenty-five.

This was stupid. What on earth gave me the harebrained idea that Georgina—or anyone else in the art world—would be interested in hiring me? *Get a job!* But doing what? I make terrible coffee and I can't even wear a miniskirt anymore. (According to Naomi, I never could.) I spent sixty thousand dollars on a college education to major in medieval art with a minor in women's studies. About the only thing I'm qualified for is writing a Wikipedia entry. It's a miracle that the Addison Gallery hired me in the first place.

All I want in the whole wide world right now is to get out of here—but no such luck. Georgina's got me secluded in the insiders-only back office.

"Sit down and take off your shoes," she commands. She snaps her fingers and yet another in the seemingly endless supply of gallery assistant appears with a basin of water. "Now sit back, relax, and soak those pretty feet."

"That's okay, I don't really want to . . ."

"Soak them!" Georgina orders. The gallery assistant shrugs helplessly and clamps her hands on my heels. The water is pleasantly warm and soothing, but within moments I feel a tickling sensation.

"What the heck!" I exclaim, hastily retreating from the basin—and at least a hundred tiny fish that are nipping at my feet. "This isn't what I meant by dipping my toes back into the water."

"Don't tell me this is your first fish pedicure?" Georgina chuckles, motioning for the gallery assistant to force my feet back into the tub. "Asian carp, natural exfoliators. They just love dead skin! A little something extra for Addison Gallery clients that I think you won't find anywhere else."

A little something extra for Addison Gallery clients that keeps them forcibly glued to their chair while Georgina makes her pitch, is more like it. Having a hundred marine animals snack on your toes takes some getting used to. Still, it's nothing compared to a ferocious assault by one hungry-to-make-a-sale piranha. Georgina walks over to a custom-designed chrome file cabinet and rifles through a stack of candy-colored photos.

"I simply won't take no for an answer," she says, wagging her finger, a bony metronome of determination. "If we have to stay here all night, I'm going to get you to take one of these fabulous pictures. Steve Martin collects them. You know what that means, don't you?"

"That he's into soft porn?" I dip my fingers in the water to try to swat the fish away. But to the cuticle-eating carp my hand is just another meal.

"Silly girl, it means that you simply have to have one!"

"Georgina," I say, pulling my wrinkly toes out of the tub. "Can I please get something to wipe my feet?"

Georgina ignores me. She's focused her laserlike concentration on flipping through the photos, and like Jack the Ripper, she won't be sated until she's nabbed her next victim. Finally, she settles on a close-up of a dancer's leg wrapped around a pole with just a hint of red satin G-string. "This is it! Forty-eight hundred dollars, that's as low as I'll go. All right, for old time's sake, forty-five. You always did drive a hard bargain." Georgina turns to another one of the overtaxed, overtired gallery assistants. "Wrap it up!" she says with a grin. "And bring Tru a towel."

Four

Another One Bites the Dust

"You bought a picture?" Sienna hoots, when I tell her about my unimpressive attempt at job hunting.

"Georgina thinks I did. But I ditched the photo by the gallery doorway and then I made a quick getaway."

"And the fish pedicure?"

"Not bad. But until they train the carp to apply polish, I'm sticking with the nail salon."

I've come over to Sienna's studio straight from the gallery. I couldn't face Peter and the girls without any good news. Sienna points to a canvas-back chair and tells me to take a seat. "I just have a quick rehearsal, then we'll get a bite to eat," she says.

In person, the high-ceilinged set—littered with booms, tangled wires, and all shapes and sizes of monitors—always looks a little cheesy. The lighting is way too bright, the backdrop of towering skyscrapers is the same view of midtown Manhattan you can buy on any fifty-five-cent souvenir postcard, and the curved "wood" desk is actually particle board covered with a veneer of plastic laminate. But somehow on camera it all comes together. The assistant director cues up the show's theme song and the TelePrompTer operator rolls the script for Sienna and her cohost to run through their lines. Sienna's new cohost is the very blond, early-thirtysomething Tom Sandler, a golden boy replacement for the veteran newscaster who, until he was unceremoniously fired last week, had been Sienna's partner for fifteen years.

Tom straightens his tie and smoothes a palm along the mountain of moussed hair that rises onto his forehead in a gentle slope. "Good evening, I'm Tom Sandler," Tom Sandler reads off the screen, as if he might not get it right without a prompt.

"And I'm Sienna Post," she purrs. Simultaneously, Sienna reads her lines, sorts through some mail and fiddles with a nail file, until the show's executive producer, Jerry Gerard, comes storming over to the anchor desk. He's wearing a brown shirt and brown pants tucked into shiny black boots and looks just like the fascist Sienna's described him to be. Jerry Gerard yanks the nail file from Sienna's grip, and for good measure, he throws it on the floor and stomps on it, hard, with the heel of his boot.

"This is a fucking newsroom, people, get a grip! We've got fucking serious work to do. The U.S. Open scores will be coming in any minute . . . and fighting just broke out in Tajikistan . . . or Turkmenistan . . . or some fucking 'T' country. Find out which fucking 'T' country is at war!" Jerry Gerard growls to an assistant. "And get me two Dunkin' Donuts iced coffees. Fucking *now!*" Within minutes the assistant is back with the coffees and Jerry Gerard tells him to place them on the anchor desk. "With the logos on the container facing out, toward the camera, you moron!"

Tom Sandler smiles amiably and takes a sip. "Thanks for the freebie, boss!"

Sienna spins around in her chair.

"We are not, I repeat not, having this argument again, Jerry," Sienna says, snagging the cup from Tom and handing it, along with her own, to a passing assistant.

"That's right, we're not," Jerry Gerard says, snatching the cups back. "Orders from the head of the news division. Product placement is a go, honey."

Honey? He called her honey? I can't wait to see what happens next! But instead of duking it out with Jerry Gerard, Sienna puts on the kid gloves.

"Listen, Jerry," Sienna says sweetly, as her face muscles relax into her practiced newscaster smile. "I know Randy Jackson holds a big red Coke glass on *American Idol* and I'm sure the only reason they give out Doritos to those poor hungry bastards on *Survivor* is that Pringles wouldn't pay as much for the privilege. But we're newspeople. What happens if there's an outbreak of donut poisoning? Or the company president is indicted for, I don't know, stealing the donut holes? Are we going to report it while we're sitting here like idiots with their coffee cups in front of us? Are we going to *not* report it because they pay us to sit here like idiots with their coffee cups in front of us?"

"Why don't you just worry about those bags under your eyes and leave the morality issues to me?" Jerry Gerard smirks. He chucks Sienna under the chin and turns her face from side to side. "Stop by to see me on the way out. I have a name of a plastic surgeon. Could extend this little career of yours by a good four or five months."

"Fuck you," Sienna says, speaking to Jerry in the only language he understands. She unhooks the wireless microphone from the lapel of her Armani jacket, throws it on the floor, and stomps away from the desk.

"Walk away from this set and you're fired!" Jerry Gerard

says gleefully, sounding not the least bit scared. In fact, he sounds like Sienna's permanent departure would make his day.

"Talk to my agent," Sienna says, speed-dialing the number and tossing her BlackBerry at Jerry Gerard, who pitches it back.

"Already did. Your contract's up in six months anyway, there's not a chance in hell we want to renew. It's been a great run, sweetie, but this show could use some fresh blood. See you at the Emmys—I hear they reserve a special row of seats for old-timers."

"You didn't, you *did not* just call me old," says Sienna, fuming.

"No, I did not. I said you were an old-timer, one of the greats, like Walter Cronkite or Edward R. Murrow." Jerry Gerard snickers. "Take me to court and I'll stick to my story."

The crew scatters across the newsroom, too frightened to speak. Jerry Gerard's threat, *"Walk away and you're fired!"* hangs in the air like a scaffold on a frayed cable—it could break loose and crush all of them, too. Only Tom Sandler pipes up.

"Does this mean we're keeping the coffee? I think the coffee's a great idea," he says. Tom might not be the brightest bulb in the chandelier, but his antennae for newsroom politics are picking up all the channels.

"If you play your cards right they might even throw in some donuts," Murray the soundman says. "This could be your lucky day."

"Yeah, lucky day," Sienna repeats, her inflection giving the phrase a darker, more ominous meaning. She gathers up some papers from the anchor desk and stuffs them in her bag. Then she taps Jerry Gerard on the shoulder, flashes her most photogenic TV smile, and pours the milky iced coffee all over his bald head.

"HIT ME," SIENNA says, sliding her beer glass across a weathered wood table for the waiter to refill. "And my friend here's allergic, give her another mocktail." She giggles.

"At least we don't have to call them Shirley Temples, anymore," I say.

"And we don't have to *be* Shirley Temple anymore, either," says Sienna, who's had one too many of those beers. "Child star, ambassador, the first woman to say the words 'breast' and 'cancer' together on television. The woman is a paragon, a paragon." Sienna takes another swill of beer. "Do you think those curls of hers were real?"

"Just another one of the great mysteries of life. What did Ben Affleck ever see in JLo? How can you call them the New Kids on the Block if it's their twenty-year reunion? Did Shirley Temple use a curling iron?"

After Sienna dumped the coffee on her arrogant idiot producer she left an SOS for her agent and we headed across the street to the local watering hole. Sienna's been staring at her BlackBerry as if she could will it to ring for over an hour, and finally, it does.

"*You knew. . . . Uh-huh . . . You've called all the other channels. . . . Nothing, not a nibble, no one's interested? Not to worry, of course not, no. A pet food commercial? National? Oh, tri-state . . . but not New York. Not definite, a few other candidates . . . You'll call.*" Sienna puts down the phone and blows at the foam around the top of her beer. "My agent says that in newscaster years I'm about a hundred and seven. But apparently in Connecticut, New Jersey, and Pennsylvania I might still be young enough to shill Puppy Chow."

"Old? What are you talking about? We're the very same age."

"Right, and over forty is over the hill in the entertainment business."

"But what about Barbara, Diane, and Katie?" I ask, ticking off the names of three of the news industry's biggest—and oldest—stars.

"Anomalies," Sienna says, swirling a finger into her beer to play with the bubbles. "Sure, a few women squeak past the age thing, but the reason that everyone talks about them is that they're the exceptions to the rule."

"But that's nuts. I want to see women my age on TV, and I have the money to spend big bucks on advertiser's products." Then I pause. "Well I did, until Peter lost his job."

"And until I became a *sinking* anchor," Sienna says glumly. "Jerry Gerard has been gunning for me ever since he came onto the show. He humiliates me every chance he gets, like making me do these dumb soft news spots. 'Sienna Post Goes Skydiving!' 'Sienna Post, Live Today from the Bronx Zoo!' An elephant's first birthday and we gave him a party. A party, with balloons and a beach ball for a present and a coconut cake decorated with peanuts! Did you ever hear of a news show giving a beach ball or a coconut cake with peanuts to a *forty-one*-year-old elephant? No siree, you did not! Even the goddamned elephant birthday party is aimed at the youth market." Sienna wipes tears away with a scratchy napkin.

I never heard of a news show giving a party for an elephant of any age, but right now that seems as irrelevant as Paula Abdul's praise.

"It's going to be all right," I say. "There are all kinds of opportunities, we just have to think outside the box. Molly was reading me something the other day about how stores hire people to shop undercover so they can rate the salespeople."

"But you have to give back the merch. Besides, it would be like sending an alcoholic to work in a liquor store."

"Point taken. If you sign up to be a nurse in Czechoslovakia for three years they'll give you a free face-lift or breast implants."

"Talk about job perks. But I faint at the sight of blood."

"And I suppose Molly's other suggestion is totally out of the question," I deadpan. "I don't think my womb's quite up to the task of being a surrogate mother."

Sienna pauses. Then she laughs so hard that a spurt of beer trickles down her chin. "I've always wanted to try my hand at writing. And then there's my secret passion—to take up botanical painting."

"Wow, all these years, I never knew! You'd paint a mean geranium."

"You bet your ass, I would!" Sienna says. She reaches for the mustard dispenser and starts doodling leafy plant designs on a paper place mat. "You know, work kills," Sienna says, making swirly flowers now with the ketchup. "I did a story on it. More people die on the job than from drugs, alcohol, or war combined. 'Course most of them are lumberjacks, or fishermen. Did you know that the most dangerous job in the world is to be a crab fisherman in the Bering Strait? We're lucky not to be crab fishermen. We're lucky not to be working. We have to get more people not working!" She slams her fist against the table and splatters ketchup-paint on her Armani shirtsleeve. "And we have to get people to stop wearing sneakers, too. There were 71,409 sneaker accidents in the United States last year. Don't you think sneakers look tacky when people wear them to work?"

"Not if they're that Olympic runner from Jamaica, Usain Bolt."

"Do you think that's his real name? A runner named Bolt?"

"What I think is that it's time to get you home now," I say, reaching into my pocket to leave a five-dollar tip for the waiter.

Always generous, Sienna adds another twenty. "Maybe a local pet food commercial wouldn't be the end of the world," she says as I hold out her suit jacket so she can find the armholes.

"Of course not. It might even lead to something bigger. Teri Hatcher's our age and she's got a contract with Clairol."

"Yeah, who cares that it's for a hair color product to cover up her gray?"

As we step out onto the sidewalk Sienna bundles her collar around her neck against an early September chill. The early nip in the air is just a reminder that any day now, the girls will be asking for new Uggs. Ugh! Just one more thing we won't be able to pay for. Sienna's hugging me goodbye when our waiter comes rushing out after us.

"Thanks, but you're going to need this more than I do," he says, pressing Sienna's twenty-dollar bill back in her hand. "It's all over the Internet. Sorry about your getting canned."

⚜

LATER THAT NIGHT, Peter and I are snuggling in bed. "Why do they call it getting canned?" I ask, stroking his arm. "Bumped, bounced, kicked, booted—sounds more like a Lara Croft action sequence than a description of being fired."

"Being fired is pretty brutal," Peter says. He sits up and throws off the comforter, swinging his legs over the side of the bed. "It's not just my company, the markets are going crazy. I may never work again. You wouldn't understand, Tru. I've been going through this hell for three months."

From the tone in Peter's voice I know that he's just stating what for him is a simple fact. Still, every hair on my body stiffens.

Maybe I would have understood if you'd told me about your getting fired when it happened, buddy! I start to snap. But in-

stead, I hold my tongue. Even if Peter had no right to keep this
a secret from me, I will not, I will absolutely, positively *not*
turn into Naomi, bitter and belittling my father for everything
that went wrong. "I want to understand," I say. "Next time, if
something awful happens, talk to me about it. I'm supposed to
be your partner, remember?"

"We are partners," Peter says, turning around to face me.
"You're doing a great job with the girls. It's just that I don't
feel like I'm holding up my end of the bargain."

"Stop that. They're *our* girls. It's *our* life. We have to be able
to support each other."

Peter shrugs. "I know you support me, Tru, it's nice that
you're in my corner. But I didn't want to worry you. It's not
like there's anything you could have done."

"Maybe yes, maybe no, but at least we could have tried to
do something together. And I want to do something now. I'm
going to get a job," I say with false bravado. Because really,
what exactly is it that I think I'm going to do at this stage of my
life? Start a rock band? Stock grocery shelves at the A&P? Volunteer to test hemorrhoid medications?

"I don't want you to have to go to work. Besides, you could
never earn the kind of money we need." Peter shakes his head.
"I'm sorry, honey, I didn't mean for this to happen. I was
happy with things the way they were."

"It's nobody's fault. It's the economy, stupid," I say, trying
to lighten the mood. And then, hoping that as on the night
after the benefit I can make us both feel a little better, I push
Peter back toward the pillows and run my finger across the
front of his white cotton Jockey briefs. Tugging at the waistband, I slip off Peter's underwear and brush my fingers across
his hip bone. Peter sighs contentedly. And then, I hear a familiar snore. I nudge my husband's shoulder, trying to get him to

revive, but it's not happening. Although Peter thinks something already has.

"Hm, thanks, honey, that was nice," Peter says drowsily.
He stretches out, rubs his feet against mine, and falls back into
a deep sleep.

I try to sleep, too, but it's just no use. I start thinking about
the time, a couple of months ago, when I unexpectedly ran into
Paige after school and I barely recognized my own daughter.
She'd ditched her prim blazer and knee socks, rolled up her
plaid school uniform skirt into a kittenish costume no wider
than a belt, and the pretty, unadorned face that she'd left for
school with that morning was positively gothic—transformed
by smudgy black eye makeup, purple lipstick and a cheek
piercing that (thank heavens!) was attached to her face by a
magnet. I didn't embarrass her in front of her friends, but
when she got home that night I'd started to read her the riot
act. "Geesh, Mom, don't have a nervous breakdown. I'm a
teenager, I'm trying to figure out who I am," Paige had
protested. "Some days I dress like Hannah Montana. Other
days I dress like Miley Cyrus."

Ever since I found out that Peter's unemployed I've been
struggling to figure out who I am, too. I try to picture myself as
something other than a bag lady, searching for an image, any
image, of what my life could look like if I'm not a shopping,
charity-fund-raising, stay-at-home-mom. But as I spend the
rest of the night tossing and turning, absolutely nothing comes
into focus.

Five

%

The Shot Heard
'Round the World

TEN DAYS LATER I step out into the street in front of our building and pull out my cellphone to call Sienna to say I'm running late. As I distractedly jaywalk through traffic, a monster
eighteen-wheeler truck comes to a screeching halt within
inches of my body and a conga line of cars going up Park Avenue narrowly avoid crashing into one another. I'm so badly
shaken that the only parts of my body capable of moving are
my hands, which fly up in front of my face. Terrance sprints
from the lobby to safely shepherd me back to the curb, and the
driver jumps down from the cab of the truck.

"Lady, you gotta look where you're going, this rig weighs
forty tons. Do you think it's a piece of cake to try to stop it on a
dime like that?" the driver barks.

"Sorry, you're right, I should have been paying attention,"
I say, as I reach into my purse to finger one of the half dozen
St. Christopher medals that I carry in each of my pocketbooks.
Even if you're not Catholic, it can't hurt to have the patron
saint of travel keeping an eye out for you. Especially if you're

an attention-deficit New Yorker who's never doing fewer than three things at the same time.

Terrance pats my hand. "Mrs. N, you're still trembling. Want to do a meditation?"

"Or medication?" a female voice sings out. "I have a whole bottle of Ativan, it's a lovely anti-anxiety drug." I look up and spot the driver extending a helping hand to a blond bombshell as she daintily steps out of the truck's cab. Even from twenty feet away I can see that her legs are longer than Heidi Klum's and her eyelashes are thicker than Bambi's. She's dressed in five-inch heels and a sexy bandage dress wrapped so tightly that I momentarily wonder whether she's wearing Herve Leger, or if she's been in an accident herself and left the hospital in traction.

"That's okay," I say, as my breathing gets back to normal. I send a quick text message to Sienna to let her know that I'm all right and I'll be there as soon as I can. "I guess if my thumbs are working well enough to use my cellphone there's no permanent damage."

Terrance and the driver laugh, but the vixenish blonde just stares at me blankly.

"You must be Ms. Glass," Terrance says, stepping in to introduce us. "Welcome to the building. Most people don't make such a dramatic entrance."

"I'm known for my entrances." She giggles flirtatiously.

"Mrs. Newman, meet our newest tenant, Ms. Glass. Ms. Glass bought the three MBA, EIK, CVAC, FISBO with BLT BC on the third floor," Terrance says. Which, to those who don't speak the one language common to all New Yorkers—real estate—is a three-bedroom, master suite with bath, eat-in kitchen, central-vacuum equipped, for-sale-by-owner apartment with built-in bookcases.

"Yes, yes I did. But call me Tiffany," she says, still locking eyes on my muscular doorman.

"Tiffany, Tiffany Glass?" I chuckle congenially. "I bet a lot of people ask you about your name. I know a little bit about that myself. I'm Truman Newman."

"Well, how about that?" Tiffany blinks.

Terrance tells the driver to take the truck around to the side entrance. "And Mrs. N, I want you to pay attention to where you're going," he scolds me affectionately.

"Will do." I glance at my watch and hurry off in the direction of the train. "Welcome to the building," I shout over my shoulder toward Tiffany. "If there's anything you need, just let me know."

"Okay, um, thanks," she says, winding up our clever conversation and turning her attention (which, let's face it, never really left) back to Terrance and the truck driver. "Now which of you boys is going to help me find my ThighMaster?"

⁂

I'M STILL RATTLED as I sit down next to Sienna—and it's not just about my near accident. Sienna's and my legs are dangling side by side over the edge of a medical examining table in our beloved Dr. B.'s office. When Sienna pooh-poohs my opposition, I give her a little kick.

"You're out of work and I'm broke," I say guiltily. "This is wrong."

"Nonsense," says Sienna as a nurse wipes our faces clean with astringent-soaked cotton balls and then frosts them with a thin coat of numbing cream.

"No really," I try to insist. "I'm supposed to be putting food on my family's table, not poison in my forehead. Getting Botox is shallow and frivolous."

"In times like these it's shallow and *practical*," Sienna argues. "Just today a job counselor told me that older people can't find work. Besides, I'm paying for it out of my severance package. That fucking Jerry Gerard is responsible for at least half of these wrinkles; it's only fair that he should foot the bill for smoothing them out."

I dab at the numbing cream to make sure that it's working and squirm around in my chair. Maybe it's too much to expect a mountain climber to scale Everest on her first try. Or to ask me to give up trying to look my best after having spent a lifetime in Naomi's shadow. Besides, now that Tiffany Glass is living in our building, it's going to take a lot more than a Sub-Zero refrigerator to keep up with the neighbors.

"Thank you," I say emotionally. "This is very generous."

"Don't mention it. I mean really, don't," Sienna says, patting my hand. "But if you happen to know a cute guy you'd like to introduce me to . . ."

"Cute guys, was somebody talking about cute guys?" Dr. B. asks cheerily, bouncing into the room on the balls of his gray ombre alligator loafers.

"Never mind that, love the outfit," Sienna says, running her hand admiringly down the skinny lapel of Dr. B.'s black Prada suit with a nipped-in waist.

"I know, and look!" Dr. B. says pulling the flaps on his shirt pocket opened and closed. "Velcro!"

I hate going for a physical, you have to drag me to my yearly mammogram, but despite the fact that he sticks dozens of syringes in my face, I look forward to seeing Dr. Brandt—his needles are like magic wands, not to mention that he's endlessly entertaining. I'd never trust my worry lines to anyone else, and neither would half the world's most fabulous faces. Gwyneth flies him to London, Madonna has him on speed dial and *New York* magazine anointed him the architect of the New New Face—which looks like what your old face used to look like, only better.

Sienna and I settle back in our seats. Dr. B. pulls on a pair of gloves and traces what used to be the hollows under my eyes. "Looking good. This Perlane's really holding up," he says. The nurse lines up a row of clear bottles and hands Dr. B. a set of hypodermic needles on a silver tray. He stabs a syringe into the top of one of his magic potions and plunges it into my cheek. Again. And, ooh, here it comes, again. "Just another little squirt, to pump up the volume," Dr. B. says, pursing his lips as the needle goes in, yes, again.

I pick up the mirror and see, despite a few pricks, that I'm already looking so much more fresher and relaxed. My mood, along with my face, immediately lifts. "Can you imagine what Picasso would have done with Perlane?" I giggle.

"You mean crossing women's eyes, flattening their heads, and reassembling their body parts?" Dr. B. laughs. "That old goat did enough damage with a paintbrush. But imagine what Michelangelo could have done with collagen!"

Over the next several minutes Dr. B. changes needles, choosing from an arsenal of modern beauty ammunition that includes Botox to freeze forehead muscles and hyaluronic and fillers like Juvederm to fill in lines around our mouths. As he loads another syringe to zap the folds between my nose and my mouth—unfunnily referred to as "laugh lines"—the good doctor lets out a whoop.

"This is the Evolence, it's made out of pig and a rabbi blessed it. Not exactly kosher." Dr. B. laughs. "But it works."

Sienna always says that Botox is like face cocaine. You get a little, and you just want more and more. Today, I'd swear it's a muscle relaxant. Dishing with Sienna and Dr. B., I can feel the tension absolutely drain from my whole body. The radio is tuned to the lite FM station, programmed for contemporary soft rock to appeal to the over-forty crowd who can't stand rap, but who don't want to spend the next decade listening to the greatest hits of the eighties, either. I'd always thought of music as a great equalizer, bringing people together—but I defy any parent to spend five earsplitting minutes with their teenager listening to Kanye West before they run screaming from the room. Sienna and Dr. B. are bantering about the latest *Dancing with the Stars* contestants when all of a sudden, a newscaster breaks in with an announcement.

"Bankruptcy . . . emergency loan . . . housing market . . . shit!"

I don't catch every word, but I hear enough. Peter had warned me that his company was just the tip of the iceberg, but in my wildest dreams—or nightmares—I'd never imagined that the whole economy was going down.

Three more nurses come rushing into Dr. B.'s office, followed by a line of patients in various stages of treatment—and distress.

"The market's crashing," a woman whose hair is tied back in a high ponytail cries. She clutches the latex glove filled with frozen peas that you usually hold against a bruise, to her heart.

"How much to do my eyes today and not the lips?" asks another woman, already in economy mode.

Sienna's reaction is pure newscaster. "Did the announcer really say 'shit'?"

"Everyone, ladies, take a deep breath," says Dr. B. "Get your head out of your hands, Millie," he says, going over to the frozen-pea-holding woman, who's burst into tears. "You don't want the CosmoDerm getting all lumpy, now do you?"

Ready to jump on the story, Sienna grabs for her BlackBerry and punches in the news desk's number. On the seventh unanswered ring, she punches the phone. "Goddamn it, they see my caller ID and won't pick up. The biggest story of the

decade and I've nobody to report it for!" She pauses as the reality of the situation hits closer to home. "This probably
wasn't the best time to quit my job."

There are wails and frantic phone calls to husbands, brokers, therapists, and who-knows-who-else. With people's anx-
iety levels rising in direct proportion to the falling Dow, Dr. B.
emerges as a King-of-Collagen-post 9/11-Rudy-Guliani, offering strong leadership and taking control of the situation.

"Okay, everyone. Heads high, put away your phones. Glo-
ria," he commands, turning to a receptionist, "get everyone
a bottle of antioxidant pomegranate water. And, ladies, stop
fretting, it causes wrinkles. Today's injections are on the
house."

The house? I'd love to stay for more Evolence but I have to
get back to the apartment to see Peter and the girls. I give Dr.
B. a quick kiss, grab Sienna, and head toward the waiting
room. It's not until we're out of the subway and the anesthetic
wears off that I realize we never finished filling in my laugh
lines. At the moment that doesn't seem so terrible—they're a
reminder of happier times.

❧❧❧

PETER'S STANDING SLACK-SHOULDERED in the entranceway
of the apartment, bouncing a red rubber ball against our
Venetian-plastered sky blue walls. Our twenty-nine-year-old
boy-wonder lawyer, Bill Murphy, is trying to get him to turn
on the lights, but as soon as Bill flicks them on, Peter stops
bouncing the ball long enough to turn them off.

"I got here an hour ago, as soon as I heard the news, but I
can't get Peter to focus on anything but that damned ball," Bill
says, patting his hair, which isn't so much slicked back as plastered, Alfalfa-style, to his baby-faced head. His suit, as al-

ways, is slightly rumpled, and although he's over six feet tall, Bill's the kind of guy who doesn't stand out in a crowd. Still, while Bill's style isn't sharp, his mind is—he got his degree less than five years ago and already he's considered one of New York's best tax attorneys. And he's awfully sweet.

"It was nice of you to come over. Why don't we go inside and I'll fix you both a drink," I say, guiding Bill and Sienna past my shell-shocked husband and dropping my bag on the now-flowerless Georgian table. "I think Peter just needs some alone time." And as I step into the living room, I can see why.

The peripatetic financial analyst Jim Cramer is waving his arms manically, shouting out blow-by-blows of the economic meltdown from the sixty-five-inch plasma TV screen. Naomi, dressed head-to-toe in black, is rocking back and forth with her hands on either side of her head like a Sicilian widow at a funeral. "It's a perfect storm, a perfect storm," wails my mother, the Al Roker of tragedy. Sitting next to Naomi, patting her arm protectively, is Dr. Barasch, P-H-D, her dancing partner from the benefit.

"Dr. Barasch, what are you doing here?" I ask, more than a little taken aback to see the headmaster of the girls' private school sitting on a folding chair in my living room. I had no idea that he and Naomi had even seen each again after the global warming benefit, let alone that they were so intimate. I want Naomi to be happy, but if she messes this one up, her granddaughters may not even get into community college. Still, for the moment, Dr. Barasch is gently making little circles between Naomi's shoulder blades, which actually seems to be quieting her howls.

"When we heard the news about the markets Naomi and I were at her apartment, er, we were just getting out of the movies," Dr. Barasch says, eyeing the twins and switching to the G-rated version of his story. "Your mother wanted to come right over to see what we could do to help."

Paige is sitting at a card table (Molly's already auctioned off the dining room set). In front of her are a large stack of dollar bills.

"What's all this?" asks Sienna, going over and kissing the top of her goddaughter's head.

"Moneygami," says Paige, holding up a one-dollar bill that she's folded into a spindly legged crane. "If I'm not supposed to *spend* money anymore, at least I can play with it."

Sienna and I exchange amused glances. Even in the grimmest of times, Paige can always make me laugh. Bill Murphy goes over to look at Paige's handiwork and picks up a bill that she's folded into an angel. At least I think it's an angel; with those ginormous wings it could just as easily be an oversized bug. "That's the spirit, kiddo!" he says.

Paige scrunches her eyes and I see the start of one of her famously contemptuous Paige Newman stares, the stare that says you do not deserve to be taking up oxygen on this—or any other—planet. But Bill's good cheer is so obviously well-meaning that, despite herself, Paige smiles. Sienna smiles, too. "Nice guy," she mouths, pointing in Bill's direction. As for Bill, I catch him giving Sienna an admiring glance.

I turn off the television. "Look at the bright side, Mom. Now you don't have to worry about buying a whole new spring wardrobe. Sounds like we're going to see a wave of 'Recessionista Chic.' "

"That's ridiculous," chides Naomi, straightening the seams of her stockings. "Isn't that silly, Gordon? Recessionista Chic. That's like jumbo shrimp. It's an onxy, oxy . . . cotin . . ."

"Oxymoron, dear." Dr. Barasch chuckles. His eyes twinkle, and he leans in to give Naomi a small kiss.

"But Grandma. . . ." Molly starts to say. Then realizing that she's not allowed to used the G word—" 'Grandma' is so aging. Besides who'd believe it?"—Molly begins again. "There is Recessionista Chic, Naomi, they were talking about it today on *Tyra.*"

I raise an eyebrow at my daughter's viewing habits.

"Light homework day." Molly shrugs. "Anyway, take this scarf, for example." Molly unties the silk Hermès draped over my mother's shoulders. "You can wear it as a belt, or even a halter."

"A halter?" asks Paige, making a beeline for Naomi— because what could be more challenging to Paige's newfound folding skills than figuring out how to hold her grandmother's boobs in place with nothing more than a thirty-six-inch square of fabric?

"Why don't we just tie this around Naomi's bag," Molly says, wrestling the scarf back from her sister.

"Girls, stop playing," bleats Naomi. "Doesn't anybody in this family take anything seriously? Tru, this is a catastrophe, why aren't you hysterical like everyone else? You never did know how to behave appropriately!"

Before I have a chance to answer that I feel as wobbly as the Dow but that I'm sucking it up for the girls, Peter comes into the living room dribbling that damned rubber ball.

"I'm upset enough for the whole country!" Peter yowls, slamming the ball so hard against the wooden floor that it ric- ochets onto a table, barely missing a lamp.

"Honey," I say, patting the cushion on the sofa next to me and trying to get him to calm down, "it's going to be all right. We'll figure something out."

"Figure out something? Like if you try really hard enough, you'll come up with an answer I haven't thought of? Let's get Tru to figure out something! Maybe she can call Ben Bernanke and give him a few tips on how to save the whole economy while she's at it, too. I'm sure he'd be grateful. Here's the phone," Peter says, thrusting the receiver within an inch of my nose. "Why don't you call right now?"

"Stop it! Just stop it! Stop being so goddamned full of yourself for once in your life, will you, Peter? You'd think you were the only one who was suffering!" I blurt back angrily.

There's an audible gasp in the room. It isn't like me to speak so sharply. And how could we ever, no matter how angry we are, have let the girls hear us attacking each other?

"I'm so sorry," I tell Paige and Molly, at a loss for anything else to say. Bill Murphy puts his hand on Peter's shoulder and he turns toward the twins.

"With everything that's happened today, everybody's emotions are running pretty high," Bill says evenly. "Sometimes parents just need to let off some steam." Then Bill guides Peter toward the den. Several moments later he comes back to say that Peter wants us all to know that he's sorry to have made a scene and he just needs a little time to decompress.

Sienna comes over to stand next to Bill. She squeezes his arm. "Thank you. That was very nice."

I tilt my head to the ceiling, trying in vain to fight back a round of tears. Dr. Barasch reaches out awkwardly to try to comfort me and even Naomi—tactless, thoughtless, unfiltered Naomi, who in the forty-four years I've known her has never had an unexpressed thought—knows not to say a word to me about Peter. Although that doesn't stop her from stumbling like a bull in a china shop into other territory.

She leans in toward me and traces her finger along my nasolabial laugh lines. The one that Dr. B. filled with Evolence— and the one that he didn't. "Tru, why is the right side of your face so much smoother than the left? Look, Gordon." She laughs merrily. "Tru's a walking before and after!"

"Yeah, Mom," asks Paige, moving in for a closer look. "Naomi's right, you look all lopsided. And what are those pin-pricks on your cheek?"

"War wounds," I say, wrapping my arms around a pillow and giving it a little hug. Suddenly, life seems like a constant battle.

Six
❦

Let's Get Fiscal

I HAVEN'T HAD A drop of alcohol since the sip of piña colada
Naomi gave me when I was fifteen that sent me racing to the
hospital with hives. Still it's five A.M. and I feel the way I've
read a hangover feels. My mouth is dry and my skull feels like
it's the size of Mr. Potato Head's. My palms and my feet itch,
too, which can only mean one of two things. Either I'm coming
into some money—or I'm leaving my husband. Although neither seems like a real possibility.

Naomi and Dr. Barasch left after it was evident that Peter
had holed up for the night in the den and wasn't coming back
for a rematch. Sienna and Bill stayed around to talk for a while,
but at a certain point I just wanted to be alone—there's only so
much you can chew over a husband's bad behavior before you
feel like throwing up. Besides, I couldn't help noticing there
was a frisson between the sweet, slightly disheveled lawyer and
my gorgeous, sophisticated best friend. Good for them, I hope
they enjoyed a nice evening together, although never in a million years would I have thought to set them up—Sienna's a

woman of the world, while Bill looks and acts like the boy just out of college that he practically is. Still, there's no accounting for chemistry. Or understanding it, either, apparently. I'm trying to talk myself into getting up and out of bed when Paige appears before me holding a textbook.

"What are you doing up at this hour of the morning?" I ask, heading toward the guest bathroom to brush my teeth.

"Test," Paige says succinctly.

"Now?"

"You're always saying I should come to you to study."

You'd think after being a mother for fourteen years I'd have learned that kids are like vampires—they strike under the cover of darkness. When was the last time a baby got a raging fever during the doctor's regular office hours? I don't have to ask, I know by the look on Paige's face that the test is today— and she probably doesn't know a proton from a pretzel. "Paige Newman," I begin, between gritted teeth.

"I know, Mom, I know. You think I *like* asking? Swear, just this once? I'll never ask you again."

"Oh yes you will." I splash some water on my face, and slip into a pair of jeans and sneakers. "Let's get some breakfast."

Luckily for me Paige doesn't have to understand Stephen Hawking—because honestly not even Stephen Hawking understands Stephen Hawking—she just has to memorize symbols, and she's already got most of them down pat. " 'Ca' for calcium, 'Zn' for zinc," Paige recites. She even knows that "Na" is sodium.

"Our teacher said it's not good to have too much salt," Paige says proudly. "So the way I remember it is that sodium is 'Na.' "

I look at her curiously.

"Na, Mom. As in 'Nah, don't have the salt.' And I know that 'Au' is gold, because Ashley Unger—her initials are AU, get it?—is the richest girl in the class and she's always wearing armloads of these awful gold David Yurman bracelets. Ugh, she thinks she's so cool."

It's always been hard for Paige to compete for grades with her twin sister. Doing well in school comes so easily to Molly that I think in past semesters, Paige just gave up. But maybe things are changing. "Good job, honey," I say, pouring some milk into a bowl of cornflakes and handing Paige a spoon. "Glad to see you taking a real interest in school."

"I've become *very* interested in school, especially science," Paige says, ignoring the cornflakes and searching around the bread box for something in the B, C, or D food groups—bagel, coffee cake, or Danish. Ever since Rosie left and Peter and the girls have been helping with the shopping, the cupboards are stocked with sugar. Paige settles on a Pop-Tart and stares dreamily off into space. "Brandon Marsh is my lab partner and he's the cutest boy in the world, Mom. I can't wait until we study black holes together."

I don't know who this Brandon Marsh boy is, but I suppose I should be grateful if he helps get Paige's marks up. Love certainly seems to be in the air—Paige and Brandon, Sienna and Bill. And you could have knocked me over with a feather when I saw Dr. Barasch and Naomi in my living room, mooning over each other like a couple of teenagers. Maybe if I just took a deep enough breath I could fill my lungs with some of the same intoxicating elixir that they're inhaling. Or maybe not. It might take more than a few whiffs of O_2 mixed with L-O-V-E to get things back on track with Peter.

My husband shuffles into the kitchen with the *New York Times*. Without so much as an *I'm sorry,* or even an *Are you okay?*, he hands me the morning paper as a peace offering. "I thought you might want to read this. I know you hate how I grab it first every morning."

"Thanks," I say dispiritedly, separating the arts section from the rest of the news. Today of all days, I can't face reading about anything more depressing than a review of Adam Sandler's latest movie.

"Okay then," Peter says, moving right along and pouring himself a glass of orange juice. "Maybe after breakfast I'll do the wash."

"Oh no, Dad, no. Mom, please don't let Daddy do it. My Juicy Couture sweatpants will be absolutely ruined," Paige cries.

"Will not," says Peter. "Who do you think did my laundry when I was in college?"

"Mom," Paige says.

"We did it together. Every Saturday afternoon we'd bring our books to the laundromat to study while we watched our clothes co-mingling in the dryer."

"Geez, talk about a cheap date. You sure know how to romance a girl," Paige teases.

"You don't know the half of it, right, Tru?" Peter asks.

"Not the half," I say softly.

"I'm going to leave you two alone now," Paige says, heading back toward her room to get dressed. She turns around in the doorway and waves her textbook. "Thanks for the help, Mom."

"You're welcome, sweetie. Good luck with the test."

Peter reaches for a coffee mug. "Paige studying for a test?"

"Well, she's studying for a test to impress a boy, but at least it's a start," I say, falling into the familiar rhythms of marriage—ignoring the larger issue of our fight in favor of talking about school and children. Normally property values would be on the list, too, but these days that's a sore subject.

From the bedroom, I hear Molly turning on the shower. Above the morning crackle of coffee percolating, Paige singing out her chemistry symbols as if they were the ABC song, and Peter noisily opening and closing the kitchen cabinets in search of cups, spoons, and bowls that are right under his nose, somehow I hear the phone ring. "Drop whatever you're doing, you have to get over to my apartment *now!*" Sienna cries.

I hand Peter the carton of milk he's been searching for everywhere but in the refrigerator door where we always keep it. "I'll be back, well, I don't know exactly," I say, explaining that Sienna needs help.

Peter leans forward to tuck a stray lock behind my ear. "How about we make a pact, no more secrets? I know it was pretty upsetting when you found out that I'd been out of work for so long. And that I hadn't even told you. I won't keep anything like that from you ever again. What do you say?"

It's hard to argue that honesty isn't the best policy, and even if I wanted to, I have to get to Sienna's. "No more secrets," I promise. Peter smiles, appreciative that I haven't made it hard to say he's sorry, which just for the record, he's never actually said. Then as I turn to leave, he taps my shoulder and hands me a Pop-Tart wrapped in a paper napkin. My husband's never been a virtuoso at apologies or sweet talk—but he's still a master of the sweet gesture.

❧

LESS THAN TWENTY minutes later I'm sitting in Sienna's living room, looking out the floor-to-ceiling windows at her spectacular Central Park view. Sienna pushes a button to start the fake fireplace—so authentic that you'd swear those crackling flames really were coming from the cement logs—and we sink into her beige suede couch. The elegant, impossibly impractical beige suede couch that announces louder than Sienna's lack of a wedding ring that no messy husband—let alone children—live here.

"Look at this, will you just look at this!" Sienna says, waving a check in front of my face.

"Calm down. What's got you so upset?" I stare at the check that's made out to "Cash." "Whoa, five thousand large, that's a tidy little sum. What did you do, rob a bank?"

"Worse," Sienna says ominously.

"What do you mean 'worse'? I was joking."

"Well, I'm not. Worse. Imagine the very worst thing you could possibly do."

"Invite Jennifer Aniston and Angelina Jolie to the same dinner party?"

"I slept with Bill Murphy" Sienna says, biting her lower lip.

I pause and try to suppress a giggle. Sienna's a grown woman. A grown woman who enviably, I've always thought, knows how to seize the moment. Besides, after everything else that went on in the world yesterday, I'd almost have been more surprised if she hadn't slept with the puppy-doggishly cute Bill. Why, for goodness' sake, would she be having morning-after regrets?

"Is that all? What's the problem? Sure he's a little young, but Bill's a sweet guy. Don't beat yourself up about it. Yesterday was brutal. The whole country's feeling panicked and confused. It's only natural that you two would end up in the sack together, it was Emergency Sex. I remember reading that after 9/11 there was a population explosion the following June." Then I pause. "You did use birth control, didn't you?"

"Of course I did. That's not the problem."

"You mean the sex wasn't good?"

"No, actually it *was* good. What Bill lacks in experience he makes up in enthusiasm," Sienna says and I swear I see a faint blush rise in her cheeks.

"That sounds promising. Isn't it every woman's fantasy to

teach a younger guy the ropes? So what in heaven's name is wrong?"

"The money, this money," Sienna wails, slamming her fist on the coffee table. "It wasn't until after he left that I noticed the check on the nightstand. I don't know whether to take it as a compliment or an insult."

"I'd say compliment. I would have thought that boat had sailed. I mean, it's too late to be a ballerina or a basketball star—how many women our age get paid for sex?"

Sienna shoots me a withering look. "Stop kidding around. It's like he thinks I'm a common hooker," she says, sounding angrier by the moment.

"Well, not common," I say, brandishing the check. "High-class courtesan, at least. Look, sweetie, I'm sure he didn't mean anything by it. Peter's always said that Bill's brilliant but a little socially inept. Maybe the guy doesn't know the number for 1-800-FLOWERS. I'm sure he was just trying to be nice."

"Nice is dinner at Per Se or a sexy teddy from La Perla," Sienna says. I decide not to point out that either of those more traditional gifts could be construed as a more subtle form of payment, but payment nonetheless. Instead, I try arguing that the money could be useful. It's no time for any of us to be looking down our noses at five thousand dollars.

"If you don't want this, I'm sure Paige would be happy to fold it into a flamingo. Or we could pay our mortgage. Or you could use it to pay for another two weeks in your apartment."

Sienna's been putting on a good face about getting fired, but at the mention of her rent, she bursts into tears. I scan the living room, which is entirely clutter-free. No knickknacks or photos from her world travels disrupt the space's sophisticated, serene lines. Just possibly, there's a tissue tucked away somewhere upstairs in a built-in closet, but instead of trying to hunt one down, I rummage around my purse and I hear a buzzing. I reach for my cellphone, only to discover that it's not ringing.

"Damn it, this has been happening all week. Maybe I do have ringxiety."

Sienna looks at me quizzically.

"Ringxiety—Dr. Phil called it a genuine twenty-first-century malady, kind of like phantom leg syndrome. People are so connected to their cellphones that they hear them ringing even when they're not."

"At least you're not hearing voices, then you'd be schizophrenic," Sienna says, smiling for the first time since I got here. "That buzzing's the intercom; I'm expecting a package. Just tell the doorman to send it up."

Sienna swipes the tissue across her face and I go into the kitchen to get us a couple of bottles of water, which, it turns out, are the only thing in her refrigerator besides a container of French vanilla yogurt and two bottles of champagne. With its Miele appliances and satin-finished glass backsplashes, Sienna's kitchen looks like something out of a design showroom, and it gets about as much use. Though today an uncharacteristic trail of toast crumbs leads me toward the coffeemaker, which is still half-full. This affair with Bill Murphy is more serious than I thought. Sienna doesn't let guys sleep over until somewhere around the umpteenth date, and then it usually spells the death knell for her relationships. She likes the sex and romance parts of dating, not the daily grind.

"You let Bill spend the night? And you let him leave a mess?"

"I'm sorry, I usually clean up after myself," says Bill Murphy, all six-foot-two-inches of him, stepping into the apartment. "Door was unlocked." He takes the coffeepot from me and empties its contents into Sienna's custom-designed sink. Then he taps one of Sienna's handleless cupboards and pulls out a scrub brush and a can of Comet.

Sienna tosses back her thick mahogany hair and marches over to turn off the spigot. "That won't be necessary. And neither," she says coolly, holding out the offending check, "is this."

Bill has at least a hundred pounds on Sienna (probably 107 at the end of her monthly juice fast)—and he's a good six inches taller. But it's no contest. Standing toe-to-toe you'd swear that Bill was the ninety-eight-pound-weakling to Sienna's sumo wrestler. He wipes his hands on a linen dishtowel and meekly accepts the check. Sienna turns on her heel and stomps out of the room. Bill waves his arms helplessly and goes trailing after her.

"I got your email, I know you're upset but you have to let me explain. It's just that you said you were worried about money and I have some, that's all."

"And you decided to pay me for a job well rendered?"

"Well, it was well rendered," Bill says, a small smile crossing his face. "But no, I mean, I wasn't paying you. . . ."

"You mean, let's be friends with benefits, and the benefits you're offering are in cash."

There's a pause in the conversation and Bill looks lost in thought. Professionally, he and Sienna are an interesting match—the newscaster and the lawyer. Each of their livelihoods depends on their way with words. Bill may be wimpy when it comes to women, but to his high-profile clients, he's a winner. And as the lawyer in him emerges over the lover, Bill takes command of the argument.

"It's a simple case of economics," he says, drumming his finger on his chin. "I have money and right now you don't. I'm just redistributing the wealth."

"But you redistributed it after sex, as if you were paying for a service!" Sienna exclaims.

"Well, that's not how I was thinking of it. I just wanted to help out a friend. If you don't want the money, you don't have to take it."

"I certainly won't be taking it."

"That's your choice. But would it be so bad if I were?"

"Were what?" Sienna asks impatiently.

"Paying to spend time with you? Because you're a beautiful, smart, funny, charming woman, an older woman who knows her way around the world, one of the most fascinating women I've ever met in my life."

"Then Sienna would be right," I declare, jumping into the conversation. "It would make her a working girl."

"Well, she's been a working girl all of her life. What's the difference between being paid by the network and being paid by me?"

Sienna's face goes from ashen to beet red in about thirty seconds.

"Because when I whore for the station I get to meet heads of state and—and interview *elephants!*" Sienna says indignantly. Then she grabs Bill's check and tears it into a zillion pieces, which she scatters at his feet.

"That's what I think of you and your money and your, your economic theories," she shrieks. "Don't email, don't call, I never want to see or hear from you, not ever again!" Sienna pushes the boy lawyer out the front door and slams it shut behind him. Sienna may be incensed. But suddenly, I'm inspired. Though I can't decide if the plan that's hatching in my brain is the best or the worst idea I've ever had.

Seven

❦

Indecent Proposal

DID ISAAC NEWTON SAY "Aha!" when the apple fell on his head? Did the ophthalmologist—whose patient reported that the Botox the doctor injected her with to treat a rare eye disorder had also smoothed out her wrinkles—do a little jig? By the morning my heart is beating wildly and I'm sure that my idea is *sheer brilliance*. True, it's outrageous. But drastic times call for drastic measures. And it just might make enough money to keep us from getting kicked out of our apartment.

I was so jazzed up about doing some research that I arrived at the main branch of the New York Public Library a half hour early, which gave me ample time to appeal to the library's stone lion mascots.

"Hi there, Patience, hello, Fortitude," I said, using their nicknames. "I'm going to need your help to make things work." I closed my eyes and rubbed their marble manes for luck.

"They ain't Aladdin's Lamp, miss," the guard shouted as

he opened the library's towering bronze doors and caught sight of what I was up to.

"We'll just see about that," I said, giving Fortitude one last pat. Then I bounded up past the guard toward the Reading Room.

I found a seat at a long oak table, switched on a brass lamp, and marveled, as I always do, at the library's shimmering crystal chandeliers, massive arched windows, and soaring gold-leafed fifty-two-foot-high ceiling—with its painted blue sky mural, it's amazing that everyone doesn't spend all of their time looking up, instead of burying their noses in books. Still, I'm on a mission. I called up about a dozen titles and I've been flipping through them furiously, taking notes. After about an hour, Sienna slips into the seat beside me. She takes a look around and blinks.

"No wonder Oprah's Book Club is such a success. How else could anyone ever choose?"

I laugh and thank her for coming.

"No problem. I don't have that much else to do these days. Even the pet commercial fell through. My agent says she's got a list longer than her arm of clients looking for work—and my agent's a tall woman, her arm is pretty long. Didn't Peter's cousin go out on a date with the niece of the sister of the CEO of Costco? Maybe if I pull in all my connections I can get a job as a food demonstrator."

"I think we can do better than that," I chirp. I thumb through a beautiful art book of works by the Venetian painter Tintoretto until I find the picture I'm looking for. Then I slide it over to Sienna.

Sienna looks at the portrait of a pretty, pink-cheeked young woman with full bee-stung lips and traces her finger along the neckline of the girl's lavish lace gown. "Nice outfit," she says.

"Yes it is."

"Like the pearl choker."

"Say the word and it can be yours."

Sienna looks up. "For heaven's sake, what are we talking about? I know you love books the way the rest of us love Twitter, but why did you insist on meeting at the library?"

I take a deep breath. I know that Sienna's going to be a hard sell, my idea *is* unconventional. But who ever made it big without taking a few risks? Can you imagine what Steve Jobs's parents had to say about it when he wanted to drop out of college?

I point to the caption and Sienna reaches for her glasses, the ones she almost never wears in public. I watch her carefully as I wait for the words to sink in.

" 'Veronica Franco, 1546 to 1591, Venice. Courtesan and Poet,' " Sienna reads. "Well, that's certainly an unusual job description." Obliviously, she skips ahead a few pages to look at Tintoretto's *The Last Supper*—a much more energetic version than the famous Leonardo da Vinci painting, where the diners are sitting in repose. Seconds later, Sienna furiously flips back to the lovely Veronica.

"*Courtesan and poet?* What's going on in that brain of yours?" she asks suspiciously.

"I'm thinking that Veronica Franco had a good life. She was intellectual and artistic and elegant and witty. She published two books of poetry."

"And she slept with men to get what she wanted. Isn't that what a courtesan does?"

"Well, technically, yes. But for goodness' sake, one of them was the king of France, a girl could do worse!" I pause. "Have you ever thought about all the men who could have helped us whom we didn't sleep with because we were too high and mighty to trade sex for power? And then have you ever thought about the guys we *did* sleep with who didn't give us anything—and ended up being jerks anyway?"

"Are you out of your mind?" Sienna yelps. "You and Peter have been together since college—is there something you forgot to tell me? Who exactly were these men who could have helped you who you didn't sleep with? And better yet, who were the jerks you did?"

"Okay, so I'm only speaking hypothetically about myself. But we had some pretty heated conversations about this in my women's studies classes. Look at these," I say, pushing an impressive stack of biographies in Sienna's direction. "Coco Chanel, Madame de Pompadour, Sarah Bernhardt, all of them were paid by men for the pleasure of their company."

"So you're suggesting that I should have taken Bill's money?" Sienna asks disbelievingly.

"Well, not just Bill. I mean, that's what gave me the idea and if you do something about his cowlick, I have a feeling you two could be good together. But I was thinking of something a little more ambitious. I was thinking that we could form a company to arrange for lots of different men to meet wonderful women. Act as a kind of matchmaking service."

Sienna arches an eyebrow—then she laughs. "Tru, honey, have you gone completely around the bend? A matchmaking service for men to sleep with women? There's a name for that. Besides, it's illegal."

"Is not," I say quickly, offering the results of my research. "There's nothing illegal about introducing men to women. What they do after the introductions is totally up to them. It would be a service business, like any other service business."

"A service business. You mean like being a personal shopper? Except instead of a new tie, we help you find a blow job?"

"Something like that. Although if the men want help picking out their ties I'm sure that could be arranged, too. There must be lots of men like Bill, good respectable guys who are a little shy with girls. We'd be doing them a favor, helping to turn social nerds into datable dudes."

"I don't know why you think Bill is shy. He's been leaving messages on my machine every hour."

"He adores you, he's called me a dozen times to ask what he could do to get you back."

"He's sent so many flowers that my house looks like the Duggar family's on Mother's Day."

"At least flowers are pretty. Remember the billionaire who gave you that awful six-carat diamond pendant in the shape of a gecko?"

"It was a turtle."

"Whatever. Do you remember what you said? 'I wish he'd just given me the money,' those were your very words! So why not just get the money and pay off our bills? Frankly, I need to do something or we're going to find ourselves living on the sidewalk. Besides, I think I'd be good at running a business. I'm well organized and detail oriented. And after years of dealing with impossibly demanding benefit committee members like Avery Peyton Chandler, I have pretty good people skills. This could be my calling."

"Your calling, to be a madam?"

"No, not a madam, I'm not going to be running a brothel. More like Madame Chairman of whatever we call our corporation. And you'll be the CEO. Or if you want *you* can be Madame Chairman and I'll be the CEO."

Sienna's mouth drops open and she shakes her head. "Ooh, no, no, not 'we,' Lucy. I'd rather stomp on grapes or sell Vitameatavegamin. This Ethel is not taking part in your cockamamie scheme!" Sienna stands up to leave, but I tug at her skirt and pull her back into her seat.

"First of all, missy, *you've* always been Lucy. This would be the first time in practically our whole relationship when we did something that was my idea. You owe me. Remember the April Fool's Day I helped you scratch out letters on the faculty parking sign so that it read '*Cult* Parking' and we got suspended for three whole days? Wasn't it you who suggested those glycolic peels that left us swollen and blistered right before the Women in Film Luncheon? A director at the party invited me to be in a documentary she was making about burn victims."

"Jessica Alba goes to that same facialist, I still can't imagine what went wrong. Besides, those peels were harder to get than tickets to the Inaugural," Sienna says, applying the peculiarly New York logic that the longer you have to wait for something, the more precious it becomes.

"Well, today's your lucky day, no waiting at all for your next appointment." I throw on my coat and take Sienna's arm, assuming a take-no-prisoners managerial style that's new but coming remarkably easily. "I can't do this without you and I won't take no for an answer. We're swinging by Dr. B.'s office to get my face fixed and then we're meeting Bill for lunch. He's already working out the details."

⊰❦⊱

BILL'S SITTING IN the back booth of a dark Midtown spaghetti joint, looking and acting like a character out of *The Godfather*. He's wearing mirrored sunglasses and instead of his usual lawyerly Brooks Brothers suit, white shirt, and red tie, he's sporting a black shirt and an even blacker shiny tuxedo jacket. As Sienna and I approach the table he brings an oversized goblet of wine to his lips, takes a sip, and whirls his hand in the air, motioning for us to sit down. Sienna had balked about coming, but at the sight of Bill's goofy transformation, in spite of herself, she can't help smiling.

"Ladies, welcome," he says, folding his hands on the table and speaking like a marble-mouthed Marlon Brando. "I'm here to make you an offer you can't refuse." Then he takes off his sunglasses and turns to Sienna. "I'm really sorry, I didn't mean to offend you. I'd do anything in the world if you'll let me make it up to you."

Bill takes Sienna's hand and despite her warning to me that nothing would come of this meeting, she doesn't pull it away.

"This is an awful lot of trouble to go through," she says.

"I would climb the highest mountain, I would swim the deepest river, I would—"

"Okay," Sienna laughs. "Now you're getting me worried. Quit while you're ahead. I forgive you." Then her eyes narrow and she swivels her head between me and Bill. "But just to set the record straight for both of you nutcases, I'm not going into business with either of you."

Bill puts his sunglasses back on and gestures for us to do the same. When Sienna protests, I fish out a pair of Ray-Bans from her pocketbook and plant them on the bridge of her nose. Then I put on my own Persols, the ones I bought last spring when we were still spending money on luxuries. I read once that if you're depressed you can trick your body into feeling better by looking at yourself in a mirror and grinning. If Sienna's in costume, maybe she'll recite the lines Bill and I want to hear. Besides, Bill's wacky presentation is a lot more fun than a PowerPoint—and it's already helped him worm his way back into Sienna's good graces.

Bill takes out a yellow legal pad scribbled with notes and places it squarely on the red-and-white checkered tablecloth. He picks up a book of matches, and reading by the light of a candle stuck in the top of a Chianti bottle, he proceeds to make his case. The three of us will draw up a partnership agreement to run a "temporary help agency." Since Sienna and I are broke, Bill will put up the initial investment money and he'll take out his share of the profits first. We'll have a corporate bank account, a Federal ID number; we'll even be taxpaying citizens. The women who work for us will be independent contractors. They'll pay our agency a commission and be responsible for their own withholding taxes. We'll recruit the ladies through perfectly legal magazine ads, and only accept clients by referral.

"I know dozens of guys, guys like me who are smart but a little backward when it comes to their social skills. Better yet, they're the hotshots negotiating bailouts and bankruptcy filings. They may be the last people in the universe to still be making tons of money. And I can't tell you how many of them would pay a fortune to meet a woman."

"What's a fortune?" Sienna asks, running a finger around the lip of her wineglass.

"Eliot Spitzer was ponying up fifty-five hundred dollars an hour to his escort service, but the Luv Gov was only interested in quickies. We're offering a more refined service. Clients and escorts will enjoy parties and dates and hopefully develop longtime relationships. With that in mind I'm thinking fifteen hundred an hour. With a four-hour minimum."

"Six thousand dollars?" Sienna asks incredulously.

"Right, for the basics. Blow jobs, deep French kissing, swallowing—those will all be extras. And we'll offer discounts for more extended dates. Why don't we say ten thousand for overnights?"

"Twelve thou," I say.

Bill laughs. "Twelve thousand it is. And our commission is forty percent."

"But why would these guys—or anybody—pay that much money to be with a woman?" Sienna quibbles.

"Exclusivity," I tell her. "Why do you pay four hundred

dollars for designer jeans that are made from the same denim as the thirty-eight-dollar ones you could get at the Gap?"

"It's the same reason that people are willing to pay a premium for good sushi. Clients want to know that what they're paying for comes from a reliable source," Bill says. "Our women will be attractive, smart, the kind of woman you could take to a dinner party with your boss or home to meet your parents. Then in bed, she'll be a man's total fantasy."

I can see from the look on her face that Sienna's starting to toy with the idea. Until, that is, Bill adds one last detail.

"And by the way. Everyone who works for us will be at least forty."

"Forty? Forty-year-old hookers?" Sienna shrieks, pounding her fist on the table. "Now I know the two of you have both lost your minds!"

"Not hookers, courtesans," Bill says patiently. "And I'm quite serious. To be successful in today's business world you have to have a niche, and my gut tells me that this could be ours. Inkjet printers, bamboo flooring, one of my clients is a psychiatrist who specializes in CrackBerry addicts—each of them filled a need in the marketplace that wasn't being met."

"Older women and younger men. It's a trend, just look at Hollywood," I say. "Courteney Cox Arquette is seven years older than her husband, David; Demi is sixteen years older than Ashton; and Katie Couric is seventeen years older than her boyfriend."

Bill pulls off his sunglasses and reaches over to take off Sienna's, meeting her gaze as if they were the only two people in the room. "What I love about you, Sienna, is that you're smart and sexy and worldly. It's not like being with a girl—I feel like we could be together forever and I'd never be bored. And I think other men would feel that way, too. I mean they'd feel that way about other women," he adds quickly, lest Sienna get the impression that he would be willing to share her. "The guys I know are successful and smart, but they've spent too much time focusing on their careers. They need an experienced, sophisticated woman to teach them about life in the outside world."

What I love about Bill—oh, let me count the things I love about Bill at this moment. That he thinks this is a viable idea and he seems to have figured out how to make it work. That after knowing my best friend for all of forty-eight hours he guilelessly used the L word that it sometimes takes months and a crowbar—to wrench out of a guy. And that for a seemingly meat-and-potatoes American dude, his tastes are delightfully European—he appreciates an older woman and all she has to offer. As luck would have it, Sienna's phone beeps and she reaches expectantly for her BlackBerry—the same BlackBerry that used to chirp with news scoops and dinner invitations and that since her firing seems to have gone silent. Except to deliver bad news.

"My broker, he leaves a message every time the market goes down another hundred points. Which is about once an hour. I'm worried that he won't be able to afford his phone bill," Sienna says wryly. "Not to mention how I'm going to pay mine."

"The company will pay for your phone, your Con Ed bill, your cab rides, and those silly little luxuries you've gotten used to, like food," Bill says, seizing the opening to reassure Sienna that our plan offers financial security. "I think we could be highly successful. If everything goes according to my estimates, you should be able to rebuild your nest egg and buy that apartment of yours within the next couple of years."

"And it would be fun. You've said yourself how now that you're out of work you don't know what to do with yourself,"

I add, knowing that more than anything, Sienna likes to be going one hundred miles a minute.

Sienna looks at me, and then Bill, and then back at me. Optimistically, Bill crosses his arms in front of him and reaches for each of our hands in a Three Musketeers–like handshake, a move that no one but our Bill, as I now think of my new business partner, could get away with.

"Oh hell. It's not like I have anything better on the horizon. My TV career's in the toilet, the rent's due, the whole world's on the brink of financial disaster, and the way the two of you make it sound, this is practically my feminist duty. Count me in," Sienna says gamely. "What do we have to lose?"

✧✧✧✧✧

ON THE WAY home I stop at Chelsea Market to buy lobsters, double-baked potatoes, *haricot verts,* and a bottle of sparkling cider to celebrate. It's the same meal that Peter and I ate when he got his first big promotion and when I found out—after years of waiting—that I was pregnant with the girls. Fueled by the flush of yet unachieved but as far as I'm concerned inevitable success, I spring for chocolate truffles and two pounds of ripe red cherries.

I hop in a cab and despite the fact that it's rush hour, I enjoy a charmed trip uptown—if there are potholes, we fly over them, and miraculously we make every light. My timing today is impeccable. The driver is hooked up to a friend at the other end of his telephone headset—a driving hazard to be sure, but less deadly than the old days, when, starved for conversation, they insisted on sharing everything from rants about the mayor to raves for Dr. Laura.

Terrance offers to carry my packages upstairs, but I tell him it's not necessary.

"It's good exercise," I say, hoisting the heavy bags effortlessly in the air as if they're filled with sunshine.

I put my groceries down beside the antique umbrella stand outside the apartment and dig around my pocket for my key. Unnecessarily, because Molly hears me and yanks my arm inside.

"Mom, you have to see this, Dad's making dinner," she says, pulling me into the kitchen where Peter—who doesn't know a blender from a box of macaroni—is dumping a bag of precut lettuce into a big wooden salad bowl. There's a collection of pots on the stove and from the corner of my eye, I spy a pouch of ninety-second Minute Rice. It takes thirty seconds longer to make, but you can put it in the microwave.

"Hm, honey, smells good in here," I say reflexively, though after a moment I realize that there aren't actually any food aromas—good or bad—wafting around the room.

Peter winks and points to a package of frozen lasagna. "Nothing like a home-cooked meal."

"It's the thought that counts." I reach into the refrigerator, open a jar, and playfully swipe a fingerful of mustard onto his pristine chef's apron. "A touch of authenticity."

Peter grins and whirls me around, pulling me closer for a kiss.

"What's all this about?" I say, feeling a flush of relief and excitement to see Peter happy after weeks of moping around. "Don't tell me you saw Halle Berry today on *The View*?"

"Better," he says, running his hand caressingly down my hip.

Paige comes into the kitchen and rolls her eyes. "Oh, please, would you two just cut it out? Don't you know that PDAs can scar your children for life?" Then she filches a carrot from the salad and twirls it in the air. "Daddy got a job," she says as matter-of-factly as if she were announcing the train schedule.

"Yes, Daddy got a job!" sings Molly, wrapping her arms around Peter and giving him a congratulatory hug.

"Tell Mom who he's working for, why don't you?" says Paige slyly.

"Yes, tell me everything, I want to know all the details."

"It all happened so quickly," Peter says, searching for the right words. "I hardly know where to begin."

"Oh I'd start with the gorgeous single woman," Paige says. "You know, Mom, that woman Tiffany who moved into 3A?"

"Tiffany, Tiffany Glass? The woman in the skintight mini-dress whose moving truck almost flattened me like a pancake?" I ask with a start. "She just moved in! How did you two get to know each other well enough for her to even borrow a cup of sugar?"

"Actually it was detergent, she needed a cup of detergent." Peter laughs nervously. "I met her in the basement and she asked me to show her how to use the washing machine. We got to talking and she invited me up to her apartment for a cup of coffee. She said we seemed simpatico."

"I told you not to let Daddy do the laundry," Paige mutters.

"What will you be doing for this Tiffany Glass?" I ask as equably as I can.

"Tiffany has a line of makeup that's been selling well in Seattle and she wants to expand the business. I'd be head of New York operations. The job doesn't come with the kind of paycheck I'm used to, but there's huge growth potential."

"Her makeup's called BUBB," says Molly, encouragingly. " 'Be U But Better,' cute, right? I read about it in *Teen Vogue*."

"And she hired you because?"

"She doesn't do animal testing and she needs your two beautiful teenage daughters and your middle-aged wife to be her guinea pigs!" Paige says sarcastically, since it's obvious to all of us that Peter knows as much about makeup as he does about heating up dinner. Which is apparently nothing, since I smell the lasagna burning. I fling open the oven door and Peter steps in front of me to seize the remains of the ruined frozen casserole. As he slaps the pan on the top of the Viking range he yells "Oh shit!" and sucks on the tip of his now-burned finger.

"I need this job," Peter says tightly. "It doesn't matter if I'm selling stocks or makeup or widgets, whatever the hell widgets are. I'm a successful businessman with—up until a few months ago—a stellar track record."

I open the kitchen cabinet stocked with Advil, Band-Aids, and other emergency medical supplies (including four cans of chicken soup) and take out a tube of aloe vera to rub across Peter's hand. Being unemployed has been quite a blow to Peter's ego. Getting this job could be just what we all need to restore some equanimity around here.

"The last few months weren't your fault. This is great news; I'm sure you'll do a terrific job," I say, putting aside my suspicions about Tiffany. Just because she's a beautiful woman is no reason to think this isn't a bona fide offer. Or that she zeroed in on Peter because he's the most attractive man in the building.

"I think it's a terrific opportunity," says Peter, with an excitement in his voice I haven't heard in a long time. "I've already started mapping out strategies and working on financial projections. Tiffany's taking care of the back-due mortgage and maintenance on the co-op as an advance against my salary. My earnings will be barely enough to live on for the next year or so, but I think this cosmetic thing could really be big and at least you won't have to go to work. I know you'd rather be home with the girls. And from the looks of it," he says, laughing, tossing the lasagna remains into the garbage, "we need you back."

"It's nice to be back," I say hesitantly. Just a few hours ago I knew the thrill of being charged up with plans of my own. Still, Peter doesn't know that, and I don't want to eclipse his news. Besides, he's right, it will be good to get back to some semblance of normalcy. Peter kisses my cheek and goes into the den to TiVo the Mets game while the girls set the table. I open up the refrigerator, defrost four small steaks in the microwave, and dither between making green beans and broccoli. I take out the chopping board and, going for broke, mindlessly dice all of the vegetables, every last carrot, cauliflower, and celery stick in the crisper. "It would never have worked," I say to myself as I'm hacking away at a particularly tenacious Brussels sprout. Sienna was right, my plan was crazy. She'll be so relieved when I call in the morning to put the brakes on this thing. Still it was fun to be back in the library; I'll have to go there more often. And maybe I'll call Pamela and Melissa to see what charity events are on the docket. It's always good to be busy. I put the steaks under the broiler and pile the vegetables into the wok—and I do mean pile; they're spilling out all over the place. I tamp them down with a big splash of teriyaki sauce and set the flame on high. Then I sit down at the kitchen table and slip off my shoes. Suddenly I'm very, very tired. It's been a long day and it's still not over, though all I can think about is putting my head down for a few minutes, just a little rest.

Moments later Paige and Molly come running into the kitchen and shake me awake. "Mom, are you okay?" asks Molly, putting on a pair of oven mitts to pull the burning wok off the stove and retrieve the charred steaks.

"You're no better at this than Daddy," says Paige, nabbing a folder of take-out menus from the kitchen drawer. She reaches into her pocket for her cellphone. "I guess I'm the only one in this family who's capable of getting us fed."

We end up eating pizza and it's not until the middle of the

night that I remember the celebratory lobsters, which are still sitting bagged in an ice-filled Styrofoam container outside the front door. I put on a robe, take the elevator downstairs, and hand over all the grocery bags to Terrance. "Enjoy," I say, without even waiting around for a thank-you. It's too late for me to cook the lobsters and, suddenly, anything sparkling, even a bottle of cider, sounds positively exhausting.

Eight

Win, Place, Showdown

WITH NOTHING BETTER TO do the next morning than worry about Peter's new working arrangement with the vampish Tiffany Glass, I threw myself into the task of reorganizing my closet, dragging every skirt, dress, and pair of paisley hip huggers I'd ever owned off their hangers and hurling them into piles of "definites," "maybes," and "what was I thinking?" Then, when I still couldn't bear to part with anything, I wrapped all the clothes I knew I'd never wear this season in tissue paper.

"Ew, that looks like a coffin," Paige said, when she saw the cedar-lined box where I was storing my sartorial treasures.

"You're right, but you never know when fashion is going to rise from the dead."

"Lame, Mom. Can I have some money to go shopping after school with Heather to buy some stuff that I might actually wear?"

"Daddy just got a job last night and already you want to go shopping?"

"With my birthday money, from last year. I still have some left over."

I fanned out a white shirt with wide puffy sleeves. "One day you're going to be *thrilled* that I saved this poet's blouse."

My daughter looked at me pityingly and I reached for my purse.

"Okay, but you have to pay me back from your savings account," I said, handing Paige three twenty-dollar bills. "Let's see what your kids have to say in twenty years about those toe-less boots you're all so crazy about."

"That I'm cool. C-o-o-l." Paige laughed as she thanked me and headed off to school while I went back to my thankless sorting. By the time I was fingering a stash of fashion mistakes with the tags I'd never even cut off and the slinky size-4 Badgley Mischka gown that I'd never be able to wear again (at least not sitting down), I was grateful to get a call inviting me out to lunch. Even if it was from Naomi.

"Can you and Sienna meet me at noon?" she asked and I readily agreed. It's always easier to see my mother with my best friend in tow. And afterward, I could tell Sienna that I was putting a kibosh on that harebrained idea to start a call-girl operation.

❧❦❧

THREE HOURS LATER, sitting in a Japanese restaurant, Naomi reaches for a white ceramic cup to take a sip of sake. "I'm considering having my pelvis tightened. What do you think?"

I squirm in my seat and pull a second napkin off the table to cover the first one already in my lap. I may be Jewish but I believe in the Immaculate Conception—I refuse to imagine my mother is actually having sex. But Sienna's intrigued. She props her chin onto her hands and leans in to get the scoop.

"Laser or radio frequency?" asks Sienna, who's clearly on top of the latest breakthroughs in pelvis maintenance.

"Electrostimulation to improve the muscle tone," Naomi says, as I try—unsuccessfully—not to imagine a volt of current running through my mother's vagina.

"You do know about the exercises?" Sienna asks.

"Of course, I'm thinking about hiring a personal trainer." Naomi giggles.

"Ladies," I say, tapping a chopstick against a water glass and trying to get their attention. "I already have my hair straightened, my eyebrows threaded, and I'd let Dr. B inject me with unborn virgin male whale sperm if I thought it would make me look fifteen days younger. But you have to draw the line somewhere. Couldn't you just settle for a nice, old-fashioned bikini wax?"

Naomi's eyes narrow. She spears a piece of sashimi and points it in my direction. "Youthful-looking genitals make a woman feel more confident."

"Mom, if you were any more confident you'd drive Ann Coulter into therapy. Is this because you're sleeping with Dr. Barasch?"

Naomi pushes a piece of yellowtail around her plate and wrinkles her nose. "Well that, and we're having a Miss Subways reunion. I haven't seen any of the girls in twenty years, and if you must know, it's rather intimidating."

For one brief, shining moment nearly half a century ago, Naomi had her picture—with her big brown eyes and her short dark hair pinned and permed into brush-curls—tacked up in every subway car in New York. The picture that held out the promise of a spectacular life and instead led to spectacular disappointment. When I was a kid, I used to wonder what it would have been like to have an average-looking mother, one who hadn't expected her looks to propel her into fame and fortune. One who didn't see me as a poor reflection. But whoever that woman is, she isn't my mom. In Naomi's ledger book the Miss Subways contest was the biggest thing that ever happened to her, and I can imagine why the reunion would make her anxious. Though not why she'd need her pelvis toned to prepare for it.

"Mom, I know you girls were always competitive, but I can't imagine there's going to be a crotch runoff."

"That's true," Naomi concedes, pushing the plate away and pouring herself another cup of sake. "I just can't think of what else there is to fix."

The woman puts on a good face and I would almost believe her. If not for the crack in her voice.

"You're beautiful," Sienna says, patting Naomi's hand.

"I know," she says. "It's just that I haven't done all of the things that I meant to. Some of the girls went on to big modeling careers. One of them became a famous lawyer. Another, she even makes jewelry for Johnny Cash."

"Did, Mom, she *did* make jewelry for Johnny Cash," I say, as if somehow that softens the blow.

"Does, did, the point is, what do I have to show for the years? Winning the contest meant something. I rode the subway every day just to see the expressions on people's faces. One fellow was so excited when he realized I was the girl on the poster that he fell forward and bumped his head." Naomi sighs, as if the herky-jerky movement of the train had nothing to do with the accident. And as if the ability to cause injury is the measure of exceptional beauty. "Sienna's lucky, she has a career. Or at least she did have a career. Tell me, dear, do you think you'll ever work again?"

"As a matter of fact, yes," Sienna says.

I shake my head to caution Sienna not to say another word. Even if she sticks to the cover story about the temp agency, my mother will be all over me with unwanted advice. And besides, now it's just not true. I can't wait to hear Sienna's sigh of relief when I tell her we're ditching the project. Though right now, the sighs are coming from Naomi—and they're directed toward the dishy waiter.

"Thank you, thank you very, very much. You're very kind," Naomi says to the waiter as if he were giving her a blood transfusion and not merely clearing the table. That's my mother, feeling down one minute, pulling herself up the next.

"You're very welcome. And may I say, ma'am, how flattering that red suit is?"

And may I say how smart the waiter is? He's just earned himself a 30 percent tip.

Naomi stands up and smiles flirtatiously. "I'm heading off to my Bikram yoga class, it's 105 degrees in there and ooh, it leaves you soooo flexible." The waiter winks and as Naomi heads toward the door, he pours us two cups of tea.

"Your friend's a pistol," he says, mistaking my mother, as people so often do, for my contemporary.

"That she is, a pistol. Just make sure you're not on the other side of her trigger finger."

Sienna laughs. "My mother won't even discuss dental floss."

"*Pleeze.* Can we just get through the rest of the conversation without talking any more about my mother's privates?"

"Privates? Is that what you call them?"

"Yes. And I still say 'number one' and 'number two,' in case you're interested."

"Very," says Sienna. "You're going to make a very provocative madam. More like the proprietor of a Chinese restaurant. 'Get a thirty-seven for the guy in the black suit.' 'Fifty-two for the man with the tan.' 'Bald fellow wants a forty-nine.' "

"Sixty-nine." I laugh. "I think it's the sixty-nine that's so popular." I blow on the edge of my cup of tea and take a sip. "That's actually what I wanted to talk to you about. . . ."

"I know, me too. Look at this," Sienna says, reaching into her bag to show me what she's reading on her Kindle.

"Fanny Hill?" I'm surprised to see that Sienna, whose passion is current events, is reading a bawdy piece of historical fiction that was written almost 250 years ago.

"Fanny Hill," Sienna says, taking back the Kindle and running her finger down the screen. "The story of a poor country girl who takes a succession of lovers to survive . . . and 'has a rollicking good time!' I'm doing my homework, just like you. Last night I stayed up watching *Pretty Woman*. And I put *Mighty Aphrodite, Irma la Douce, Klute, Belle de Jour* and *Never on Sunday* into my Netflix queue. Who knew there were so many movies about working girls?"

"Well, not *Working Girl*, I mean, *Working Girl*'s not about a working girl, it's about Melanie Griffith pretending to be her boss so she can climb up the corporate ladder. But Melanie Griffith did play a working girl in *Milk Money*. Which was weird. But not as weird as *A Stranger Among Us*, when she played a cop who goes undercover as a Hasidic Jew."

"Melanie Griffith as a Hasidic Jew?" Sienna hoots, stopped in her tracks by my encyclopedic knowledge of movie trivia. "Next you're going to tell me that she had her boobs done halfway through the filming of *The Bonfire of the Vanities* . . ."

". . . and if you compare the first to the last half of the film it looks like someone attacked ol' Melanie's chest with an inflatable tire pump!"

Sienna laughs. "We go back a long way. I'm glad you convinced me to do this, we're going to have so much fun! Why don't you come over tonight and we'll have a minimarathon? Popcorn's on me."

I take a gulp of water and play with a napkin, mindlessly

folding it into the same pyramid as the linen at the Global
Warming banquet. Some night, that banquet—hard to remember that there was a time, not that long ago, when my
biggest worry was the shape of a piece of fabric. Still, I didn't
expect Sienna to be so gung-ho about the new venture. And
now I feel guilty about backing out.

"Good news," I say, avoiding eye contact. "We're not going
to have to start the business after all. Peter's got a job."

Sienna's whole body visibly stiffens as she takes a moment
to digest my news. Then she rubs her hands together, pressing
her palms in front of her face like a nun who's about to pray—
or a prosecutor on *Law & Order,* ready to move in for the kill.
"I see," she says somberly. "Peter's got a job so you don't need
to work anymore. Or you think you don't need to work anymore. Well, bully for you."

"I'm sorry, I didn't mean," I mumble, flustered. "It was a
crazy idea. You're such a sweetheart to have gone along with it
just for me. But now, well, I can go back to looking after the
girls and I know you're going to find a job of your own. Really
soon."

"That's very supportive. In fact half the newsrooms in New
York have been decimated, so no, I don't think I'll be getting a
job anytime in the near future. Maybe not ever."

"What about your severance?" I say guiltily, thinking how I
blithely let Sienna pay for our Botox.

"If you mean that golden parachute I was supposed to get
when the station fired me, it never opened. Didn't get a cent. I
only told you that because I knew you wouldn't go see Dr. B.
any other way and I thought you needed a pick-me-up. That's
what friends do, support each other."

"I do support you," I say sheepishly. "I just don't see now
how we can go ahead with the business."

"Because Peter's working?"

"Yes, he's part of a new start-up. He won't make much at first but he says there's real potential. And I think he needs to feel like the head of the family again. He's been an absolute beast since he lost his job."

Sienna taps her finger on the table impatiently. "Didn't you hear what Naomi was saying about missed opportunities? Don't you ever feel like you need something of your own? When you talked about starting the business you were as excited as I've heard you in years."

"Oh, I was just being crazy," I say, downplaying the rush of adrenaline I'd felt, now willing to take a backseat to my husband's plans. "Besides, Peter's starting something new, too. It would be like we were in competition."

"Not if you don't tell him."

"But I promised, Peter and I promised we weren't going to keep any more secrets," I say, thinking about how I accepted a Pop-Tart instead of a proper apology, but that I gave my word. "Besides, I couldn't start this company now even if I wanted to. My first responsibility is to take care of my family. The girls need me," I try to explain. "Do you remember when Woody Allen was suing for custody of his son and the judge asked him to name the boy's teachers?"

"He couldn't come up with even one name."

"And neither could Peter." "There must be one with an 'A,' right?" he'd said with a laugh when I tested him.

"So you'll leave him a list," Sienna says. "You'll leave lots of lists. Girl Scout's honor, we'll work out your schedule so you're home every day when the twins come back from school."

On the days they come back after school, I think. Between Paige's soccer practice and endless after-school dates and Molly's commitment to the school paper and saving the world, sometimes I barely catch sight of them before they go to bed.

"They're getting so big now, they have lives all their own." I sigh. "The whole point is to raise happy, independent children, but then one day you turn around and you have happy, independent children—children who want to go to the new Kate Hudson movie with their friends instead of you."

"Say the word and we can start watching movies tonight. Even Kate Hudson movies—though not the Matthew McConaughey ones, okay? I like a bare chest as much as the next woman, but does that man not own even one shirt?"

I shift in my seat and line up the chopsticks so they're perfectly parallel. "Okay," I say slowly, trying to convince myself that I'm making the right choice. "I'll do it."

"You will?" Sienna flings her arms around me so enthusiastically that she nearly knocks over my teacup. "What changed your mind?"

"The girls are aging me out of a job. In a few years they'll be going away to college," I say, stabbing a chopstick at the tablecloth to emphasize my point. Sienna puts her hand over mine to get me to stop before I poke a hole though the linen. "And?" she asks, knowing me well enough to realize that there's something else on my mind.

"Oh, nothing, it's just silly," I say. "When you said that about the Girl Scouts I thought about their motto, 'Be prepared.' For just the tiniest moment I thought about what would happen if Peter up and left me, too. I mean he never would . . ."

"No, he wouldn't," Sienna says staunchly.

"But what if he did?" I bite my lip, sorry to have said such a terrible thing out loud. "Anyway, as much as I've loved being an M&M it doesn't seem like a viable job option in today's economy."

Sienna looks at me encouragingly. "And . . ."

"Let's go for it!" I say, lightly slapping my hand on the table. "Any thoughts about what to name the company?" Before I have a chance to change my mind, Sienna fishes out her BlackBerry, logs on to her electronic Memo Pad, and starts typing in ideas. I doodle with a pen on the back of our lunch check.

"Bill said he liked older women. How about the Cougar Club?" she asks.

"No, we don't want to give anyone even a hint of what we're up to," I say cautiously.

"SPTN?" she says, combining our initials into what sounds like a new sports franchise. "Tru, Truce, SeeTru, SeeThrough, Newman-Post?"

"Or 'Post-Newman.' " I laugh, waving my hand through the air like a banner. "The next generation of great salad dressings."

We bounce ideas back and forth for several minutes, until Sienna comes up with the solution.

"I've got it!" she says, "The Veronica Agency! And you and Bill and I will be the only ones who know that it's named after our late great sixteenth-century sister, Veronica Franco, the inimitable poet and courtesan."

"The Veronica Agency. That's great!" I agree enthusiastically— throwing caution to the wind when it comes to tempting the fates. Not to mention the risky undertaking of going into the world's oldest profession.

❧❦❧

NOW THAT WE'RE really going into business I have a million things to do. My closet organization might be going to go to hell, I think merrily, as I walk up Madison Avenue with a buoyancy I haven't felt in weeks. Although I'm still careful to look down at the pavement. Can you imagine Naomi ending up with a broken back because *my* high heels slipped on a crack?

I stride past a bistro where a few jeans-and-suede-clad M&Ms are lingering after long lunches and the collegiate grouping of luxury shops that are each recognizable by a single name—Giorgio, Donna, Oscar, and Hermès—though these days, the stores are appreciably less crowded and I notice too that the line for the hotdog vendor on the corner of Sixty-fourth Street is unusually long. Once the business gets going, I'll be back, I think, stopping to see what's new at Missoni, and as I catch my reflection in the window, I reach for my cell-phone. I've been telling myself that my dark roots are hip, like Sarah Jessica Parker's in the third season of *Sex and the City.* But my stripey mane reminds me more of a raccoon with a bad dye job than the spunky star. I'm just speed-dialing Angela Cosmai to see if the city's most fabulous colorist can possibly squeeze me in, when I spot Molly walking toward me. And she's not alone.

My older, wiser, studious daughter, the daughter I count on to be reasonable, reliable, and uncomplicated, is walking down the street, holding hands with a young man—a young man with chiseled good looks framed by spiky blond hair, wearing khakis and a navy blue blazer and looking as if he just stepped out of an episode of *Gossip Girl.* Molly's ditched her owlish black glasses and pulled out her elastic band to let her dark locks cascade over her shoulders. As Molly tilts her head toward the teenage Adonis, a goofy smile spreads over her face. What is it about the first, ethereal stages of ro-mance that could turn even Condoleezza Rice into a grinning idiot? I call out a cheery "Hello!"

Molly looks furtively at me, shakes her head almost imper-ceptivity, and continues walking.

"Who was that?" I hear the young man ask as they brush past me and I recognize the emblem on the boy's blazer, identifying him as a student at Molly's school.

"Don't know, just some woman," says Molly, looking over her shoulder, raising her palm in a signal that tells me not to say another word. I watch as the boy takes Molly's backpack and loops his muscular arm through hers. Molly laughs and buries her head in his shoulder. "Thanks for the cheeseburger," I hear her say as they slip around the corner. "I'm having the most fun ever, Brandon."

❧

LATER THAT NIGHT Paige is in her bedroom working on a history term paper when I hear Molly's key turn in the door. I've been waiting for her to get home all evening, and she comes into the kitchen full of excitement and excuses.

"I'm sorry, Mom, I know it was dumb not to say hi, I was just so embarrassed to, you know, introduce my date to my mother," she says, grinning as she slides her backpack off her shoulder—the very same backpack that just a few hours ago had been held by the golden-haired Brandon. The very same Brandon—I now know from checking the school directory the minute I got home—whom her sister has a crush on.

I don't know if Molly knows that Paige likes this boy or if Paige knows that Molly had a date with him, and I have to figure out a way to make each of them aware of what's going on without hurting their feelings or turning it into an Olympic-sized competition. Not so easy when you're dealing with twins who've been scrutinized and sized-up against each other since the day they were born.

We've always told the girls, "Celebrate your uniqueness!" But how could you not make comparisons? When Paige started walking at ten months, it was nearly impossible not to push Molly to try to follow in her footsteps. Molly was only a year old when she started speaking in full sentences, which made us worry about why Paige was still babbling. And while Molly has the budding-but-undeveloped poise and beauty of Anne Hathaway in the opening scenes of *The Princess Diaries* or *The Devil Wears Prada,* Paige was born as sleek and confident as a blond version of the actress in act two.

Molly's always been shier and more hesitant in social situations, more likely to watch from the sidelines than her outgoing twin. So despite my resolve to be as neutral as Switzerland, I'm secretly rooting for her. As long as this Brandon Marsh isn't playing my two girls against each other.

"A date, huh?" I ask as nonchalantly as possible, rinsing off some plates and stacking them in the dishwasher.

"Mom, you never do this right," Molly says affectionately, coming over to make sure that the bowls and salad plates are on the top of the machine and that the larger plates are properly spaced and facing each other on the bottom.

"So this boy . . ."

"Oh Mom, we had so much fun! We went for chocolate shakes and cheeseburgers at Jackson Hole and when the bill came I offered to split it but he said, 'Here, let me get that,' so I did, even though I said, 'Okay, but next time I'll pay,' and then we walked through the park and he carried my backpack and I know I should have introduced you. I'm sorry, it was just so weird to run into you and I wanted to seem cool, though next time I promise I'll say hello. And oh yeah—" she laughs as she interrupts sorting through the silverware look up and flash a radiant smile "—his name is Brandon Marsh."

"That's sounds great, honey, hmm, Brandon Marsh," I repeat carefully, as if I'm trying to place a vaguely familiar name. "Isn't that the boy who's in Paige's science class?"

A small shadow crosses Molly's face and she turns her back

toward me to plunge a group of forks into the wire dishwasher basket, tines down. Some might argue that placed in that direction the forks could nest, running the risk of their not coming out clean, but in our family, we're more concerned about nobody getting stabbed to death when they're unloaded.

"So what if Brandon is in Paige's science class?" Molly asks. "For once a boy likes me!"

"A boy likes you, what boy like you?" asks Paige, sauntering into the kitchen with one earplug dangling out of her iPod, obviously having heard only the last part of Molly's declaration.

Molly and I lock eyes.

"Brandon Marsh likes me and we went on a date today and had cheeseburgers," Molly says with a brazenness I haven't heard in her voice before. Whether from inexperience or exuberance or a desperate attempt to mark dibs on this Marsh man, she puts Paige, who needs no provocation, on the offensive.

"Big deal," Paige says, toying with the twist top on a package of English muffins. She opens the cellophane wrapping, fingers all of the muffins in the package so that no one else will want to eat them, and then reties the bag and puts it back in the bread basket. "So Brandon bought you a cheeseburger. Woo, woo, headline, let's call the *New York Times*. Brandon buys sodas and French fries and salads and anything else they want for girls seven days a week. He's a serial snack dater," she says dismissively. "But Brandon and I have something deeper and more meaningful. He studies with me. We have an intellectual connection."

At the thought of Brandon and Paige entering the Intel science contest—or even leaning on each other to get a C-plus—Molly lets out a whoop.

"I see," she says, barely able to suppress a giggle. I would have thought Molly would shrink from competing with her sister, not to mention the news—news to me anyway—that this Brandon is a player. But far from it, she's holding her ground. "You're just jealous that a boy likes me and not you," she says, pitching the last knife into the dishwasher with just a little too much verve.

"Jealous? Of you? I don't think so. By the way, if you're interested I heard about a new dandruff shampoo," Paige says, walking by her twin and brushing some imaginary flakes off Molly's sweater.

Molly swats away her sister's hand and makes a show of sniffing. "And I heard about a new deodorant."

"Girls, stop it, I won't have you two fighting over some ridiculous boy."

"He's not ridiculous," Molly snaps.

"And we're not fighting. Fighting would mean that there's a match of wills, a worthy opponent. You two think I'm the family idiot, but I pay more attention in my classes than you give me credit for. No, Molly and I aren't fighting," Paige says airily, plugging her iPod back into her ears as she makes an exit. "When it comes to who'll be Brandon's girlfriend there's no contest."

Nine
❦

Afternoon Delight

A LOT CAN HAPPEN in a week, especially when you're dealing with feuding daughters, a husband who's working with a sexy neighbor, and two business partners who make the Energizer Bunny look like he's on Quaaludes. Not to mention that in preparation for the Miss Subways reunion, my mother had sweet-talked Dr. Barasch into taking bodybuilding classes with her.

"I want to be ripped," Naomi had explained at dinner the night before, describing the demanding weight-lifting regimen she'd signed up for, which would tax a person half her age. And then turning toward her seventy-two-year-old lover, my mother cooed, "Don't you want to be ripped, Gordon?"

Molly broke into a spasm of giggles, spewing a mouthful of water onto the damask tablecloth. "Dr. Barasch in a Speedo?"

"With oil-slicked skin?" Paige laughed under her breath. Then she straightened her back and fixed her stare on Molly. "It's not over," she said darkly.

"Not by a long shot," Molly answered, as the twins settled

back into the stony silence that had descended like a storm cloud ever since they declared war over Brandon.

Ever since that fight my usually Chatty Cathys (who would absolutely *kill* me if they heard me call them that) have barely grunted at each other, except to record their progress in their battle for Brandon, the teenage heartthrob. They seem to have nabbed him for an equal number of lunches—two each— but being his lab partner gives Paige a tactical advantage. The green chalkboard in the kitchen has been turned into a scoreboard, tallying FACE TIME WITH BM. So far Paige's exuberant "15!"—which she decorated with a circle of hearts and arrows—trumps Molly's "9." Not only have the twins been silent, but my motherly advice is falling on deaf ears. Neither wants to hear that no boy is more important than your sister— especially a boy who is toying with at least two girls. Who knows how many others this Clearasil-using Casanova has on the hook?

As for Peter, Naomi's exercise regimen intrigued him. Of course these days he seems to be open to all kinds of new experiences.

Ever since my husband started working with the glamorous Tiffany Glass he's been paying a lot more attention to his appearance—trading in his conservative pinstripes and knotted silk ties for open-necked shirts and slacks cut to flatter a muscular pair of thighs. Thoughtfully, oh so thoughtfully, whipped up by Tiffany's personal tailor.

Peter says he's dressing more fashionably because he's in the beauty business now and clients expect to see him showing a little more pizzazz. A more mistrustful wife might argue that he's showing all the classic signs of a married man who's infatuated with someone other than his wife—a new wardrobe, an interest in shaping up, and a genial demeanor that borders on the unseemly. Last night Peter actually seemed to be enjoying

Naomi's company, which can only mean that his endorphin level is off the charts. But after my flash of insecurity the other day about him leaving, I made a decision—a very grown-up decision, I might add—not to let my imagination run wild. Tiffany isn't a threat unless I let her be. And I plan to keep telling myself that and telling myself that and telling myself that until I genuinely believe it.

Still, for a man who used to feel naked in anything but a three-piece suit, last night Peter sounded suspiciously ready to start stripping down and slathering on the bronzer.

"Bodybuilding . . . sounds like something I might like to try," Peter said, eschewing the chicken marsala on his plate to dig into a butterless serving of broccoli. "Did you know that before Arnold Schwarzenegger was the governor of California or *The Terminator* he was crowned Mr. Universe?" he asked the twins.

"The whatenator?" asked Paige, who was talking again, at least to us.

"*The Terminator,*" Peter said with an exaggerated sigh. "Can somebody tell me why we send you girls to that expensive private school?"

"What do you think about the bodybuilding classes, Tru?" my mother asked in an attempt to bring the focus of the conversation back to her.

"I guess that tightening your abs is more reasonable than tightening your pelvis. But it seems like an awful lot of effort to go through to get ready for a gathering of ex–beauty queens. Whatever makes you happy, Mom," I said, and as the words left my mouth, I realized they sounded condescending.

"Happy? It's not a matter of happy," Naomi snapped. "It's a matter of pride." And then, as I reached for a second helping of mashed potatoes she added, "I guess you wouldn't understand."

But Naomi's wrong. I *do* understand. I'm feeling very proud these days, although never in a million years would I tell my mother why.

Once we decided to go ahead with our plans to open the Veronica Agency, things moved quickly. The one (and probably only) good thing about the stock market crash is that it made it easy to find an office space at a rock-bottom rent—even if our requirements were unusual. Most new businesses are looking for a flashy building with a doorman, but given the nature of our work (and its illegality), we wanted an anonymous building with no one stationed in the lobby who might track the comings and goings of our employees or clients. As promised, Bill picked up the tab for all our initial expenses; if his projections are right, the agency should be able to pay him back in less than two months. We brought in desks from home and scored a Ligne Roset couch for half price at a showroom sale, and Sienna loaned us a deep burgundy and black Barnett Newman lithograph and a bust of Mozart to give the outer office a sophisticated air. The espresso machine was a splurge, but a good cup of coffee can be crucial to office morale. Even if for now "the office" is just the three of us.

Next we divvied up the workload. Bill will be vetting clients and overseeing the budget. I'm in charge of anything that has to do with our employees. And since everyone recognizes Sienna from TV—and we need to keep our identities anonymous—my famous friend will handle the company's paperwork and make bank deposits. It took Verizon an extra two days from when they promised for us to get our phone and computer lines, but even that seems like a minor miracle in New York, a city known for its speedy pace except, ironically, when it comes to installing the Internet. Then at the end of last week, we took the step that's going to turn our fantasy business into a reality, placing a discreet ad in the back of the *Village Voice:*

> The Veronica Agency seeks attractive, articulate,
> well-educated women over 40 for part-time work.
> Knowledge of sports and finance helpful
> but not a necessity.

We've already had more than a hundred responses.

I settle into the ergonomically correct chair that my two partners insisted we spring for. When I'd objected to the price, Bill had argued that the right chair keeps your neck muscles from getting all tense. And when Sienna added that it was a boon to your posture—that we'd look leaner in these chairs than if we were hunched over in some run-of-the-mill seat—I was sold. I'm just about to start calling job applicants, when I realize that I don't know what to say. I don't want to give away too much on the phone, but I don't want a bunch of gals who are expecting to work in the library of a nunnery to show up for interviews, either.

Bill combs his fingers through his hair, which is no longer plagued by unruly tufts. I don't know if, as some people say, love can help ward off the common cold, but it certainly seems to have tamed Bill's cowlick.

"Tell them we're looking for escorts," Bill says, standing over Sienna and giving her shoulders an affectionate squeeze. "Charming, lovely, well-dressed women who would enjoy going out on the town with an attractive man."

❧❧❧

FRANKLY, GIVEN THE job description, I'm surprised that half the female members of eHarmony didn't show up. Three days after we started screening applicants and having them email in their pictures, our office is crammed with possible candidates.

I look around the room. The thirty-five folding chairs we borrowed from the superintendant won't be enough, I think, as I see all shapes and sorts of women—tall women, short women, women with button noses and women with prominent cheekbones—scrambling for a place to sit. They pop Altoids, pull out pots of gloss and bullets of berry red lipsticks to freshen their color, and try to figure out what to do with their coats—some fold them onto their laps and others sling them over the backs of chairs. A redhead in the first row slips her arms out of a faux-rabbit jacket, crumples it up, and shoves the furry ball under her seat. As it nudges the woman behind her, the second woman lets out a bloodcurdling shriek.

"It's a rat, it's a rat!" she screams, running from the room.

"Works every time," the redhead mutters, and as her prospective employer, I try to decide if her cunning is a pro or a con.

Bill summons the meeting to order and turns the floor over to me. Sienna's working from home today and to be on the safe side, we're even using aliases. Because we're the Veronica Agency, Bill and Sienna have dubbed themselves Archie and Veronica, after the comic books. They've suggested that I could be Betty, the steadfast, less glamorous friend. But after years of being stuck with Truman, I'm picking my own name, thank you very much.

I stride to the front of the room. "Good afternoon, ladies, thank you for coming," I say in the same poised voice I've used dozens of times to chair charity-event committees. "Let me introduce myself: I'm Anna Bovary."

I admit it was an unusual choice. But can I help it if my two favorite heroines just happen to be Anna Karenina and Madame Bovary?

A lanky woman with an alligator purse in the front row puts her hand to her mouth to stifle a chuckle. But the literary reference seems to have eluded the rest of my audience, who pepper me with questions about what the job pays, how many women we'll be hiring. And oh yes, what exactly it is they'll be doing.

I've rehearsed this part for days.

"We're a very exclusive escort agency," I say, gazing out steadily at the sea of faces. "We're looking for a few special women to match up with our clients. Successful businessmen who spend too much time at the office and need some help relaxing."

"Relaxing, is that code for jerking them off?" a busty blonde bluntly asks as half a dozen women hurriedly excuse themselves from the room.

"Can you tell me how to get to Al-Anon? Or any 12-step program?" asks a brunette, nearly tripping over her feet.

"*Yo no hables ingles,*" mutters a woman who I swear is Irish-looking.

"That's perfectly all right," says Bill, smoothly. "That's why we're here today, to see which of you ladies is a good match for us and vice versa. We expect that our clients will want to get to know our employees more intimately, although you never have to stay with a man if you don't want to. But I know all of the men personally and I think you'll enjoy their company. The pay is excellent and we're hoping to help you develop long-term relationships, not one-time dates."

"Anna," a voice rings out from the back of the room and it takes me a moment to realize she's addressing me. "I'm a little confused. The ad said that you're looking for women over forty? I thought that these kinds of jobs went to younger women."

"We're looking for women of character and experience," says Bill. "Our clientele are the kind of men who appreciate a fine wine. . . ."

"My ex-husband always said I had a fine whine," cracks the faux-fur-wearing fireball, who introduces herself as Lucy.

"And mine said no one would ever want me," a fine-featured woman in the back, named Rochelle, says quietly.

"You'll show him!" Lucy says, encouragingly. "Forget about that jerk. The idiot's your *was*-band."

"Do we have to sleep with the men?" someone calls out.

"Hell, do we *get* to sleep with the men?" Patricia, the woman with the alligator purse asks, eliciting another round of generous laughs.

One by one, we ask each woman to step into the back office for a private interview. Bill and I answer their questions, and we rate each applicant for PAL—personality, attitude, and looks.

We eliminate one with a strong *New Yawk* accent, and another who asks if she can get an advance on her salary "to have my tits done." I don't think it's a good idea to give an employee money she hasn't earned yet. Or—unless we're going after a different type of clientele—to hire an escort who's going to spend a month on the job in bandages. One potentially promising candidate has red runny eyes, which she admits is a permanent condition. "Can you believe it? I used drops every day for about a year, and now I'm having a rebound effect—no matter what I do, I can't get my eyes to look normal. Who'd have guessed?" she says mournfully, putting on her coat and thanking us for our time. "You can kick heroin, but you can't kick Visine."

By the end of the afternoon, we've hired ten attractive, well-educated women I'm looking forward to getting to know better—like the lanky Patricia, an out-of-work money manager with a master's degree from the Wharton business school, and Rochelle, the recent divorcée whose husband dubbed her undesirable, but who in fact is an avid Knicks fan with a thirty-six-C chest. And we hire the rabbit-jacket-wearing Lucy, too. She seems like a team player and I admire her moxie.

As our new employees file out the front door, Bill apologizes for having to rush off to a meeting with another client. Until we're operating in the black he's keeping his day job. "Great start," he says. "I can't wait to tell Sienna all about it tonight."

"Give her a hug for me, will you? And tell her I'm really sorry she couldn't be here today. Working with the woman is going to be half the fun."

"I know, but you can't be too careful. Besides, she's in charge of keeping all our clients' records—their contact information, credit card numbers, hobbies, allergies, likes and dislikes—and she'll track what our escorts are paid. There'll be plenty for Sienna to do."

"That's true, but Sienna's not one to take a backseat in anything," I say, thinking how my best friend has spent a lifetime in the spotlight, and wondering how she's going to adjust to being behind the scenes.

Bill laughs and tells me not to worry. "Everything's under control," he says, planting a light kiss on my cheek and heading out the door. "Don't borrow trouble."

⁂

BACK AT THE apartment, things seem to be under control, too—Tiffany Glass's control. While their new office space and warehouse are being renovated, Tiffany and Peter have set up headquarters in our apartment. Just when I'd started to enjoy the peaceful ambience of our eBay-induced, clutter-free living room, Tiffany's boxes, brochures, and hundreds of pots of BUBB face cream have transformed my home into a mini-storage.

"Where is everybody?" I ask, surprised to see a wildly extravagant orchid on the Georgian table in the entrance hall and following peals of laughter across the apartment into my bedroom. There's a crack of light coming through the slightly opened door of the master bathroom—the master bathroom that's been out of commission for weeks.

"Tru, you're home, I didn't expect you back for a couple of hours," Peter says uneasily, as I swing open the door and survey the scene. The broken tile floor has been artfully restored, the Carrara marble tub that the workmen had refused to install is now magically in place and Tiffany Glass—in all her gilt-blond glory—is, infuriatingly, sitting in front of my vanity, admiring her own reflection.

"Surprise!" she says, standing up and clapping her hands. "When I came in to use the bathroom and I saw that you didn't have a tub in the master bath, I just had to have it fixed *right away!* I couldn't have Peter living that way. Or you either," Tiffany adds, almost an afterthought. "No, no, no, no, *no!*"

Tiffany has the unbridled enthusiasm of a kindergartner gifting a painted Popsicle-stick picture frame, although her present is much less welcome.

"How sweet," I say, pursing my lips. What was Tiffany doing in the master bathroom in the first place when she could have just used the one in the hall? And why the heck didn't she stop playing around in my bathroom after she'd swapped out the tubs? I'm irritated to see that Tiffany's replaced my discreet round magnifying mirror with a curved three-foot-long wall fixture that makes every crow's-foot and wrinkle look deeper than the San Andreas Fault. "And what happened to my Roman shades?" I wail, walking over to the once elegant window that is now draped with a red Swiss dot fabric and an upholstered cornice with comic-book-sized stars.

"I know, don't you love it?" Tiffany exclaims, coming over and playfully twirling a piece of the diaphanous fabric. "It's

Tilly and Milly. They did Tori Spelling's nursery! It was quite a coup to get them to do an adult's bathroom, but for me— well, let's just say that I helped one of them clear up a certain acne problem though I'll *never* say which one. No, no, no, no, *no*! But they owe me! And you do *not* have to thank me. The look on your face is gratification enough."

I swivel around to catch my stern, tight-lipped reflection in the CinemaScope-sized mirror. Either Tiffany is totally clueless and thinks I actually do appreciate her unwelcome bathroom overhaul, or she's playing blond-bombshell-dumb to steamroll her way into getting what she wants— which I'd be a fool not to see includes my dimpled, blue-eyed husband. Either way she's a formidable adversary. But only if I let her be, I think to myself, remembering my pledge not to be thrown by Tiffany's tactics.

"That was very kind." I walk over to put my arm proprietarily around Peter's shoulder. "And I guess I should thank you for the beautiful orchid in the entryway, too?"

"Actually that was my contribution," says Peter, beaming, relieved that I'm not upset by the renovation—or the invasion of my personal space by his bodacious blond boss.

"Yes, Peter's always very thoughtful," says Tiffany, coming over and chucking my husband under the chin.

"Yes, he is!" I tighten my grip on Peter's shoulder and press a kiss on his cheek. Tiffany counters by taking Peter's hand. I move my fingers sinuously down his body and let my fingers dance across his bum. Tiffany eyes me and considers her next move. I know we're in the bathroom, but I'm praying we don't get to the point where one of us has to lift our leg to leave our scent.

Tiffany, it turns out, has a better move up her sleeve. Make that Manolo mule.

"Oh dear me, I slipped," she says, pretending to have

gotten her heel caught on the new tile and falling backward toward Peter—who wriggles out of my embrace to catch her.

Tiffany wraps her arm around Peter's neck and leans tightly into his body, as if her tiny waist and his broad chest were matching pieces of a jigsaw puzzle.

"My hero!" she cries, and my husband actually blushes.

"Oh no, no, no, no, *no!*" Peter echoes Tiffany's trademark protest as both of them giggle.

For a moment, I'm frozen, unsure of what to do.

I could knock Tiffany over the head with a pot of her BUBB face cream and see if she can actually stand on her own. (Like *that's* in question.) Or I could kick her in one of her well-turned shins and hobble her for real. Instead, I clear my throat and edge a shoulder between them. "Here," I say, clapping my arm on Tiffany's and steering her toward the door. "Let's get you back to your apartment and off your feet."

"I'll take her," says Peter gallantly, and although I agree to let him help, I insist on coming along.

Inside her apartment, Tiffany makes a show of limping to a hot pink chenille daybed. Once she realizes I'm not leaving without Peter, she tells us not to worry. "Go home to your family." She sighs theatrically. "I'll be fine here all by myself. I'm used to being on my own. Even if my ankle is sprained— or possibly fractured."

"Okay, well bye, take care," I say, wheeling Peter around. And then stupidly, I add, "Anything you need, just let me know." Damn my Hebrew School training! Fifty-two times a year for seven years I was told that the Torah commands us to help our neighbors—not to mention that it forbids murdering them.

"Well, now that I think of it, Tru, I could use just a teeny-weeny bit of ice. And maybe a couple of magazines. And oh yes, there's a fuzzy-wuzzy blanket on the top of my closet that would make me feel ever so comfy."

"That's okay, I'll get them," says Peter, who unlike the doggedly oblivious Tiffany can read the expression on my face and knows that I'm losing my patience.

Moments later Peter returns with Tiffany's essentials. I slap the ice bag unceremoniously on her foot, wrap the blanket Egyptian-mummy-tight around her body so that she can barely move, and prop up a copy *US Weekly* on her chest, two inches away from her nose. Tiffany perfunctorily thanks me for my help. But of course she doesn't miss a chance to gush over Peter.

"If you hadn't caught me I don't know *what* I would have done!" she oozes.

" 'Twern't nothin', ma'am," Peter says with a bow. Then he promises to call and check in on her later.

We leave the apartment and silently walk toward the elevator. My mouth is clenched and my arms are hanging stiffly by my sides. Peter smiles and reaches out to take my hand.

"I know, I know, I know," my husband says with a chuckle. "You don't have to say it, Tiffany *is* a little bit over the top. You hated the bathroom, didn't you?"

"Uh-huh," I say, as we step inside the cab and I punch the "penthouse" button. "And that thing with her foot, it wasn't a very original move."

"Tiffany can be a little flirtatious," Peter says, in a masterpiece of understatement. Next he's going to tell me that Henry VIII has commitment issues.

I cock an eyebrow.

"Okay, Tiffany's very flirtatious. But that's just the way she is. And despite her looks, she's a surprisingly good businesswoman."

"Maybe it's because of her looks," I say petulantly.

Peter looks into my eyes and cups his hand underneath my chin. "You know you don't have to worry about me, right, honey? I'm yours, all yours. Although I was pretty turned on when the two of you started fighting over me."

Fighting? Over him? Before I get a chance to act all innocent and tell Peter that I don't have any idea what he's talking about—or that I'd wrestle Tiffany to the ground before I let her come between us—Peter gets a mischievous twinkle in his eye. He throws his jacket over the security camera and hits the stop button on the control panel. Within seconds, the elevator comes to a bumpy halt.

"What?" I ask as Peter presses me against the back wall of the elevator and kisses me hard, impeding my ability to speak—or even think.

"Good thing the co-op board never installed that new elevator they were arguing over," Peter says, brushing his lips against mine. "The one that has all sorts of alarm buttons." Then he pulls my sweater over my head and hungrily reaches for my breasts.

Ten

♣

A Change of Heart

LIKE A COUPLE OF preteens with their first tampon, Sienna and I are sitting cross-legged on the zebra-print rug in her living room, trying to figure out how to use the Lumigan she's scored from her eye doctor.

"Why didn't you just get him to give you a prescription for Latisse?" I ask, twisting the bottle's rubber-top stopper and wondering why Sienna didn't buy the beauty-strength version of the new eyelash-enhancing drug instead of the glaucoma medicine from which it's derived.

"It's not going on sale until December. Besides, we're on budgets now, remember?" Sienna says, batting her lashes, which look entirely lush to me. "The glaucoma medicine sells for half the price."

"Interesting. The American consumer is only willing to pay so much to stave off blindness, but the sky's the limit for longer, thicker, mascaraless lashes?"

"And this is a surprise?" Sienna laughs.

"What would be a surprise is if this actually works." Sienna turns to her laptop and Googles for instructions. Bill passes through the living room with a cup of coffee and the *Wall Street Journal* and bends down to give Sienna a kiss.

"See you at two o'clock, Tru?" Bill asks, confirming our shopping expedition with the Veronica Agency's new hires to pick out work clothes. Then he plunks his coffee mug down—without a coaster—on Sienna's prized triangular glass Noguchi coffee table and makes his way toward the door.

Since Bill's been with Sienna he looks happy and relaxed and I'd swear, he's even standing taller. As for Sienna, she's radiant, and why not? Good sex is better for your skin than even the priciest carrot-and-sesame body buff. More impressively, she seems completely unfazed that the perfect order and symmetry of her living room has been upset by the intrusion of this errant coffee mug—or this man.

"Looks like it's going well," I say, reaching across the zebra area rug to rap my fist on the blond wood floor. Sienna shrugs.

"We'll see. My longest intimate relationship to date is with the woman who gives me my colonics." Sienna scoops up the mug and I follow her into the kitchen where she busies herself piloting a foamy cloth across a spotless counter. "I will tell you one thing about Bill, though," Sienna says, wringing the wipe with both hands as soap drips onto the counter and a big smile spreads across her face. "We're having terrific sex."

"Me too!" I've been waiting all morning for an opening to describe my hot elevator tryst with the man I've been married to for more than twenty years. "Peter was thrusting inside me. The back of the elevator cab started shaking and I was scared to death the whole time that the wires on the cab might break loose or that the elevator would open and someone would catch us!" I feel my face flush and I cover my mouth with my hands. "It was great."

"Elevator sex? You and Peter? Like in *Fatal Attraction*?"

"Well, it was deliciously illicit but I'm not going to end up boiling a bunny." I smile.

"Maybe just a simple sauté? I thought that kind of thing only happened to us single gals. Doesn't the marriage license come with a clause about trading passion for security? It doesn't seem quite fair that you should get them both."

"I know, I mean, it just came out of nowhere, I can't imagine what got into Peter." Although one particular explanation has been haunting my thoughts all night. "You don't think Tiffany was the foreplay, do you?" I ask anxiously.

"What? Of course not," says Sienna, slamming down the sponge.

"Well, Tiffany couldn't keep her hands off Peter and Peter certainly looked like he was enjoying the attention. And my husband and that woman spend hours every day alone, holed up together in our apartment until the girls get home from school."

"So what? You're the one Peter . . . Well, what *would* be the word here? Plundered? Ravished?"

"*Schtupped* is what Naomi would say. But really, do you think Peter's passion for me was all about his wanting Tiffany?"

"Of course not," Sienna says loyally, because even if she believed otherwise, what else could she say? "You're sexy and beautiful and desirable and your husband lustily *schtupped* you in an elevator. The other thing? That silly Tiffany girl? Forget about it. Why borrow trouble?"

Sienna's right: There's nothing to be gained in my fantasizing about Peter fantasizing about Tiffany. Though I'd still like to know how Tiffany Glass came to be in my private bathroom, the one that's attached to my private bedroom, in the first place. Still, at the moment another, more pleasurable picture is forming in my mind—Sienna and Bill making a cozy home together. Because whether or not she realizes it, something pretty seismic is happening to my best friend.

"Just before, when you said, 'Why borrow trouble?' You know Bill says that, too," I hoot. "Better watch it, Ms. I'm-Never-Going-to-Get-Married Post. That man's getting to you in more ways than you know."

❧

IT WAS PATRICIA, our ex–money manager, who suggested that we bypass Madison Avenue and hunt for lingerie bargains on the Lower East Side. My parents used to take me there every Sunday when I was a kid, but as I emerge from the subway to meet Bill and our new employees for our shopping expedition, I see that a second wave of immigrants—the hip and trendy—have arrived. Brand-new balconied apartments jostle turn-of-the-century tenement buildings. Cute little designer shops and cool-looking after-hours clubs have sprouted up along the area's narrow streets, like dandelions poking through cement. My walk down Orchard Street turns into a stroll down memory lane as I pass a store where I used to buy penny candy that now sells forty-dollar candles, and just a few doors down from Russ & Daughters (where my father always went for "the best" sturgeon), I spot the Landmark Sunshine Cinema, so chic that they have red-carpet premieres. Still I'm glad to see that Patricia's lingerie shop is one of the last of the old-fashioned hosiery stores, the kind I remember shopping in with Naomi.

As our little group crowds into the store, a man who identifies himself as Morris rises up from behind a wooden counter. Morris is wearing a once-white shirt that's now yellow with age, baggy suspenders, and a yarmulke—he's about as sexy as a Geo Metro. But he knows his underwear. And his clients.

Morris takes our measure and matches each of us with the perfect "bit."

Patricia snags a dark blue underwire number with a ribbon bow. For Rochelle, Morris selects a bustier with crisscross straps and Swarovski crystals dotted across the cups.

"A good piece of lingerie, it brings so much happiness," Morris sighs, as Rochelle returns from the dressing room, grinning.

"Maybe you could suggest something for me?" a willowy blonde named Georgy, steps forward to ask. "I was wondering, do you have that pantyhose that eats cellulite?"

"No, but I have a bridge I could sell you." Morris laughs. "Sweetheart, a dimple here or there, who cares? It's women who worry about the cellulite, not the men. You wear the black bra and panties with the semi-sheer baby doll that grazes the thigh, I promise, no man will be able to resist."

I finger a delicate crushed-silk camisole. I'd promised myself that after the benefit I was going to buy some pretty lingerie, but so much happened that I never got around to it. Still, now that Peter and I are having elevator sex—and Tiffany Glass is hovering—I'm going to do my best to make it worth my husband's while to want to take off my clothes. And a sexy nightgown puts me more in the mood, too. A luscious satin teddy makes you feel like hitting on your hubby. Not like those sweatpants and T-shirts I've gotten into the habit of wearing, that are better suited to attacking the bathroom with a scrub brush.

Morris wraps up our purchases and Bill puts the charges on his credit card. "You can pay me back after you start working," he reassures the women. "No rush." At $1500 an hour our employees will be earning more than some top runway models and, according to Bill's research, clients enjoy watching their escorts undress. "Most of the guys I know saw their first naked woman in *Playboy,* just like I did, wearing fishnet stockings or some kind of frilly panties," Bill says nostalgically. Then he picks out a gorgeous embroidered bra for Sienna and a lacy peekaboo corselet.

"That was so much better than when I went shopping for my first bra," I say with a laugh once we're outside the store. "This saleslady screamed out in a big loud voice like she was announcing a lottery winner, 'Thirty double-A, do they even make a double-A?' I think my chest shrank another three inches along with my confidence."

"Honey"—Lucy grins—"that's nothing. Just imagine being a twenty-eight double-A—even my brother had bigger nipples."

Bill peels off from our group. Either we're starting to embarrass him or he really has to get back to his law office. The rest of us—heartburn be damned—are on our way to Katz's Delicatessen, the restaurant where Meg Ryan had her fake orgasm in *When Harry Met Sally.* Bill Clinton has eaten there, too—though after his quadruple bypass surgery, the management removed his picture from the wall. But as we stroll past an innocent-looking awning, Patricia suggests a shopping detour before lunch.

"Toys in Babeland? I used to have so much fun shopping for the girls when they were little," I say wistfully as Patricia pushes open the door.

"Tru, sweetie, these aren't the kind of toys a mother buys you," Patricia says, picking up a very large, very purple acrylic dildo. I blush, and she hands me a slightly smaller, less flashy pale-pink-colored model.

If you didn't look closely you really might mistake the brightly lit store filled with open shelves of colorful toys for FAO Schwarz. A gamine student fingers a clitoral massage toy tagged BETTER THAN CHOCOLATE. A grandmotherly type in Crocs asks for "a vibrating penis ring, the rechargeable kind—we don't want to be running out of batteries at a critical moment," she says with a wink. If I didn't know better I'd think that grandmother was shopping for a head, er, of lettuce.

Georgy picks up a strand of blue pop-it beads and starts to fasten it around her neck. Lucy comes over to explain that the graduated rings of plastic are worn lower down and inserted inside the body. "*Ick,* I think I know what you're talking about, but I don't want to think about it," Georgy says, dropping the beads like a hot potato.

Patricia recommends that everyone buy the Rocket Balm cream. "It makes your John's penis more sensitive. He'll have the orgasm of his life, which means you'll get a bigger tip." But I'm more intrigued by a toy that has the esteemed Good Housekeeping Seal of Approval.

"I love the Naughtibod!" says a young saleswoman who sees me eyeing the vibrator. "You can plug it into an iPod or a CD player and it pulses to the music. I like to do it to the 'William Tell Overture.' "

I laugh. "Hm, music to accompany a vibrator? How about 'My Boyfriend's Back'?"

I hem and haw for a few minutes, but when the salesgirl assures me that she'll pack my purchases in a plain brown paper bag, I take the Naughtibod and a tin of Rocket Balm along with the sexy teddy. This certainly isn't the Lower East Side that my parents used to take me to. Then again, I'm not the same girl that my parents used to take to the Lower East Side.

❧❦❧

"POSTURE," I SCOLD good-naturedly as I walk into the office and find Sienna sitting at her Knoll desk, hunched down in her ergonomically correct chair. I toss the brown bag filled with my exotic new lingerie and toys on top of my own perfectly serviceable IKEA workstation, kick off my shoes, and pad barefoot to the kitchen, which Sienna was supposed to have stocked with drinks and nibbles. I open and close the refrigerator door. "No Fresca—or anything?" I ask as a quick check reveals that the cupboards, too, are bare.

"I didn't have time to get to the supermarket," she says with an edge of defiance.

"That's okay, I've probably had enough to eat today," I babble, still exhilarated from the afternoon's fun. "After we went to Katz's we found this adorable little pastry shop. Lucy, remember, she's the beautiful gal I told you about with the rabbit jacket . . . ?"

"That must have been nice," Sienna says, cutting me off. "I spent the day fielding phone calls, returning the folding chairs to the super, and trying to make sense of this bloody accounting system. How did I ever get saddled with that job? I don't even balance my own checkbook." She snatches my paper shopping bag and pulls out the musical vibrator. "But I'm glad to see your afternoon was so productive."

"Bill bought something for you too. Two somethings. They're really beautiful, he's going to surprise you with them tonight," I say, standing over Sienna's chair and this time running my hand soothingly across her back. "Tough day?"

"I guess." She shrugs. Sienna nudges a small pile of papers toward the edge of the desk with the eraser on her pencil until they topple onto the floor. Then she sighs, and we both bend over to pick them up.

"Sorry. I'm used to being in the newsroom, stories breaking, people running in and out all day long. It's a little weird to suddenly be on the sidelines. I think I'm probably just going through reinvention pains."

"Hey, switching your career, opening a new business, and

falling in love with a guy for the first time in umpteen years has got to get your heart rate pumping."

"Falling in love? Who said anything about falling in love?" Sienna asks stubbornly. And then, she can't help it, the corners of her mouth turn up into a little grin. "Let's just call it 'like,' okay? That way when it's over I won't feel so bad."

"Okay, 'love,' 'like,' I'm not going to say anything to spook you. Though I think our Bill is a keeper. But to tell you the truth, I'm feeling a little overanxious these days myself. I mean, so much is changing. Peter's working with that ridiculous Tiffany Glass person and she spends so much time at our apartment that I'm thinking of charging her rent. Of course, she's paying our mortgage, which may be why she's acting like she owns the place."

"Don't worry, her office renovation has to be finished sometime. Even the Taj Mahal only took twenty years to build. Besides, you're going to be able to pay your way all on your own soon. We start working with customers in just a few days."

"I know, I've been thinking about that." My voice drops to a whisper. "I don't want to send any negative thoughts out into the universe. But do you ever worry that something could, you know, go wrong? Like somebody finds out what kind of business the Veronica Agency really is and we end up going to jail?"

Sienna shakes her head. "No, Bill's very careful. He knows all of the clients personally."

"Well, let's just make sure that no one gives out our phone number to Charlie Sheen. Or Eliot Spitzer."

"Agreed. Although come to think of it, maybe you wouldn't mind giving out your own number to your husband? I had two calls from him today wondering where the heck you were. He said it was important. Don't tell me you forgot to charge your cellphone again?"

"Damn." I reach into my bag to retrieve my red Nokia, which is in fact dead. Sienna laughs at my predictable disregard of all things electronic and hands me her BlackBerry, which is never more than half an inch away from her fingertips.

As I punch in Peter's number, I'm already thinking up excuses for where I've been all day. I'd like to be able to say that I categorically hate lying to my husband, that it's bad and that I'm going to stop doing it soon. But my whole world has always revolved around Peter and the girls, and having a "secret life"—a life in which I'm a businesswoman with plans of my own and where no one knows me as "Peter's wife" or "Paige and Molly's mother"—is turning out to be surprisingly satisfying. Besides, how much do I really know about what Peter's up to these days? How much did I ever know? My husband was out of work for three whole months and I didn't have a clue. Maybe that's why I'm keeping this from Peter now, to get back at him and prove that he's not the only one who can have a double life. Besides, I'm not actually lying to him about having a business. . . . If my husband comes right out and asks, "Tru, are you running an escort agency?" I've promised myself that I will absolutely, positively say yes. But until then, or until I'm ready, there are some things that I'd just rather not talk about.

Peter picks up on the second ring and before he has a chance to say a word, I'm blathering an explanation.

"Sorry I was out of touch, I forgot to charge my cellphone again, it's a good thing my brain doesn't have to be plugged in, or my head would constantly be beeping like one of those smoke detectors whose batteries are wearing down. Anyway," I say, trying to keep the rest of the story simple, so I don't get caught in some trap of my own making, "I'm with Sienna now. I was shopping, I got—"

Peter gives up waiting for an opening and plunges into the reason for his call.

"Tru," he says, "I'm at Mount Sinai. You've got to get over here right away. Naomi had a heart attack."

❧❦❧

"HEART ATTACK, MOTHER," I repeat numbly as Sienna and I practically knock over a woman with two young children to elbow our way into a taxi. "Emergency," Sienna says, and the cabbie puts his pedal to the metal to get us to the hospital stat.

Having watched every hospital TV show from *Doogie Howser* to *House*, I thought I knew what the inside of an emergency room looked like—but I was wrong. Instead of the fast-paced drama that it takes to keep viewers glued to their TVs, in real life an air of torpid resignation hovers over the hospital waiting area, and there's not a George Clooney or a Hugh Laurie in sight. Vacant-eyed patients are slumped down in thinly padded metal chairs that are bolted in place to the floor. (Not that anyone seems even remotely as if they'd have the energy, never mind the inclination, to steal one.) Children are wheezing, people are clutching their heads and stomachs, and there are enough runny noses to make Kleenex seem like, if anything can be these days, a good investment.

I'm the only person on line to talk to the nurse at the information desk, but she refuses to look up from her paperwork. "It's an emergency. Naomi, F-I-N-K-L-E . . ." I start spelling my mother's name after having said it—and gotten no response—twice.

"Yes ma'am, they're all emergencies, that's why this is the *emergency* room," she says curtly, still declining to make eye contact and talking to her desk full of reports.

I'm just about to threaten to call the head nurse, the head of the hospital, or the head of CNN when Paige and Molly come rushing over. And with them is Brandon Marsh.

"Mrs. Newman, your mother's all right," says Brandon. His take-charge tone is meant to be calming, but frankly, coming from Brandon, I can't help but hear an edge of imperiousness.

Molly leans in and gives me a kiss. "She's okay, Mommy, really. The doctor says Naomi's heart attack was mild, more like a warning." Paige gives my hand a little tug and the three of them guide me and Sienna through a short maze of corridors so I can see for myself.

My mother, God bless her—and he or she obviously has— is lying on a narrow cot. She's hooked up to an IV, and draped over her ears is a thin plastic blue oxygen tube that leads to a prong fastened around her nostrils and a series of saucerlike electrodes wired from her chest to a bleeping EKG machine. Naomi looks like a weird science experiment, albeit one with a good manicure. She lifts her head slightly and motions us toward her bedside—where she's already holding court with Peter, Dr. Barasch, and Tiffany Glass.

"The Dalai Lama couldn't make it." Naomi smiles weakly, straining to speak above a whisper. "But all of my other loved ones did. They came like lemmings."

"Not lemmings, dear," Dr. Barasch says nervously. "Family."

"Lemmings, family, everyone came. Except you, Tru. You are a little late," Naomi says reproachfully.

"She's here now," says Peter, taking my hand and placing it in Naomi's.

I'm not sure when Tiffany or Brandon became "family." But it's no time to quibble about bloodlines. Naomi looks exhausted. Her naturally high color is washed out and I'm not used to seeing my mother, who's usually a whir of motion, lying quietly in a bed. But she's lucid (not to mention complaining), and I can tell by everyone's face and the tone in the room that she's going to be all right. Still, I feel my eyes well up with tears.

"Mom, what happened? Are you sure you're okay?" Peter steps behind me and anchors his hands on my shoulders.

"We were at the bodybuilding class," Dr. Barasch says, and then, overcome with tears himself, he pauses to wipe his eyes.

"Your mother was bench pressing," says Tiffany, "*symmetrical* bench pressing, right, Naomi? So one side of your body doesn't look more developed than the other."

"Yes, biceps," Naomi murmurs, as she makes a fist with her left hand to show us her muscle.

"Naomi got a little chest pain, then it got bigger. She was having trouble catching her breath. I called 911," says Dr. Barasch. "In the ambulance, they put that little nitroglycerin pill under her tongue."

"She's had aspirin and a beta blocker and the doctor says that according to her EKG, there was no significant heart damage," Brandon reports as efficiently as any bright-eyed TV intern. Any moment, I expect him to grow a stethoscope.

Molly comes over and strokes Naomi's brow. "That's good news, Grandma."

Naomi had been drifting off to sleep, but suddenly her eyes are wide open. "What did you call me?"

" '*Glam-ma,*' Molly called you 'Glam-ma,' " says Brandon, barely missing a beat and making an impressive save. "Like Goldie Hawn. Only prettier." He's standing squarely between Paige and Molly and he reaches over to take each of their hands.

"Prettier than Goldie Hawn, I can live with that." Naomi

smiles, turning toward her granddaughters. "This Brandon, I like him." Then, provocatively, she adds, "Which one of you two is going to be his girlfriend?"

That's my mother—you can slow down her heart but you can't stop her tongue. I suppose I should find it reassuring that even a brush with mortality can't tame Naomi's pot-stirring ways. But frankly, nothing at the moment feels reassuring.

A stern nurse comes in to check Naomi's monitors and chases us out of the room. "This is a heart attack, people, not a party. I don't know who in the blazes let all of you in, but you have to get out of here, now! We're keeping Mrs. Finklestein overnight for observation, and if everything goes the way it's supposed to, you can pick her up after morning rounds. That is, *one* of you can pick her up." I tentatively raise my hand. "Come back tomorrow. You better plan on having your mother stay with you at least for several days."

We say our goodbyes and troop out of the room. As she's leaving, Tiffany, who was with Peter when he got the phone call and insisted on driving him to the hospital, tells Naomi she'll visit her at our apartment later in the week. "I'm there all the time, anyway. I'll bring all my samples and we'll give you a complete makeover."

As we make our way back down the corridor, the enormity of everything catches up with me and I feel the blood rushing to my head. I stop to lean against the wall and start sobbing uncontrollably. Sienna and Peter rush over to comfort me.

"Your mother's a tough old bird, she's going to be fine, sweetie," says Sienna, rubbing my arm.

"Sienna's right," says Peter. My husband must be the last man in America to still carry a hankie. He pulls a linen square out of his inside coat pocket and reaches over to gently dab my swollen eyes. "Naomi's indomitable. By next week she'll be back in weight-lifting class, bench pressing seventy pounds."

"I know, I just never imagined, I mean, it's true, Naomi's going to come out of this better than new. She'll probably convince the cardiologist to get her health insurance to pay for a tummy tuck," I say, trying to be brave.

After a few moments I pull myself together and turn around to look for Dr. Barasch. He loves Naomi. He was with her when this happened. I can only begin to imagine how horrible today's been for him, too. I see him standing by himself off in a corner, and I go over and give him a hug.

"I'm sorry, it must have been so scary. How can I ever thank you?" I say wrapping my arms around him. "I'm just so grateful that you were with her."

"Good job, Dr. Barasch," Brandon says, perhaps the only eighth grader on the planet confident—or cocky—enough to plant a hearty slap on his headmaster's back.

Dr. Barasch's shoulders are hunched, and his normally imposing frame seems crumpled, as if his bones have collapsed, made weary by the weight of the world. He pulls away from my embrace, covers his face with his hands, and starts to cry.

"The Chinese say that if you save someone's life you have to take care of them forever." Dr. Barasch stuffs his hands in his suit jacket pockets and looks down at his shoes. "I can't, I can't do it, I watched my wife." Then he stumbles down the corridor, and makes his way toward the brightly lit red EXIT sign. "Tell Naomi I'm sorry. I can't go through it again."

Eleven

❦

Death and Sex

NOT EVEN JAY LENO can put me to sleep. I flip through ten minutes of a *Frasier* rerun and wonder at a commercial for an incontinence pill featuring a group of guys in a rowboat who all need to pee. (You're on a boat, guys, why can't you just take a piss in the lake?) Peter, as usual, is so deep in Slumberland that he doesn't notice that I've been thrashing around our queen-sized bed like a lightning bug caught in a jelly jar, or that, in an attempt to get some company for my misery, I've "accidentally" jabbed him in the rib cage several times. At about two A.M. I resign myself to a sleepless night. I give Peter a peck on the cheek, pull on my robe, and shuffle toward the kitchen. Not that I could eat anything. But I can't keep lying in bed worrying about Naomi's heart, which in less than twenty-four hours—and I can't even imagine how I'm going to find the words to tell her about Dr. Barasch—has taken a double hit.

I nab a box of tea bags from the pantry and see Molly sitting at our round oak kitchen table, mechanically turning the pages of some fashion magazine without actually looking at them. She raises her arms toward me and I lean in for a cuddle.

"Why do things like this happen, Mom?" Molly asks glumly. I look down at her magazine, which happens to be open to a page of "Fashion Don'ts." But I know that Molly's question is about Naomi and not a badly chosen pair of sequined culottes.

"I don't know, honey, maybe it's sort of a warning."

"You mean that Grandma has to take better care of herself?" Before I can answer, Molly shakes her head. "I mean look at her, she does everything right. Who takes better care of herself than Naomi? She exercises, she doesn't eat garbage, if she can get sick . . ." Molly says, and her voice trails off.

". . . then Daddy and I could, too?"

"Something like that, I guess."

I brush away a curly lock of hair from in front of Molly's eyes. "Daddy and I are going to live for a very long, long time. Long enough to watch you girls graduate college and get married and to spoil our grandchildren."

Molly gives me a sideways look and scrunches her mouth. "Mom, you can't know, you can't know you're going to get to do any of those things. How can any of us know anything?"

I pull Molly closer. When the girls were little they were convinced that I possessed a sort of telepathic magical Mommy Power that told me when they'd misbehaved in nursery school and, more important, guaranteed their safety when we were apart. But my babies aren't babies anymore. Now they realize that I'm a mere mortal who can't see into the future and doesn't even have eyes in the back of her head. But I hope they know, too, that I'd throw myself under a bus to protect them. And I'll always do my best to try to calm their fears.

"You're right, sweetheart, you can't *know.* None of us can

know anything, that's part of what makes life so mysterious—and wonderful, and so scary sometimes. But you can play the odds. And the odds for me and Daddy, and for Grandma, are very good. In a weird sort of way what happened today was a good thing. Now that Naomi knows her heart is vulnerable she can take two aspirin every day and make sure she always carries a nitroglycerin pill. Daddy and I protect ourselves, too. I go for checkups, I take my vitamins. And I promise to never ever leave the house in a white velour Baby Phat tracksuit—which means I'll never die of embarrassment."

"Oh Mom, you're such a dork." Molly grins. She picks up the box of tea bags, walks over to the stove, and fills the kettle with water.

"I want to take care of myself, too, Mom. I'm going to get serious about trying out for the swim team. You always say that I spend too much time inside studying. Besides, it'll look good on my college application. And I've made another decision," Molly says thoughtfully. "I'm going to stop competing with Paige for that stupid Brandon Marsh. Yech, did you hear him today, calling Naomi 'Glam-ma'? He's such a phony, holding both of our hands. Paige can have him. I don't want any boy who isn't sure that he wants me."

"Good for you. That's a pretty grown-up decision," I say, thinking that I have forty-year-old friends who don't have as much sense about men.

The kettle whistles and Molly carefully pours water into each of our mugs. Then she leaves the tea bags to steep and walks over to the chalkboard.

"Brandon is bad news," she says, pointing to the collection of hearts, arrows, numbers, and exclamation points surrounding Brandon's name, cluttering the board. "I deserve a boy who's mine, not somebody like Brandon or Dr. Barasch, who'll leave when the going gets tough. I want to find a guy like Daddy, a guy who'll be there for me the way Daddy was there today for you, Mom." And just like that Molly takes one last look at the chalkboard, lifts the eraser, and wipes the slate clean.

ॐ

I WAS TERRIFIED that when I gave Naomi the news about Dr. Barasch she'd have another heart attack. Instead, she's eerily calm. "That's the way the cookie crumbles," she says indifferently.

"Mom, I'm sorry. It sounds like he went through a long illness with his wife."

Naomi shoots me a withering glance.

"Not that you're ill, Mom, I mean, it sounds like he's scared."

"Scared, who isn't scared?" Naomi straightens herself up and smoothes her right hand against her head. "But just in case you were planning on throwing one, I would *not* appreciate a pity party. The one thing I want in the whole entire world right now is just to get the hell out of the hospital." It's only when I realize that my mother's left hand is balled up into a fist and that she's dug her fingernails into her palm that I know for sure that Naomi understands what I've just said. Dr. Barasch isn't coming to pick her up at the hospital. Dr. Barasch won't be visiting her later at our apartment. Dr. Barasch, Naomi's salsa-dancing, weight-lifting, up-until-now totally adoring boyfriend, is never coming back.

The discharge nurse comes in with some release papers for Naomi to sign and insists that my mother can't leave the hospital unless she's in a wheelchair. "Policy," the nurse says humorlessly, crossing her arms in front of her chest.

"Fine." Naomi sighs. She climbs onto the cold metal seat and primly settles her purse onto her lap. "Let's get a move on, I'm a busy woman."

Back at the apartment, Peter and Tiffany are waiting for us with a tray of fruit, fat-free crackers, and four tall glasses garnished with lemon slices.

As Tiffany walks across the room to welcome her, Naomi shackles my arm. "Does she live here now?" my mother hisses under her breath as she tightens her grip. "Tiffany's much too pretty, you shouldn't let her live here."

"Oh no, no, no, no, no, I have my own apartment," says Tiffany, who's overheard. "But thank you for saying I'm pretty." Then Tiffany turns toward me. "I'm sorry to be camped out in your living room, Tru. But you do realize that it was because the contractor had to work on *your* bathroom that he got just a teeny-weeny bit behind on our office and our warehouse space?"

"It won't be long, honey," Peter says. "The construction manager says that both the new places are coming along nicely. And when did a construction manager ever fib about a schedule?" Peter sighs. Then he turns to Naomi. "We're glad to have you here, Mom. We hope you'll stay as long as you want."

"That's right," I say, and I mean it. I was scared out of my mind when I thought something had happened to Naomi. She might not have been Mother of the Year, but she's the only one I've got. And maybe this will be a chance to repair our relationship, for each of us to appreciate what's good about the other, instead of always finding fault.

Naomi sinks into the couch, takes off her shoes and curls her feet under her tush. For a sixty-eight-year-old woman, never mind a sixty-eight-year-old woman who's just had a heart attack, she's amazingly agile. "What, suddenly I was in the hospital for a few hours and everyone calls me 'Mom'?" she bristles.

"Sorry, Naomi," says Peter.

"And I'm sorry about Dr. Barasch," says Tiffany, leaning in to give Naomi's arm a pat.

Naomi pushes Tiffany's hand away and stares straight out into space as if she didn't hear her lover's name. Then slowly, she turns around to face the three of us.

"We shall never speak of that, do you understand me?" she says coolly. "That man is dead to me!" Then she reaches across the table for one of the frosty glasses. "This better be gin and tonic, not lemonade," she says, taking a generous gulp.

❧❀❧

THE NEXT THREE days passed in a blur. Naomi's bravado lasted about as long as a Wall Street stock rally. Between her crying jags and feedings, my mother needed more attention than a newborn baby. She burst into tears without any warning and had an insatiable appetite. "Bring me something yellow or white," she'd say, meaning scrambled eggs, mashed potatoes, a pint of ice cream, or any of the other typical comfort foods that spurned lovers crave. For one whole day she ate nothing but pasta.

And then there were her attempts to plan her own funeral. Apparently these days, it's not enough to own your own luxury condo—the ante's been upped on where you spend eternity.

"I'd like a mausoleum, with a chandelier," Naomi said yesterday, out of the blue. "Something modest, maybe twelve hundred square feet."

I was tempted to ask her about real estate—dollar for dollar, can you get a better price in heaven or hell? But I saved my smartass remarks on the subject for Sienna. Naomi was in no mood to be teased, not about dying or real estate or the computer chip tributes that she hoped we'd all record to go along with the pictures and voice-over she was planning on installing in her new crypt. And why should she be? Naomi's heart attack was no laughing matter. It's terrifying to see my usual bulldog of a mother acting like a wounded pup. I haven't been out of Naomi's sight for more than ten minutes. I've been trying to do everything for her that I possibly can. Still, today's the day that the Veronica Agency's employees are hooking up with—I mean *meeting*—their very first clients, and I just have to get to the office.

"It's all right, you can leave," Naomi says listlessly as I set a bowl of oatmeal down between her and the television that she's been staring at blankly for days and explain that I have to go out for a few hours. "Everybody leaves."

"I'm coming back, Mom," I say, and when she doesn't object to me not calling her Naomi, I know she's sinking deeper into a funk. The doctor had warned me that after a heart attack, even a small one, people get depressed. As if Dr. Barasch's breaking up with her wasn't reason enough for Naomi to be miserable.

"Mom, aren't you going to tell me not to call you 'Mom'?" I chide.

"Call me 'Mom,' 'Grandma,' 'the Old Lady of Park Avenue.' The heart attack, it was the start of a whole new chapter," Naomi says with a whimper. "What does it matter? What does anything matter?"

I'm way behind schedule, but I can't bear to go. I'm settling on the sofa next to Naomi when, mercifully, the twins traipse into the den. Molly clicks off the TV and nosily unloads an armload of samples onto the table.

"We got them from Tiffany. New lipstick, blush, and an incredible anti-aging cream that she swears will make your skin look twenty years younger," Molly announces perkily.

Paige pulls at her cheekbones. "If my skin looked twenty years younger it would disappear. I'd be minus-six years old."

Naomi picks up the remote and turns the TV back on. "What I wouldn't give to be young again," she says distractedly. "Minus six, that's a good age."

"But Grandm—I mean, Naomi. Then you wouldn't be alive."

Naomi grimaces and pulls the comforter that she's holding on to like a security blanket more tightly around her shoulders. Just a few days ago Naomi didn't want a pity party; now she's the Perle Mesta of depression. I ask Molly to turn on some music.

"Maybe the Rolling Stones. 'You Can't Always Get What You Want' always gets my mojo going. Why don't we play that?" I lift my arms in the air and wiggle my hips as I sing out the lyrics. *"You can't always get what you wa-ant. You can't always get what you wa-ant. But if you try sometimes, you just might find, you get what you ne—"*

Paige comes over and fixes her hands on my hips. "Mom, please. Don't dance. And don't ever say the word 'mojo' ever again, okay?"

Naomi picks up the remote—lifting it seems to have become her main form of exercise—and turns off the flickering screen. "I think I would like to hear some music," she says, uttering the first positive statement that I've heard cross her lips in days.

I flash my smug I-told-you-so look at the girls. "You just have to keep trying," I whisper, trying to teach them that if you work hard enough at something you can go from rags to riches—or drag your Grandma from melancholia toward merriment.

"Why don't you play that Elton John song?" Naomi suggests. " 'Candle in the Wind'? You know, the one they played at Princess Diana's funeral?"

MOLLY PROMISES THAT she and Paige will get Naomi to listen to something uplifting. But as the girls scroll through their playlists, it's harder than they thought to find an appropriate song. After nixing Carrie Underwood singing about slashing the truck tires of the guy who cheated on her and Kelly Clarkson's "Cry" just based on the title, they settle on a medley of peppy tunes from the Jonas Brothers.

Molly hands me my coat and points me toward the door. "Go, Mom. We know you and Sienna are working on some secret project."

"What?" I ask, flustered that she doesn't buy my cover story about doing some grocery shopping and having an emergency facial. "I just need to get out of the house for a little while, I . . ."

"We're not blind, we know something's up," Paige says. "I mean, you're covering your mouth and walking out of the room to talk on the phone all the time and you're not here during the day like you used to be. It took Daddy two hours to even find you when Naomi got sick."

"I know, I'm sorry. . . . My—my cellphone went dead," I stammer, not used to being in the position of explaining to my children where I've been, instead of the other way around.

"We figure it's some sort of business, right? Sienna's out of work, and we need money, so it makes sense. Paige and I think it's great," Molly, my irrepressible optimist says supportively.

Paige shrugs. "Yeah, sure, whatever. But we just can't figure out why you're keeping it a deep dark secret."

"It's just that we want to make sure it works out, not get anyone's hopes up, when it's further along . . ." Then I take a deep breath. "Sienna and I are opening a temporary help agency, but I'd like to keep it just between us right now, okay?

Let's see if anything comes of it before we make a big deal. Does Daddy know?" I wince.

"Nah, Daddy's so involved with Tiffany and BUBB he'd barely notice if we got a new puppy," says Molly, who's been angling for one, slyly.

"No puppy. The last thing we need around here is another mouth to feed or someone else to clean up after!" I say, just a little too sharply. "I'm sorry, honey, I'm just distracted. But you know this isn't a good time to add a new member to the family?"

Molly nods. "But that doesn't mean I can't keep lobbying, right? I just have to pick a better moment."

"Right," I concede. A moment when my mother's not sprawled across the sofa like a bedridden Violetta in *La Traviata*. And my husband's not so involved with his new business and his new boss that, unlike his daughters, he can't see what's going on under his own nose.

Molly tells me to get going, pledging to look after Naomi and hold down the fort.

"I'd stay to help with Grandma, but I'm going out with Brandon," Paige taunts.

"And yay, I'm *not*," Molly counters.

"Yeah, did you hear, Mom? Molly conceded. She knew she'd lose so she dropped out of the race."

"No, I decided that Brandon's no prize. He's not worth competing for. But I could have won if I'd wanted to." And then I think I hear her mutter, "Believe me, I still could win." Although I'm sure I must be wrong. Because wasn't it only three days ago that Molly, the most mature fourteen-year-old on the planet washed her hands of Brandon? Wiped him off her blackboard? Said she didn't want any guy who didn't want her?

"Girls, please, as far as Daddy and I are concerned no one's ever going to be good enough for either of you," I say, giving them each a kiss on the cheek or in Paige's case—because she swivels her head away from my motherly affection—a kiss on the air near her head. As I walk toward the elevator, music is blaring so loudly from Peter's beloved Bose sound system that I can hear it all the way down the hall. It's not the Rolling Stones or the Jonas Brothers, but it's not that drippy Elton John dirge, either. Still, I can't say it's much cheerier.

"*Yesterday*," the usually chipper Paul McCartney drones, "*all my troubles seemed so far away . . .*"

I don't have to guess who picked out the song.

❧❦❧

DESPITE THE MIDTOWN traffic I manage to get to the Veronica Agency's office building in less than twenty minutes. Navigating what should be the last sixty seconds of my trip, however, proves more daunting.

"It's those people on the fourth floor. Their workmen have been holding up the elevator for hours," the super apologizes, telling me it'll be faster to take the stairs. We're only three floors up, but the hallways are filled with construction dust and when I arrive at the agency, the din of jackhammers, drilling, and the whiny annoying sounds of screw guns whirring echo throughout the office.

"At least it's not 'Candle in the Wind,' " I say, pointing toward the ceiling. I pour a cup of coffee and snag one of the Dunkin' Donuts that Lucy has generously brought in to celebrate our opening. I can't help remembering that Sienna quit her job over that very donut company—and Lucy's buying these today of all days, seems like a good omen. We never would have started our business if Sienna hadn't gotten so riled up over product placement and I'm more than happy now to give the company a plug. "Here's to the Veronica Agency and Dunkin' Donuts," I say, passing around the sugary treats.

"To the Veronica Agency and Dunkin' Donuts," our little group sings back in unison, although most of them take a pass on the carbs.

"I'm not having anything at all," says Georgy, the rangy blonde who was searching for cellulite-eating pantyhose. "I'm starving myself to get into this hot little black number for tonight."

"Not too hot, right?" I ask, reminding our employees that we want them to look glamorous, not cheap. "Like Carla Bruni after she married the president of France—not before, when she was dating Mick Jagger."

"That's right. A man who's paying this kind of money for a date wants a woman who looks sophisticated outside the bedroom and sexy inside it," says Bill, pulling up a chair and telling everyone to do the same. "We've tried to think of everything, but let's go through some of the rules again. Why don't we consider this a dry run?"

Lucy, as always, is the first to crack a joke. "A dry run? That's not the kind of thing you want to have happen to a gang of forty-year-old hookers." Bill shoots her a reprimanding look. "I mean courtesans," Lucy says, using our insisted-upon description. "You don't want any *courtesans* having a dry run."

"I stand corrected," Bill chuckles. "So, let's do a run-*through*, okay? You'll meet your dates for dinner, and then a client may invite you back to his apartment or to one of the three hotels around the city in which we've discreetly booked rooms."

"And don't forget to call us. Archie and I want to hear from you," I pipe in, proud at myself for having remembered Bill's alias. "Let us know when the date is over so we can know how it went and how much to charge. And if you need our help anytime during the evening, you can reach us here at the office or on Archie's cellphone."

"I know some of you have done this before and for others, it's your first time," Bill continues. "But there's nothing to be nervous about and if you decide you don't want the evening to go any further, it's your call. If there's something a man wants to do and you don't want to . . ."

". . . like using pop-it beads?" Georgy asks.

"Like using pop-it beads—" I chuckle "—or *anything.* If you feel a client is pressuring you, tell him 'Anna won't let me do that.' And if that doesn't work, say you're sorry this isn't working out between you and that you'll check with Anna to see if the agency can find someone who'd be more to their liking.

"Our clients will be charging your services to their credit cards so you don't have to worry about asking them for money or carrying around large amounts of cash. You'll get a weekly check, based on the number of times you see a client and the services you perform. Blow jobs are a thousand dollars extra."

"And swallowing?" asks Lucy.

"An additional thousand."

"And about four hundred fifty calories." Georgy giggles.

"Bring condoms," I say.

"And your vibrators, and Rocket Balm cream, and your edible panties," says Lucy.

"And we expect you to be good dining companions," I remind them. "I hope everybody has boned up on current events."

"Boned up?" Georgy giggles again.

"Ooh ladies, this is worse than a sixth grade sex-ed class." I laugh.

"I think it's fourth grade sex-ed now," says Patricia, the former money manager. "And by the way, no man, no matter how young he is, wants to think about erectile dysfunction. Which is why when we're talking about current events I want to suggest that nobody bring up the fact that Mexico's answer to a flagging economy is to give away free Viagra."

"At least the out-of-work Mexicans won't have flagging you-know-whats," Lucy wisecracks. "*Mucho* better than the American stimulus package. And while we're talking about packages, don't let your date eat artichokes."

"Right," I agree. "They're messy and hard to pull apart, you don't want a guy to be embarrassed about his eating habits."

Lucy laughs and puts her arm around me. "Anna, honey, I was thinking about *our* eating habits. Artichokes are smelly and funny-tasting, you know, after they've been through a guy's digestive system. . . ."

"I think she means when you're giving them a blow job," Georgy says helpfully. "You know, the taste of the—"

"Well, yes, of course, I just took it for granted that everyone knew *that*," I say, as the girls just giggle.

"And remember," says Patricia. "A man likes to hear that his penis is big."

"What does a woman like to hear?" asks Bill.

"That her hips are small!" Lucy laughs.

On their way out, Bill hands each of the women an assignment sheet with their client's name, where and what time they'll be meeting, and a few pertinent facts.

"My guy likes baseball," says Rochelle, our divorced sports fan, happily. "Yankees or Mets?"

Bill presses a few keys on his Palm Pilot. "The Sox; Gary's from Boston. Is that a problem?"

"No, I'll be diplomatic," Rochelle says, referring to the

long-standing feud between our hometown team and
Boston's. "I can't let politics get in the way of work."

"Good," says Bill. "Any other questions?"

"Yes," says Georgy. "Who's Salman Rushdie and how am I
supposed to dress for a Literacy Partners benefit at the Man-
darin Oriental?"

"Oops," says Bill, taking the slip out of Georgy's hand and
exchanging it with Patricia's. "I gave you each other's assign-
ments. Patricia, you're going to the Literacy Partners benefit
where they're *honoring* Salman Rushdie, with my buddy Matt.
And Georgy, you're going to the Hudson Cafeteria tonight
with Gabe."

"A cafeteria?" Georgy asks, sounding disappointed.

"Don't worry, it's nothing like the Automat. It's a very hip,
happening place. And it's conveniently located in a hotel."

After everyone's sure they've got their dates straight, the
women start to leave and I stop them one last time. I can't believe we're really, truly, finally opening for business. I'm so
nervous that the butterflies in my stomach are the size of
beach balls. And I can't stop playing mother hen to my forty-
something chicks.

"Don't forget—" I begin, welling up with emotion. But before I can finish my sentence, the women of the Veronica
Agency finish it for me.

"We want to hear from you!" They all laugh. Then with
hugs and waves they head out to prepare for the evening.

Twelve

⚘

Restaurant War

I COULD GO HOME too, but I don't want to. I spend several minutes alphabetizing the four sheets of paper on my desk and go over to the refrigerator, which thanks to a few clicks on the computer at the FreshDirect grocery delivery site is now amply stocked. I rearrange containers of soy, organic, and whole milk Greek yogurt in their descending order of fat content.

Bill slings his briefcase onto his shoulder and leans over my desk. "You know this can wait, don't you? Relax, everything's going to be fine. The gals won't be calling in for at least a few hours and I have to get back to my law office to take care of a couple of things."

"You go along. I'm still jazzed up from the meeting. I'm just not ready to go back yet."

"Naomi won't be living in your guest room forever," Bill promises.

"I know. It's just such a relief to be out of the house. For years, when Peter and I had a fight or one of the girls was sick,

I was in absolute awe of the tunnel vision that allowed him to forget about everything and bury himself in his work. During the meeting today I was like that, too, totally focused. I didn't have to think about not thinking about my mother, I just didn't think about her. Of course," I admit, "now that I'm thinking about not thinking about her, I'm back to thinking about her."

Bill laughs and wishes me luck.

"Thanks. And when you see Sienna tonight, don't forget to compliment her on her small hips."

"Will do. Who knew running an escort service was going to be so educational?"

I call home and Molly tells me that Peter's gone out, Paige has left for her date and that she's holed up with Naomi, all by herself.

"It's okay, Mom, Naomi's on 'MyFace.' "

"You mean Facebook?"

"Yes, but she's got it all mixed with MySpace. Isn't that cute?"

"Adorable. Your grandmother's just adorable. I wonder what she's doing on there? Anyway, you sure you don't mind babysitting a little longer?"

"Nah, no problem, I know you're busy. Besides, I want to find out what Naomi's up to."

I go back to riffling through some papers but the constant din of the renovation work going on above us is starting to get on my nerves. I leave a message about the racket on the super's voicemail, but then I decide to go up and talk to the workmen myself. Maybe a polite in-person appeal will get the crew to hammer a little more softly.

I head to the stairwell, but the masonry particles billowing down from the landing makes the ascent seem more like a jour-ney through the Mojave than a quick trip upstairs, not to mention that I can barely see two steps in front of me. Then, somewhere about halfway between the third and fourth floors, I hear a sound that's a lot more menacing than a plaster-dust sandstorm.

"I don't care what we have to pay in overtime, you have to have this warehouse job and our offices in the building around the corner finished by Friday. My wife will absolutely kill me if I don't move my work out of our apartment by next week."

Shit! Shit, shit, shit, shit shit! There might be other husbands in the city whose wives will kill them if they don't get their businesses out of the middle of their living rooms, but how many can charm the pants off the workmen with Peter's calibrated tone of obsequious authority? Still, even if the landlord was offering an amazing deal on the rent, what are the chances in hell that BUBB and the Veronica Agency would end up renting space in the same building? I can barely make out the forms of two figures at the top of the staircase. I turn before they can see me to race back to the third floor. Then just as I reach for the doorknob, I stumble. "Damn, my heel broke!" I squeal.

"Need any help down there?" Peter calls.

I try to control my breathing, which all of a sudden is alarmingly fast. "No, thanks," I squeak, trying to disguise my voice. "Everything's okay." Then, as quickly as possible given my shoe situation, I hop back to the office and slam the door.

Inside, Sienna's hunched over her laptop, chuckling. When she sees me, she quickly snaps the cover shut, as if she has something to hide.

"Thank goodness you're here," I say, collapsing into a chair and telling her that Peter's in the building. "Peter, who has no idea that I'm working, let along what I'm doing, is here, directly above us. What are we going to do?"

"Wow, are you sure?" Sienna sounds more interested than alarmed by the coincidence.

"Of course I'm sure. After twenty years I know what my husband sounds like. And I know what he sounds like when he's really mad. As in, 'Tru, we're in the same office building and you're running an escort agency?' This is my worst nightmare!"

"No it's not. Worst nightmare, let's see, Naomi decides to never move out of your house. Or better, Paige tattoos Brandon's initials across her belly button—in thick, big, black letters," Sienna says swirling an imaginary B in the air.

I'm trying my best to have a Zen moment, but I may have to make it a Xanax one. I look over at Sienna, who's totally calm. "Why are you so relaxed?" I complain.

"Because you're going to have to tell Peter about the business sometime and it might as well be now. Listen, I know when we started I said that you could keep this whole thing a secret, but I think that was bad advice. He's your husband, you need to tell him. Think how upset he'll be if he finds out before you tell him."

"Paige and Molly have already figured it out—the part where you and I are working together, anyway. I told them we'd opened a temp agency."

"Good, that's what you'll tell Peter, too. Although I really think you should tell him the truth. Peter's not a prude, he's a businessman. I think he'll be impressed that we're addressing an untapped market."

"You mean, *undressing* an untapped market." I open the door and peek into the hallway, then before anyone—such as Peter—can see me trying to see if he's there, I slam it shut. "I'll tell him soon, really, I'm just waiting for the right moment."

"Unless you run into him first in the building."

"There is that," I say, realizing that the construction noise seems to have finally stopped. I glance at my watch. "It's after six. The workmen must have finally left for the night. I'll just give Peter a call."

I pull out my now and forever fully charged cellphone. Peter answers on the first ring.

"Hi, honey," he says. "Sorry, I'm a little winded, I just walked down a flight of stairs. Hold on a sec, I'm leaving an apology for the people in the office below ours. The super told me the noise from our renovation is driving them crazy."

I look up, and sure enough, a folded sheet of white paper is being slipped under the door. The door, which my husband is standing on the other side of, less that five feet away.

"Peter's there, right outside," I whisper. I wave my arms frantically and mouth the words *no talking*. The last thing in the world I want is for Peter to hear a noise in here and decide to meet the new neighbors.

"I, er, what?" I ask Peter, trying and failing to make conversation with my husband, who has no idea that it's his nearness that has me tongue-tied.

"What are you doing? Right now? Can you meet me for dinner?" Peter asks impetuously. "We haven't been out to a restaurant in months and I feel like celebrating. In fact, why don't you meet me first and I'll show you the warehouse and take you over to see the new office?"

"Dinner, I'd love to, let's go to dinner. But why don't we wait until the offices are completely finished, that way it'll be a total surprise," I improvise, trying to think of a reason—any reason—to get out of going upstairs.

"Okay," says my unsuspecting husband. "We'll save the tour for next week. I'll leave now. Meet me in half an hour at the Hudson Cafeteria?"

"Great," I say distractedly, eager to get off the phone and for Peter to leave. I hear the shuffle of feet in the hallway and let out a sigh of relief.

"Close one," I say, telling Sienna to call me the minute she hears a word from any of our gals about how their dates are going.

"Sure thing," she says, snapping her computer open and burying herself in whatever it was she was doing before I got here. "Have fun with your husband. Where are you guys going?"

"Hudson Cafeteria," I say, stepping out into the hallway and peeking around the corner to make sure the coast is really clear. "I've never been there but I hear it's terrific. Someone or other was talking to me about it just the other day."

WHEN I ARRIVE at the restaurant, Peter's already waiting. I look around at the brick walls, soaring eighteen-foot cathedral ceiling, Gothic chairs, and stained-glass windows.

"Like it?" Peter asks, patting the space next to him on a wooden bench at a long communal dining table. "Their website describes this place as 'an Ivy League dining room,' but I picked it because I thought the decor would appeal to the medieval scholar in you."

"The clean stained-glass windows look just right here," I say, leaning in to give Peter a kiss. Just half an hour ago my husband was making my heart beat faster out of sheer terror that I might run into him. Now sitting next to him makes it skip a beat. Amazing that after all these years his big blue eyes and crooked smile can still make me melt—when I bother to look into his eyes and he bothers to smile, that is. It's been a long time since we've enjoyed a relaxed moment together, but tonight could be the night. At least I hope so.

"You're a good husband. Sometimes," I tease.

"Not always, but I mean to be a good husband," Peter says, cradling his arm around my shoulder and pulling me close. "I'm not very good at saying 'I'm sorry,' but I am, Tru. I'm sorry that I was such an idiot about not telling you that I'd lost my job. I'm sorry for letting Tiffany redecorate the bathroom. I'm sorry. . . ." Peter pauses. "Aren't you going to tell me I don't have to keep apologizing?" He laughs.

"Just one more," I urge.

"Okay, I'm sorry for just about everything that's happened recently. Except that I married you. And the elevator sex. I'm definitely not sorry about the elevator sex." Peter slips his hand under the table and rubs it across my knee. "I'm very grateful for you and the girls. Naomi's heart attack puts everything in perspective. We have a good life, honey. I'm glad that things are back on track."

"Me too." I rap my hand against the wooden table, accidentally knocking over the crystal salt shaker. I hurriedly set the shaker back upright, and toss a large pinch of salt over my left shoulder.

"You have to blind the devil while you're cleaning up the mess," I say with a smile. I know it sounds silly, but what if it's true?

Peter laughs. He doesn't believe in all of my superstitious mumbo jumbo, as he calls it, but he's willing to indulge me. "Why not?" he says, picking up the shaker and pitching another couple of tablespoons over his shoulder, too. A pretty blond woman walking behind him lets out a little shriek.

"Sorry," Peter says, turning around to apologize for his poor aim.

"That's okay, I was just a little surprised," she says, looking down to brush the white specks off of her chic knee-length black dress and leaning into the man standing next to her, who's holding her glittery clutch. She sweeps the last granules off her bodice, looks up, and I echo her little gasp.

"Anna! Anna Bovary!" says the blonde, whom I now recognize as Georgy—my Georgy, the Georgy who works for the Veronica Agency. Now I remember why the Hudson Cafeteria sounded familiar: it was, it is, where Georgy is rendezvousing with her date.

I shake my head slowly from side to side and try to keep my cool. "Anna, no, you must have me confused with someone else," I say steadily.

IQ tests weren't part of our interview process, but now I'm starting to see that maybe they should have been.

"An-na," Georgy says insistently, pointing back and forth between us, as if she's a member of a 1950s girl group acting out the words to a doo-wop song. "It's me, *Geor-gy,* from the Veronica Agency. You know, *I* work for *you.*"

Peter looks at me curiously, but I pretend to have no idea what this crazy stranger is talking about. Then, as she finally gets it, Georgy grins maniacally and tries to backtrack.

"No, yes, of course, how silly, I'm nearsighted, or farsighted. Anyway I don't see that well without my glasses, sorry for the mistake," Georgy says with a wink. A wink so broad that even Stevie Wonder would see that something's up.

Georgy's date doesn't want to attract any more attention. He motions for the hostess to come over to escort them to a different table. "Over there," he says, pointing to a more intimate area toward the back of the darkly lit restaurant.

"No problem, sir." I watch Georgy and her agency-arranged-date settle into a cozy spot across the room, as the hostess walks back to us.

"Sorry for the commotion, folks," the hostess says, rolling her eyes. "I heard everything. Anna Bovary, that's a good one!"

"Yes, indeed," I say, reaching for my goblet of cider and taking a big swig.

Peter pulls his hand away from mine and looks at me searchingly.

"Anna Bovary, funny choice," he says, tracing small imaginary circles with his finger on the table top as he gathers his thoughts—and suspicions. "I'm guessing she's the mythical love child of Anna Karenina and Emma Bovary. Which is kind of a coincidence when you think about how those are the heroines of your two favorite novels."

"What exactly are you saying?" I ask, trying not to meet Peter's eyes.

"I'm saying that I want to know what that woman was talking about. She 'works' for you, doing what? What's this Veronica Agency she was babbling about? You never really told me where you were for those first few hours when Naomi was in the hospital and we couldn't find you," Peter says. "But you're never where you're supposed to be these days. I'm your husband, I have a right to know what's going on."

I press my palms down on the table, and push at my fingertips. Usually I'd be counting to ten or figuring out how to smooth things over. But not now. I've spent a lifetime being the good girl, the girl who tries to make everything right for everybody, the anti-Naomi who'll do anything to avoid a conflict. But now I'm Hurricane Katrina and the levees have burst.

"Well, I'm your wife, I had a right to know what's going on, too. How could you possibly, how could you have kept it a secret from me that you were out of work? For. Three. Whole. Months. Our savings were gone, you borrowed against the apartment, we were this close to losing our home!" I cry, pinching my thumb and pointer finger together so tightly together that I feel them turning red. "And all the while you were getting dressed and going off to Starbucks, and I was spending money like we didn't have a worry in the world."

"You're not supposed to have a worry in the world, it's my job to take care of you!" Peter says righteously.

"No, it's our job to take care of each other. And you didn't let me do that. You never let me do that! I'm not the same nineteen-year-old girl who used to schedule her classes around yours or who let you talk me into moving to Park Avenue when I thought it would be more fun to live in SoHo."

"You know you wouldn't have been happy in a loft, we agreed. There wasn't even a supermarket in the neighborhood when you wanted to live there. What were we going to do for groceries—grow vegetables on the roof?"

"Why not? Why not grow our own vegetables, or eat peas out of a can? Or, I don't know, but something that every other investment banker and his wife in the world weren't doing. Something original."

"What are you talking about? Have you gone crazy? How did this argument become about gardening and real estate?"

"Because you don't listen, you never listen to me!" I say, banging my fist on the table hard enough to send a spurt of cider streaming from my glass.

"Quiet down, Tru," says Peter. "People are starting to stare."

"Let them. I don't care about other people, I care about us. You make all the big decisions, you say you're looking out for my best interests but you don't know what those interests even are anymore. I've changed and you don't even see that. You'll never see that!"

"Never see what—what in hell do you mean?"

"I don't know, I just don't know," I say, starting to sob. Big, bubble-sized raindrops of misery that are salty and fierce.

Peter, my hankie-ready husband who was such a comfort

just a few days ago when I was so upset about Naomi is not only unmoved by my tears but finds them a personal assault.

"Oh, so now I've made you so miserable that all you can do is cry. Fine, I'm the bad, rotten, stinking, good-for-nothing husband, and you're the poor, put-upon wife. Glad we got that straight," he says testily.

"Nothing's straight, and nothing's right," I moan.

"You're damned right about that!" Peter says, pushing the bench away from the table. "And nothing's going to be right until you tell me what's going on. We promised to tell each other the truth, or have you conveniently forgotten that?"

"Conveniently? Forgotten?" I repeat Peter's words, letting them sink in. "You're the one who *conveniently forgot* to tell me that you were fired. Or how you and Tiffany got cozy enough in the laundry room for her to invite you up to her apartment and offer you a job."

"Is that what this is about, some trumped-up irrational fantasy about Tiffany? Don't make such a big deal about it. Tiffany's new to the city and she doesn't know who to trust."

"And neither do I!" I'm sobbing now so furiously that I can barely get the words out. I cover my face with my hands and try to press back the tears.

Peter signals the waiter for the check, and when it arrives, I snatch the black leather folder. "I'm paying," I say, stuffing my American Express card inside and handing it back to the server.

"With whose money?" Peter snickers, and then he starts to walk away. "In case you're interested, I'm going back to meet with the construction manager at our warehouse."

"I'll be in the same building," I mumble under my breath, although by now Peter's stormed across the room and can't possibly have heard what I said.

Thirteen

❧

Trade Secrets

BRAZENLY, I WAS ALMOST hoping that I'd run into Peter at the entrance to the building. That would show him! But by the time I'd ducked into the ladies' room to fix my mascara, Peter had gone upstairs first to—judging from the sounds coming from the floor above me—do something with a chain saw.

"You don't think he'll hurt himself, do you?" I ask Sienna, though I'm still smarting from the fight. "Not that I care. But I'm still his wife; I suppose I'm the one who'd have to take him to the doctor."

"Nah, one of the girls brought in a sewing kit. I'm sure we could fix him up right here. I think I even saw a bottle of mercurochrome in the bathroom—we'll pour it all over his wound and make sure it stings like hell." Sienna closes her computer and comes over to lean against the edge of my desk.

"I hate him, you know," I say dispassionately.

"Yes, I know."

"I'm serious. The man is a Neanderthal."

"Sweetie," Sienna says gently. "Peter did catch you in a lie."

I shift uncomfortably in my ergonomically correct chair. "For what this thing costs it should be padded with Mother Goose feathers," I complain.

"Tru—"

"I don't want to talk about it. Peter doesn't have to talk about things when he doesn't want to, why do I? Why do women have to be the great communicators, the person in a relationship who's supposed to go the extra mile, or ten, when a guy isn't capable of meeting you in the middle? As if a guy could find his way to the middle!" I sneer. "How many times have you been in the car with some asshole when he gets lost and refuses to ask for directions?"

"I always drive."

"That's not the point. Or maybe it is."

"Or maybe every couple just needs a good GPS. You could think of it as a marital aid."

"I love you," I say, smiling. "I hate Peter, but I love you."

"Tru . . ."

"Okay, I love you but I don't hate Peter. I just hate Peter now. I hardly recognize that man anymore."

"He's the cute one. With the infuriating ego."

"Look, I know that I have to forgive Peter for not telling me about losing his job. Or not. But I know we have to move on. I can't throw it up at him every time we have a fight. And I'm going to tell Peter about the business," I say, looking around at the smartly furnished Veronica Agency offices, which started out as nothing more than two empty rooms with peeling paint. "But I still don't know why I'm the one who has to make the first move."

"Maybe women are just emotionally superior human beings," Sienna says with a shake of her head. "Well, I'm not, but most women are."

"And men take out the garbage and schlep luggage through the airport."

Sienna gives me a hug. Then she plucks a red paper clip from the Lucite holder on my desk and unbends it. "If I were a different kind of a person I might make this into a heart," she says, as instead she zings the S-shaped piece of metal across the room.

"If you were a different kind of a person—" I start as the phone rings and we both dive for it.

"Veronica Agency!" we sing in unison. I punch the speaker button so we can listen together.

"Veronica, Anna, is that you?" a lissome brunette named Treena trills. "I'm upstairs, at the hotel, I mean, I'm calling from the *job*, it's good, everything's A-okay, mission accomplished. And accomplished and—"

"I think we get the picture." Sienna laughs as Treena recounts the high points: dinner at a restaurant she'd always wanted to go to but could never afford on her own; an easygoing conversation with her date, Timothy; and a lovely and still-in-progress night at a fancy hotel. "You're sure I'm getting paid for this?" she quips. "Not the other way around?"

Sienna and I get off the phone and start screeching like schoolgirls. Whatever problems I'm having on the home front are overshadowed, at least for the moment, by our opening night success. Bill comes in, grinning ear-to-ear, nodding enthusiastically into his cellphone.

"Tomorrow, can do . . . Wait a minute, I have another call. . . . No, I didn't know she wasn't a natural redhead. . . . You liked her anyway. . . . Threesomes? I don't think so. . . . If you like *Shrek,* she'll like *Shrek,*" Bill says, balancing his Palm Pilot to his ear while he pens notes on the back of his hand.

"Fun," "perfectly natural," "a little uptight, but not

anymore," "wants to see me again": the reviews are—
hallelujah!—mostly raves. Georgy, who's curious about who I
was out with at the Hudson Cafeteria, thought her date Gabe
could lose a couple of pounds. "I'm putting him on Atkins,
nothing but protein for the first two weeks," she says, as if her
services include nutritional counseling.

"Can we charge extra for that?" I mouth as I playfully
punch Sienna's arm.

"No, but we can for the role-playing," she whispers.
"French maid's uniform and handcuffs? He brought them in
his briefcase?" Sienna asks Georgy as she scribbles notes furiously in Gabe's file. "Twenty-five hundred dollars extra." She
whistles. "And another five hundred in the future if we pro-
vide the props."

An hour later, most of the women have checked in. Several
comment on their younger, thirty-something partners' staying
power. "I'd forgotten they can do it again, right away!" Treena
exclaimed enthusiastically. Another offers a different take:
"I'd forgotten that they want to do it again, right away," she
grouses. "I'll have to get TiVo if I ever want to see Stephen
Colbert again."

I've just snagged three bottles of water and plopped one in
front of each of my partners when we're interrupted by squeals
and a loud rapping outside the door. Bill looks out the peep-
hole and tells Sienna to hightail it to the other room. "It's Patricia and Lucy. Quick, before they recognize you."

Sienna makes a face. "I'm tired of being a silent partner. I
want to meet the women. Who cares if they know who I am?"

"We'll talk about this later. *Ssh!*" Bill says, physically es-
corting Sienna and her laptop behind a rice paper shoji screen
that separates the two work areas.

"*Ssh?*" Sienna says peevishly.

"Talk about what?" asks Lucy, flouncing into the room. She and Patricia are holding fistfuls of money, which they giddily toss into the air.

"It's raining money, honey!" Lucy sings as we're deluged in a shower of fifty- and hundred-dollar bills.

"We're so money!" babbles Patricia excitedly. "I love the color of money! Don't you love the color of money? It's sooo deliciously green!"

"Show me the money!" I say, snagging a handful of bills and clutching them to my chest.

Bill steps on a hundred-dollar bill and quickly bends over to pick it up and straighten out the creases. "We're charging our fees to our clients' credit cards, what's all this?"

"Tips!" Lucy chirps. "Hard currency, a pretty penny, legal tender . . ."

"*Illegal* tender," I say with a laugh. I'd break into a chorus of "We're in the Money," but I don't want to seem like the oldest person in the room. "This is good!" I say instead.

"Yes, it's very good!" Lucy grins and flops onto the red Ligne Roset couch. "Everything went smooth as silk. Larry was a little nervous about checking into the hotel without any luggage, but as we were signing the register with the fake credit card you gave us I took his hand and looked up at him adoringly. 'What a great anniversary surprise, sweetheart! And the sitter said she could stay until two?' The concierge even sent up a free bottle of champagne."

Patricia laughs. "I usually tell my John to go up to the hotel room first," she says. "Then I come a few minutes later and walk right up to the guy who looks most like a security guard and ask, 'Do you know where I can find the elevator to the tenth floor?' They're expecting someone in our line of work to skulk around. They never suspect a thing. By the way"—she winks—"turns out Matt's a good dancer. On the dance floor

and off. And I even ran into a former colleague at the Literary
Partners benefit who gave me a lead on a job."

"You wouldn't leave, would you?" I ask, tightening my grip
around a fifty.

"No, of course not; that other thing would be a day job. I
like this line of work. I put myself through college by having a
couple of different sugar daddies, as I liked to call them. The
only difference between me and the girls who slept with their
professors was that I earned thirty thousand dollars a year for
my trouble. And I went to bed on better sheets."

"Well how about that," I say, at a loss for words but not
questions. Why am I so surprised to learn that the elegantly
tailored Wharton Business School graduate was a college call
girl? And why, oh why, am I feeling just the teensiest bit judg-
mental? Pairing up women with a few well-chosen men is pre-
cisely what my new profession is about.

There's another knock at the door and this time, it's the shy
divorcée Rochelle, who, unlike Lucy and Patricia, looks anything but thrilled about her evening. Lucy puts a protective
arm around Rochelle's shaking shoulders and walks her
toward the couch. "What is it, sweetie?" she asks.

"I thought I could. . . . I'm sorry. . . . My husband said no
one would ever want me but Gary did and I couldn't."
Rochelle blinks, looking as ashamed as Dick Cheney should
have been on, well, who can pick just one occasion? Though
she has no reason to be embarrassed.

"Here, have some water," I say, handing her a Poland
Spring. "It's okay. Remember, we said you don't have to do
anything you don't want to?"

"I know, but Gary seemed pleasant enough and it's part of
the job. But then I started to take off my clothes in the hotel
room. . . ." Rochelle wipes her tears away with the back of her
hand. "That sweet lingerie salesman, Morris, I was wearing

the bustier with the crystals he picked out for me, but all of a sudden I was just so embarrassed, I ran out of the room with my dress still wrapped around my waist. What must Gary think? And you? And everyone? I've let everyone down."

"You didn't let anyone down," Patricia says soothingly.

"I wasn't any good at marriage and I'm not any good at being a hooker," Rochelle says dispiritedly, as if somehow not being able to sleep with a stranger for money is a moral failing. "I guess I'll have to go back to computer programming. At least I can interface with a mainframe without turning beet red."

Lucy smiles. "C'mon, Patricia and I will take you out for a drink."

"Don't be so hard on yourself. This line of work isn't for everyone," Bill says. Rochelle insists that she doesn't deserve to be paid for the evening, but my partner forces her to accept a check.

"Your date, Gary, already called. He said he hoped he hadn't scared you and that he enjoyed talking with you about baseball. And also, that he thought you were very pretty." For the first time since she got here, Rochelle smiles.

"I thought Gary called to ask for a refund? You handled that really well," I say admiringly after the three women leave.

"Thanks." Then Bill points to the paper partition that stands between us a wrathful Sienna. "Try telling that to our friend in there, would you?"

"Ooh, I'll put in a good word, but I don't think it was a smart idea to 'ssh' her."

"I know, it just kind of happened, like steam escaping a heating pipe. Maybe I'll just go out and get us a couple of coffees. . . ."

I arch my eyebrows and Bill dutifully heads toward the backroom.

"Sienna, I'm sorry, I shouldn't have pushed you out of the front office," he says as he pulls open the screen. We're both expecting Sienna to be furious, but she's so engrossed in whatever it is that she's doing on her computer that it takes her a moment to even realize we're in the room.

"What are you up to?" I ask, trying to look over her shoulder. As usual, whenever I'm within reading distance, Sienna snaps the damn thing shut.

"Nothing."

"Well it can't be nothing. If it was nothing, you'd say what that nothing is. You'd say, 'I'm emailing,' or 'reading Ashton Kutcher's Tweets,' or 'I'm on dailycandy.com, finding out all about sales and fabulous things to do.' "

Sienna holds her computer protectively to her chest. "Just because you're keeping a secret from Peter doesn't mean that everyone's keeping secrets," she gripes.

"Wow, I guess I really hit a nerve," I say, hurt at Sienna's stinging reaction.

"Sorry, I just don't get why you're being so nosy."

"Tru has a point, honey," Bill agrees. "Why don't you just tell us what it is?"

Sienna plasters a smile on her face—not the carefree smile where, charmingly, just a little too much of her gum shows. This is her professional smile. The tight, polite, practiced grin she flashes for the cameras or when someone asks for an autograph and she'd rather be finishing her dinner.

"Fine, if the two of you really want to know, I'm blogging. I wasn't really meant to be the office help. I'm a trained and highly respected reporter."

"That's great," Bill says effusively, wrapping his arm around Sienna's waist. "I know you miss the newsroom. I'm glad you're doing something you like."

"Me too," I say cautiously. "Though why would you keep it

a secret?" And then I think to add, "And what are you blogging about?"

"Just this and that," Sienna says evasively, as the corners of her mouth get a little tighter. "My life, what it's like to be a reporter, a little bit about what I'm up to now."

Life . . . reporter . . . up to now . . . it takes a moment for Sienna's words to register, but when they do, they hit me like a ton of bricks. Reflexively, I fasten the top button of my sweater and fold my arms in front of my chest as if I can shield myself from the news.

"You're blogging about the Veronica Agency?" Bill asks, alarmed, as he too starts to understand Sienna's drift.

"Of course not. I'm not an idiot. The two of you should stop looking so worried," Sienna says cavalierly. "I don't use my real name or the Veronica Agency's. My blog is called Madame XXX. There's nothing to connect us or the girls or our clients to the real business. I don't even say that we have a Ligne Roset couch—on the blog, it's from Maurice Villency."

Fourteen

✿

What to Expect When You're Suspecting

"By the time I got home I was bushed. I thought for sure Peter would be asleep, but he was waiting for me in the foyer, with his hands on his hips like a cheesy bouncer. 'You can't be serious!' I said. I just *knew* he was angling for another fight. But instead he tilted my head toward his and gave me a kiss.

" 'I'm sorry things didn't turn out the way I'd planned,' he said.

"I said I was too. But when I started to explain Peter stopped me.

" '*Ssh!*' he said, giving a whole new generous meaning to the same sound which got you into so much trouble with Sienna."

"And he carried you into the bedroom and you made passionate love?" Bill asks.

"Whoa, I think working in an all-female environment is starting to get to you, my friend! That was definitely a girly question. And no. We were both so exhausted, we fell asleep right there, sitting on the floor, leaning up against each other. If the delivery guy hadn't thwacked the newspaper against the door like he was trying to knock over a kewpie doll at a carnival we'd still be snoozing—Paige and Molly would have discovered their parents crumpled over each other in the hallway."

It's late afternoon and Bill and I are at the agency catching up on work. But so far we've spent most of our time going over current events.

"Peter and I are taking another stab at going out to dinner tonight. And I'm going to tell him all about our work."

"That's good," Bill says. "If you and Peter can't make it there's no hope for the rest of us."

I reach over and squeeze Bill's hand. "There's lots of hope. I've never seen Sienna so happy. We just have to get her to stop blogging. Doesn't she realize she could blow our whole cover?"

"I haven't known Sienna long, but I can see that she likes to stir things up."

"Or maybe there have just been too many secrets," I say, thinking about Peter being unemployed, the agency, Sienna's blog, and how distrustful I've become toward my husband ever since *I* started fibbing about where I am all day. "Okay, enough," I say, snapping myself out of my reverie and scanning my finger across an Excel calendar to check on our employees' schedules. "I'm just going to finish a few notes. I want to get home to see Paige and Molly before I meet Peter for our date."

Bill and I spend the next hour working companionably, trading a few stories about the escorts, their dates—and how much more fun it is to run the Veronica Agency than to be a tax attorney.

"It doesn't matter how many thousands of dollars I save them, everybody hates me at tax time. But here, clients shower me with unconditional love."

"That's just because our employees shower them with unconditional sex. Well, I guess it isn't unconditional." I giggle.

I'm just gathering up a few papers and saying goodbye when Bill's phone rings. He motions his hand in the air, signaling me to wait. "A buddy of mine from grad school. He needs a woman to take to his company's cocktail party tonight and his date just called to say she has the flu. Just two hours, no sex, can you check to see who's available?"

"Sorry, no one," I say without consulting the schedule, because I already know that everyone's booked.

Bill talks into the phone again, makes a face, and turns back to me. "Is there anyone you can think of? My friend says it's an emergency. Something about his boss favoring employees who are in stable relationships. Doesn't like the people who work for him to be gallivanting around. And my buddy's up for a promotion." Bill's got the hangdog look of a man who's about to ask for a favor, but before he can, I vigorously shake my head.

"Oh no, don't even go there! I'm a married woman! With teenage children! I am not a hooker!"

"Courtesan," Bill says. "And there's no sex, I promise. My friend J.T. just needs an attractive woman to stand at his side and make pleasant chitchat. A cultured woman, a woman who owns a call girl operation and who wants to ingratiate herself forever to a grateful client. A client who's willing to pay five thousand dollars. It's from six to eight. You could go to the party and be finished in plenty of time to have dinner with your husband. Please?"

WHEN I GOT home to change for my date I didn't actually get to *see* Paige and Molly, or hear their voices, either. As usual, these days, they were out, and I texted them. I've finally, if reluctantly, accepted the fact that they'd rather type than talk on the phone. (Although I worry that instead of growing their brains, the next generation is going to develop thumbs the size of corn cobs.) I took a shower and reapplied my makeup and changed into my best cocktail dress—a pretty good knockoff of a Versace that even Donatella would have to take a close look at to know it isn't the real deal. Two hours later I'm on the arm of Bill's buddy, J.T.—a short, thirty-four-year-old with the manners of a toddler. He slithers his hand down my back and despite my jerking my shoulders up and down to try to dislodge them, his stubby fingers stay firmly planted.

"Great place for a party," J.T. says, looking around the lobby of Lincoln Center's newly renovated Alice Tully Hall. It's not open to the public yet, but tonight special donors are getting a sneak peek. I take in the building's gorgeous two-story glass façade, long limestone bar, and tongue-and-groove wooden wall.

"It must have been some job building this place, but it was worth it," I say.

"Some expensive job," J.T. snickers, pointing to a wall that thanks his company, among others, for their contribution. "Nothing gets done in this town without money. Drink?" he asks, and before I have a chance to answer he's summoned the waiter, who hands me a wide-lipped glass with a salted rim.

"Looks delicious, but I can't," I say, reaching toward the waiter's tray to put it back.

"Everyone's having margaritas," J.T. snarls, through gritted teeth. "Just hold it. Maybe put it up to your lips every once in a while."

"What?"

"The idea is to fit in." And when I look at him quizzically he adds, "I'm paying you, remember?"

My back stiffens and I look at my watch. Ninety minutes to go and I am never doing this again, I promise myself. Are these the kind of assholes our employees are having sex with?

J.T. tries to move his hand down to my waist, but I discreetly slap it away. "No physical contact, that's the deal."

"Okay, okay, don't be so testy. No hands, see?" J.T. says, waving his palms. "But for five thousand bucks you better ooze an awful lot of charm." He points across the room and starts to lead me toward a table where his boss is holding court with several couples.

"Let me freshen up first," I say, leaving J.T. to cool his heels and hold both of our drinks. I open my purse and start fishing around for a lipstick and as I maneuver past a particularly crowded area near the bar, I look up, startled. Even from the back I easily recognize my husband. And if I didn't, who could miss Tiffany Glass? Her hair is swept up off her neck into a Brigitte Bardot–like beehive and she's leaning in suggestively toward Peter to wipe a crumb away from the corner of his mouth with her finger.

I drop my lipstick and let out a little gasp.

"Tru, is that you? What are you doing here?" Peter says, turning around and looking puzzled. I bend over to pick up the lipstick and smooth my hands down my hips.

"I could ask you the same question," I say, flustered. I'm not sure if I'm supposed to be on the offensive or the defensive here. Clearly, both of us have a lot of explaining to do.

Tiffany giggles. "The host of the party owns CoverGirl, They're thinking of investing in BUBB. This is a work night for me and Peter. What's your excuse?"

From across the room I see J.T. raising the margarita glasses in the air, his head darting back and forth as he searches for me.

"I, um, I'm here with a friend of Bill's. He needed a last-minute date," I explain awkwardly, not knowing what else to say.

"I didn't know you still went out on dates," Peter says, looking mildly annoyed.

"And I didn't know that your 'work' involved being pawed by Tiffany at cocktail parties," I mutter.

"Maybe you and I should get out of here before one of us says something we regret. Tiffany, are you okay with me leaving?" asks Peter.

"Whatever you need, Peter," Tiffany says solemnly. As if they're in *Casablanca,* and she's selflessly telling Peter it's okay to get on the plane.

"Do you need to tell your date?" Peter grumbles.

"No, it was just a favor. Well, maybe that's a good idea," I say, as I give Peter my coatroom check and I go to find J.T. "Sorry, about this," I tell J.T. "The agency will make it up to you. I'm having an emergency of my own that I need to deal with."

We've only spent thirty minutes together but I get the feeling that this isn't the first time that J.T.'s been ditched. He pulls himself up to his full height—all five-foot-three—and tells me, "Go on, get out of here. You weren't worth five thousand dollars, anyway."

I'd have to agree. I didn't hold up my end of the bargain. But the price to my marriage for tonight's shenanigans could be a whole lot more devastating.

❧❦❧

STILL, IN THE cab, things go a lot more smoothly than I antici-pated. I even manage to turn the story about J.T.—as much of the story as I'm willing to tell Peter, anyway—into a funny anecdote. "Just my luck. I finally go on a date with a thirty-year-old and he's shorter than Martin Scorsese—and meaner than the characters in his movies."

Peter accepts my story that Bill's friend was in a fix about someone to take to the party and that Sienna couldn't do it because she and Bill had theater tickets. And I—well, I try to, at least—accept Peter's explanation that "Tiffany's just flirtatious, it doesn't mean anything."

"I know you keep saying that," I fret. "But can you imagine what it's like to see that creature all over my husband?"

"I'm sorry. I guess it can't be very pleasant. But after all those months of being unemployed I'm grateful for the job. And it's going really well. You just have to learn not to take Tiffany too seriously, sweetheart. She'd bat her eyes at a totem pole if there was no one else in the room." Peter frames his hands on my cheeks and gives me a long, sweet kiss.

"Okay," I say, resting my head on his shoulder, wondering where I can find a totem pole—or a husband of her own—for Tiffany Glass. Peter strokes my hair and after a few moments he pulls away and turns around to face me.

"I have something to tell you and I'm afraid you're not going to like it. But please, Tru, don't read something into it that it's not. Tiffany and I are going to Hawaii on a business trip. She just told me about it today."

"You're leaving?" I ask carefully, biting my lip, which just a few minutes ago was the source of so much pleasure.

"No, I'm not leaving. I'm going out of town for ten days. We leave tomorrow morning."

"In the morning? For ten days? With Tiffany?"

"Tru, Tiffany's my boss, this is business. It's late," Peter says wearily as the cab pulls up in front of our building and we walk past Terrance to the elevator.

"I have something to tell you, too. I've started a business with Sienna," I say impulsively, as we step inside the elevator cab. Picking the worst moment and the worst way to tell him. "That woman at the restaurant, Georgy? You were right, she works for me. I don't know why I didn't tell you about it before—there are a million reasons, maybe really none. But I want to tell you about it now."

Peter is quiet for what seems like an eternity. He turns the key in the lock and walks past me toward the couch. "What kind of a business?" he asks finally.

No, not now, I can't believe that I blurted it out like that. One more complication, this is just what we need! I can't possibly explain that I'm running an escort agency, especially since Peter's just caught me out on a date. But I don't want to lie and give him the cover story about a temporary help agency, either. Because soon, very soon, I'm going to find the right moment to explain everything—and when I do, I don't want to have to wipe away one more lie.

"I don't want to say too much about it until I know that something's going to come of it," I say anxiously. "You know me, I don't want to jinx anything."

"I guess we're even," Peter says, stuffing his hands in his pockets and concentrating hard on his thoughts. "I didn't tell you when I got fired. You didn't tell me when you started a new business. We're quite a pair."

"We're quite a pair," I say, hoping that as with Peter's reading of "ssh," I can transform a pejorative into something positive by the lilt in my voice.

But not even Mary Poppins could inject a note of optimism into the state of our relationship, not with all the things that have happened in the last few weeks. And in my vast—and these days seemingly unrelenting—experience with marital problems, the best a couple can hope for after a long, exhausting fight-filled day is a temporary cease-fire induced by the overwhelming desire to just get some rest.

Silently Peter bends to untie his shoes. He strips down to his briefs and unfastens the buttons on his shirt. "I'm leaving in the morning," he says as his head hits the cushion. Then he falls into a deep, undisturbable sleep.

AFTER A FITFUL night feeling dwarfed and very alone in our queen-sized bed, I got up at dawn to make us both a pot of coffee, but Peter's already gone. I shuffle around the room straightening books that don't need straightening, plumping up pillows, bending over to pick up the glistening silver locket Paige has been searching for for weeks, which is in plain view, peeking out from underneath a wingback chair. In the kitchen, I stand frozen at the coffeepot, unable to decide between decaf and double-strength espresso.

I'm leaving in the morning. Peter's last words run unrelentingly through my head. But Peter didn't mean *leaving,* leaving. He meant leaving as in taking a train or an airplane. To go to Hawaii with Tiffany. For ten whole days.

"She's my boss, don't read something into it that it's not," I repeat Peter's words, trying to convince myself that they're true. And I really believe that whatever else is or isn't going on between us these days, whatever missteps or mistakes either of us has committed, Peter's not the kind of man to have an affair.

"He even said so once on TV," I think, unable to choose a coffee I scoop four heaping tablespoons of cocoa into a cup and sit down at the table, remembering the on-air interviews Sienna did a few years ago with three middle-aged men about monogamy. One had cheated and the second allowed that he might. But Peter was steadfast. "I love my wife, I love being married, it's just not worth the risk," Peter said, making him the poster boy for fidelity. And me, the envy of my M&M coffee klatch.

Distractedly I stir the cocoa, to which I've forgotten to add any liquid. Knowing that Peter would never cheat is a blessing. But there's a harder truth that goes along with that. Somewhere in the deepest recess of my heart I've always harbored the fear that if Peter did have a midlife crisis—if he grew tired of me, or if he was inexorably pulled toward another woman—he wouldn't fool around, and he would never have a fling. Peter, my upstanding, fidelity-thumping husband, Peter, would have to leave.

Naomi pads into the room just as I'm spitting out a mouthful of dry cocoa powder.

"Ugh!" I say, wiping the back of my hand across my lips and then running my cakey hand across my jeans.

"Tru," Naomi says reproachfully. Then, seeing my face and thinking the better of attacking my lapse in hygiene, my mother makes her way to the stove to heat a saucepan of milk. She comes back to the table with a cup of cocoa for herself, and she splashes the rest of the warm milk into my cup.

"My mother—your grandmother—used to say that cocoa was the assimilated woman's chicken soup, good for whatever ails you. Of course sometimes I would have liked a cup of chicken soup, but my mother wasn't much of a cook."

"I guess it runs in the family. But we're damned good at takeout," I say, taking a sip of the soothing liquid. "I'm sorry Nana died when I was so young. I would have liked to have gotten to know her better."

"No, you wouldn't have. She was a tough cookie," Naomi says matter-of-factly.

"Mom . . . she was your mother, I mean, there must have been some good things you liked about Nana?"

Naomi folds her hands around her mug. "She made me

strong. For a little while there, when I was Miss Subways, I think she was even proud of me. But then I married your father and had you and she never let me forget that nothing about my life was anything but ordinary."

The sins of the fathers have nothing on the mothers, I think as I look at Naomi, who's so wrapped up in her own unhappy memories of her childhood that she doesn't realize that she could be describing how she treated me. You have to be pretty clueless to be telling your only daughter that even her grandmother thought she was nothing special. But unlike Naomi, I'm past getting caught up in this family drama and meshug geners. And rather than feeling sorry for myself, I feel sorry for Naomi.

"It's too bad Nana didn't appreciate how special you are," I say, reaching across the table and taking Naomi's hand.

Embarrassed, Naomi wriggles free. She concentrates on stirring her cocoa, brings the cup to her lips, and then sets it back down. "And it's too bad your grandma didn't realize how special you are, too." Then she pauses. "I know it isn't easy to have me here, Tru. I appreciate your taking me in. I know I'm not the easiest person in the world to get along with."

"Mom, you, not easy?" I laugh, the first good honest laugh that Naomi and I have had together in . . . well, maybe ever.

"All right now, Truman, let's not sit here wading up to our eyeballs in what might have been; there's too much of that around here lately. I've decided to get on with my life. And from the looks of you sitting here sulking, it's something you might want to think about, too."

"Everything's fine, I . . ."

"Oh please, we've just had one of those icky mother-daughter moments that Oprah's so big on and now you're going to clam up all CIA-not-talking-everything's-okay?"

"It takes a brave woman to string the CIA and Oprah into the same sentence," I say with a chuckle.

Naomi gives me one of her famous steely-eyed stares, the stare that kept me on the straight and narrow all the way through high school.

"Tru, don't try to tell me nothing's wrong. You and Peter have either been sniping at each other or walking on eggshells for weeks. And that Tiffany Glass woman." Naomi clucks.

"What about Tiffany?" I say, pouncing on Naomi for any tidbits of information.

"She's beautiful, she's with Peter twelve hours a day, what more is there for me to say?"

"Nothing." I slump down in my chair.

Naomi leans over and combs her fingers through the wispy top layers of my hair. "If you got a proper haircut, I think you could conceal some of the thinning," she says.

"Thank goodness. For a minute there I was wondering if my real mother had been captured by aliens."

"I can't help it. If I criticize it's only because I want the best for you. But maybe I could learn to criticize. . . ." Naomi stops, at a loss for words.

"Less critically?"

"Yes, I could criticize less critically. It will be a challenge, and right now, I'm into taking on challenges."

I look carefully at my mother. It's barely dawn, yet to make the trip from the guest bedroom to the kitchen she's combed and styled her hair, meticulously applied lipstick and eyeliner, and although the unforgiving morning light is streaming through the window, there's barely a crease on her well-cared-for, lasered-perfect skin. Despite Naomi's bitterness, or maybe because of it, I've grown into a reasonably happy woman—a woman who's smart enough, or always has

been up until now, to treasure my children and husband. I
don't know exactly what I'm going to do about it yet, but I realize that no way am I going to sit back while Peter goes off
angry for ten whole days, especially with Tiffany Glass. If I've
learned anything from Naomi, it's about survival.

I lift my mug and reach across the table to clink it against my
mother's. "I hope Paige and Molly have your resilience. And
my sense of family. And Peter's decency," I toast. Even when I
want to strangle Peter because he's bent out of shape about
being the Man of the Family and how he's supposed to be the
one to support us, I know that it comes from a good, if mis-
guided, place.

"What, are you writing their commencement speech?"
Naomi asks with a laugh.

"No, just feeling a little emotional." Though at the moment, planning for my children's futures—or anything more
taxing than putting my head on the pillow—seems about as
likely as a Beatles reunion.

I take a sip of cocoa and feel my head bobbing toward the
cup. "It's been a long night," I say sleepily.

"Mom," says Paige, bouncing into the room, as she simultaneously pulls the straps of her backpack over her shoulder
and nabs a bottle of cranapple juice from the fridge. "It's not
the night, it's the morning! Time to start a new day!"

Fifteen

⅋

Mouth-to-Mouth

MY "NEW DAY" doesn't start until late in the afternoon—after I've napped, showered, and headed downtown to meet Sienna. Between my efforts to economize and how busy I've been lately it's been ages since I've had any kind of special beauty treatment, but Sienna says that she's heard this new one is a must. And, she adds, it's tax-deductible.

"It's called the 'Geisha Facial,' " Sienna chirps, assuring me that given our line of work, the IRS will consider this a business expense.

I start to protest. "A geisha's not a courtesan. They entertain men, they don't actually sleep with them." And more important, no one's supposed to know what our line of work *is*. But as I sink into the comfortable white leather treatment chair I'm willing to suspend any discussions about our need for anonymity or our disagreement over her Madame XXX blog for a truce-filled hour of pampering.

The lights are low, Japanese flute music is humming in the

background, and two pretty young technicians, Suki and Yuna, come over to introduce themselves.

"You relax," says Suki, as they position our chairs so that Sienna and I are lying with our heads comfortably tilted back. I close my eyes and Suki gently strokes my face with a warm washcloth. Then she taps my forehead and my cheekbones with her own fingertips so soothingly that I nearly fall asleep.

"Hmm," I sigh luxuriously. "This was a good idea."

"Now comes the best part," says Yuna as I open my eyes long enough to see her pouring a stream of white powder into a bowl. She adds a few drops of water and vigorously mixes the concoction with a porcelain pestle. When she's satisfied that the potion is perfect, she applies a thick mask of paste all over Sienna's face and neck, and Suki does the same to me.

"It tingles," says Sienna. "In a good way. What is this stuff anyway?"

"Very special." Suki giggles. "Is called *Ugui su no fun.*"

"No fun? I'm having lots of fun," I say, as Sienna, ever the reporter, presses the duo for details.

"You don't know before you come?" Yuna says. "It is the special facial of the geisha, to exfol, exfoli . . ."

"Exfoliate?" Sienna says helpfully.

"Yes, thank you. It ex-fol-i-ates, takes away the dead layers. The geishas, they wore so much heavy thick makeup, they needed something extra-special to clean the skin. It is made from the nightingale."

"From a nightingale?" Sienna, an active PETA member, asks, alarmed that an animal might have been hurt in the name of beauty.

"No, no, not to worry. It is external part of the nightingale. It is made from the nightingale's poop."

"Nightingale's poop?" I repeat, sitting bolt upright in my

chair. "I've spent half of my life in New York trying to avoid bird droppings, and now I'm paying someone two hundred dollars to smear them on my face? Holy shit!"

"Yes, yes, shit," says Yuna agreeably. "Some of my customers when I tell them too they say, 'Oh crap!' "

I don't care about Suki's assurances that the poop's been sterilized and mixed with rice bran. I sit back in my chair, trying not to move a muscle until I can get her to wash off the fecal facial. I adored my babies more than I can say, but all those mothers on urbanbaby.com who think their kids' shit smells like roses should get themselves to the Mayo Clinic to check out their olfactory senses. Not to mention their sanity. Sienna looks over and cracks up over my twitchy discomfort.

"My mistake. The facial's on me," she says cheerily. Then Sienna pretends to lick her lips and smacks them for good measure. "Mmm, mmm, mmm, tastes just like chicken!"

"Thanks," I say as we walk out to the street and I declare that under no circumstances will I ever eat chicken, turkey, or wood hen ever again—even though that last one's a mushroom and has nothing at all to do with poultry except for its inexplicable name. "I think this is the push I needed to go vegan," I say as the maître d' of a cozy sandwich-and-salad place on Madison Avenue walks us through the narrow restaurant toward a booth where Naomi is already waiting. She doesn't notice us at first because her head is buried in her computer.

"Not you, too! First the girls, then Sienna, now I can't even pry my own mother away from the Internet." I sigh, as Sienna glides in first and I slip down opposite Naomi.

"It's very interesting all the things you can find here. Molly showed me how to go on My Face."

"Facebook," I correct her.

"My Face, Facebook. They could call it Spacebook, for all I care. The point is, I'm getting myself ready to go to the

Miss Subways reunion. I'm getting the lowdown on all of the girls."

Naomi has been talking and worrying and downright obsessing over the Miss Subways reunion for months. It even contributed to her heart attack—she never would have been pumping iron if she hadn't been so overzealous about getting into shape.

"Mom, it's just a party," I protest.

"It's not 'just a party,' " Naomi sneers. "Is the shuttle launch just another road trip? This reunion is like a marathon, it requires preparation and endurance. I'm going in there armed to the teeth with all the information I can get, and a new haircut." Naomi puts on her glasses and moves to within an inch of Sienna's nose. "Your skin, it's very clear. Maybe that facial you two had today is something I should do, too?"

"Well, it does give you *excremental* changes. . . ." Sienna says, giving me a wink.

"You always look wonderful after those facials at Elizabeth Arden, Mom. You don't want to be trying anything radical with your skin just a week before a big event."

"You're right. How did my only daughter get so smart?" For a moment, Naomi seems to look at me with new admiration, and then she adds, "Well, why wouldn't you be smart? You're a chip off the old block."

After last night's heart-to-heart I'm almost relieved to know that some things will never change—Naomi can't even issue me a compliment without congratulating herself. A week ago it might have gotten a rise out of me, but today it only makes me laugh.

The waiter comes over with menus. Naomi orders a three-ounce burger without the mayo, I ask for a Waldorf salad without the mayo, and as a joke, Sienna requests "a jar of mayo with a spoon."

"A jar of mayo . . . Oh, I get it, very funny." The waiter snickers, then recognizes Sienna and asks for her autograph. After years of attention Sienna's missed being in the public eye, and as she scribbles on the waiter's order pad she smiles as broadly as if she were signing her name in cement at Grauman's Chinese Theater next to Brad Pitt's.

"Thanks, I'll get you that jar of mayo," the waiter says, as he stuffs the paper into his pocket and heads for the kitchen. "Now that you're not on TV anymore I guess the ol' diet can go to hell."

Sienna's nostrils flare and she throws back her head. "The 'ol' diet' is not going to hell, and for your information, you haven't heard the last of me, buddy, not by a long shot," she sneers, taking the waiter's feeble attempt at a joke a little too seriously.

Naomi, ignoring the dustup, goes back to clicking on her computer. After a few moments she triumphantly points the screen toward me—and now it's my turn to feel bad. "If you want to know where Peter's staying, this is the hotel," she says.

I look down at my left hand and nervously twist my wedding band. I'd awakened from my nap blessed with the numbing temporary amnesia of a post-traumatic stress sufferer. I vaguely remembered that something was wrong, but I pushed it to the back of my mind and hurried off to meet Sienna. Now the crushing feeling that my marriage is in trouble comes rushing back to me. I massage my temples with my fingertips, pressing the facts back into focus.

"What do you mean you know where Peter is?"

"Whoa, ladies, back up a minute. What do you mean, Peter's gone?" Sienna asks. "Why didn't you tell me?"

"I forgot. And he's not gone. He's just traveling. For business. I'm sure he'll be stuck in a boring conference room the whole time."

"This doesn't look boring to me!" Naomi trills, pointing toward her computer.

I stare at the tropical setting Naomi's pulled up on the screen. Palm trees and pink stucco cottages dot a sandy white beach that stretches toward a glistening blue-green ocean. WELCOME TO PARADISE reads a pretty banner written in girly purple script across the idyllic picture. *Meet Tiffany Glass and her team of BUBB cosmeticians for free consultations every day this week.* Google, I hate you! Did I have to be reminded that Peter and Tiffany are spending ten days together on a sexy, exotic island while I'm all alone in New York?

"A few lessons on the computer and I'm a regular Columbo," Naomi crows.

"And I'm nauseated," I say, burying my head in my hands and cursing my geographical fate. "He really is in *Hawaii?* Couldn't it have been Kalamazoo? I hear they're in desperate need of eyeliner in the Arctic Wasteland."

"It's good that it's Hawaii, *bubbala,*" Naomi says confidently. My mother only resorts to Yiddish when she wants to seem sage, and while it doesn't have the haughty authority of Latin, I find the familiar cadences lulling. "Hawaii's romantic, the weather is sultry. It'll totally regurgitate your marriage."

"Mom, I think you mean 'resuscitate' it."

"Regurgitate, resuscitate, it will make things better." Naomi's painting a pretty picture and I'm with her, imagining myself on that endless white beach walking hand-in-hand with Peter into the sunset. Until, that is, my mother adds one more visual image to the mix. "Of course, you'll have to get a new bikini. Maybe a one-piece bathing suit and a nice sarong. Or a caftan. That Tiffany woman . . ." Naomi's voice trails off as having brought up the competition, she finds herself at a loss to explain exactly how it is that she thinks I can trump the beauteous, buxom Tiffany Glass.

"Maybe I should just get a burquini, one of those Iranian swimsuits that covers everything but your face," I say glumly. "I need a plan."

"No, what you need is an airline ticket," Sienna scoffs. "Peter loves you; you just have to fly over there and drag him back home."

Fly, drag, buy a bathing suit—the amount of physical and emotional energy required to save this relationship seems daunting.

The waiter arrives bearing my salad, Naomi's sandwich, and an extra-large jar of Hellmann's with thee spoons. "A plan wouldn't hurt, *bubbala*," Naomi says, scooping out a large dollop of mayo and smearing it expansively over her burger. "Let's see what we can cook up."

I STOP AT the supermarket on the way home to get all the ingredients for chicken cutlets, the girls' favorite dinner. When Molly and Paige were little I'd let them dip the strips of chicken in eggs and roll them around on a plate of bread crumbs; while the chicken was baking, they'd squirt honey and mustard together to make a spicy sauce, getting as much on themselves as they did in the cup. Maybe the twins will even be around this afternoon to help. If I have to explain that their father's off on an unexpected business trip—and that I'm leaving them with Naomi so I can go off to join him for a few days—I want everything to seem as normal as possible. Although it's been so long since I've made a meal that doesn't involve an aluminum freezer tray or a waxy white takeout box, that that could be a red flag in itself.

The lights are off in the apartment, and as I step inside I nearly stumble over a backpack carelessly thrown by the front door.

"Paige Newman! How many times have I told you not to leave things around the house for people to trip over?"

I set down my shopping bag, turn on the lights, and march toward the girls' room, which is empty. I open and close the door to the den and as I head to the library, I hear the faintest flurry of activity. Without warning I throw open the door and spy the silhouetted heads of a boy and girl. Barely an outline, in the darkness they look like one of those black construction-paper Colonial cutouts. Except these are twenty-first-century kids—their hair is wildly mussed and their lips are locked. I flip on the light and the two flushed, startled teenagers turn around to face me.

The top two buttons of my daughter's blouse are unbuttoned, and she bunches the material together to hold it closed. Then she buries her face in the shoulder of the boy who's got his arm wrapped around her. Brandon, the little pissass lothario, who has a shit-eating grin on his face.

"Brandon, you get out of this house immediately!" I scream, barely able to control my temper.

"Sure thing, Mrs. N," Brandon says with a smirk. He grabs his tie and navy blue blazer off the floor and—goddamn him— blows an air kiss in our direction.

Shaking, I put my arm around my daughter and pull her toward my chest. I sit there for what feels like an eternity, trying to figure out how I can reach her, not wanting to make everything worse by saying the wrong thing. Finally, I put my hands on her shoulders and look searchingly into her tearful blue eyes.

"Molly Newman, what in hell were you thinking?"

Molly sits on the couch quietly for a few moments. Then she buttons her blouse and gets up to leave the room.

"What, don't tell me you have nothing to say for yourself, young lady," I say, channeling every bad sitcom parent I've ever seen on TV Land. How is it that I've found my fourteen-year-old daughter with her blouse half off making out with a boy on the couch—a boy her sister is dating—and I'm the one who's groping for the right words?

"I'm sorry," Molly mumbles with her back to me. Then she turns around and her voice becomes bolder. "Don't you get it? For once a boy likes me. He said he was breaking up with Paige to be with *me*. And he's not just any boy, he's popular, he's Brandon Marsh," she says as if somehow that explains everything.

This is my comeuppance, I think guiltily. All those weeks ago when this whole thing started, I was secretly rooting for Molly—and now look what's happened: I got my wish. Of course Molly wants to be popular; who doesn't? Life is just like high school, a constant struggle to belong. For goodness' sake, in the TV business, viewers rated Sienna's likeability every single night. But somewhere along the way, if we're smart, if we're lucky, we populate our lives with the people who love us just the way we are. Not for what we could be or what we do for them—such as making out in a darkened den or pumping up their egos by competing for their attention. I have to make Molly understand that by being with Brandon she's not only betraying her sister, she's betraying herself.

I pat the cushion on the couch beside me. Warily, Molly folds her arms in front of her chest and sits down.

"So," I say softly. "It must feel good to have Brandon like you."

Whatever Molly was expecting me to say, this isn't it. "It does," she says tentatively.

"I remember the first time I kissed Daddy. . . ."

"Oh, Mom, please, you're not going to make me listen to that story again? About how you'd go out to coffee with him after your study group and you got to know him and trust him before you two really got together? That was like centuries ago. Things are different today."

"How so?"

Molly shifts uncomfortably on the sofa where just five, ten minutes ago she was sprawled out with Brandon. "Well, for one thing, kids today don't wait so long. I mean if you want to have a boyfriend you have to show him that you like him."

I suspect that Adam tried to get Eve to give it up by trying that one on her, but I hold my tongue.

"Did you want to make out with Brandon?" I ask carefully.

"Well, of course I wanted to make out with Brandon. What girl wouldn't?"

The girl I knew just a few days ago who said she only wanted to be with a boy who wanted to be exclusively with her, I think, and for the second time in as many minutes I censor my thoughts. Instead I ask, "Did you like kissing Brandon?"

Molly crosses her right leg over her left, then recrosses them in the other direction. "Well, yeah, of course," she says unconvincingly. "I mean I don't have anything to compare it to."

"Molly . . ."

"Okay, yeah, you're going to say that I was just kissing Brandon to make him like me."

"And?"

"Maybe a little. But I was curious, too."

"You know you can say no, right? I mean, even once you've started kissing a boy, you don't have to—"

"*Ohmygod,* Mom, next you're going to be quoting that retard list they gave us in the sixth grade. 'No, I'm not ready.' 'No, I don't want carpet burn.' And oh yeah, my all-time favorite, 'No, I'm allergic!' What, the guy's going to be afraid that you'll end up in anaphylactic shock?"

"It could happen," I say unconvincingly, because rationally I know that you're more likely to die from allergies to peanut butter than sex, although I'd do anything to get Molly to switch her affections from Brandon to Skippy.

Molly shakes her head and stands up to end the discussion. "I could also get hit by a bus," she says, quoting her father, who seems to believe that the dangers of crossing the street will make me less worried about whatever it is that I'm focused on, when in truth it just gives me something else to be anxious about. "Stop turning this into the End of the World. Why does everything in this family have to be such a big deal?"

"Because I love you! Because I want to protect you! Because you're too young! Because it is!" I say, in frustration, abandoning my politically-correct-be-understanding-and-open-minded-with-your-kids tact. "And by the way," I say, as Molly picks up her iPod from the floor and storms noisily out of the room, "you're grounded. For about a hundred and fifty years."

Sixteen

Analyze *This*

"MOLLY, IT WAS MOLLY, not Paige," I groan, unable to make sense out of yesterday afternoon's events.

"Maybe that's the problem. Molly's always been so low-maintenance. If it'd been Paige you'd be sore but not surprised, probably not fair to either one of them. Here," Sienna says, breaking off a piece of chocolate and handing me a square. "The guy at Whole Foods told me that each batch of this stuff is exposed for five days to the electromagnetically recorded brain waves of meditating monks."

I roll the chocolate around in my mouth. "Did he tell you they were praying for world peace and zero calories?"

"Actually he said they were praying to raise enough money to buy an air conditioner for the monastery."

I smile and reach for the rest of the bar. "Maybe I'll stop and buy some on the way home. As fellow small-business owners it's practically our moral obligation to eat as much of this as we can. And Molly always likes to support a good cause. Maybe I can get her interested in something besides Brandon."

Sienna raises an eyebrow but refrains from saying the obvious. No matter how many endorphins are crammed into a bar of chocolate it can never compete with the thrill of being with a boy. Especially a boy who I've now declared off-limits. I'm furious with Brandon. And myself. And with Peter. I'm so mad at Peter I might have to rip the shoulder pads out of his sports jacket. What the fuck is he doing in Hawaii at a time like this? He's supposed to have been here to threaten that moron Marsh boy that he'll chop him up into a million pieces with a meat cleaver if he ever so much as comes within a hundred feet of either of the girls ever again. And then Peter was supposed to have climbed into bed and made me believe that everything's going to be all right.

I crumple up the candy wrapper and toss it into the wire wastepaper basket. Sienna and I are sitting behind a two-way mirror, waiting for a focus group that Bill's organized with Veronica Agency clients to begin. The room where the meeting is taking place has a pale green carpet, soft lights, and comfortable-looking armchairs. On the other side of the wall, Sienna and I are perched on metal folding chairs. A fluorescent fixture makes me feel as if we're the ones under investigation.

"I can't even get hold of Peter," I say sullenly. "He sent one email yesterday from Miami. Something about how when he got fired the company took away his BlackBerry and when he replaced it, he hadn't wanted to spend the extra money for the world plan. 'Didn't think I'd need it, never expected to leave the house again.' The damn thing doesn't work outside the continental U.S."

"Did he leave a hotel phone number?"

"Yup, but the phone lines are down. I tried calling all night."

"I'm sure you'll talk tonight. And you're going to see him Saturday, right?"

"Maybe," I say, rummaging around my purse for my phone. Still no messages from Peter. And nothing from Molly, either. "I'm not flying off to Hawaii until things are settled at home."

Sienna leans forward on her chair and runs her hand comfortingly across my back. "I shouldn't be giving advice. I'm not the mother of a teenager, or anybody's mother, for that matter. And I'm not even very good with plants. Everybody says you can't kill a cactus, but somehow I managed to."

"You're a great friend. And it seems like you're becoming a pretty good girlfriend," I say, looking through the two-way mirror at Bill, who's just entered the room. He smiles up toward where he knows we're sitting.

"We'll see," Sienna says, issuing a small wave back to her beau. "But the one thing I know is that you're a terrific mother. Molly's not screwing up her life. . . ."

"She's just screwing around?" I say, distressed by Sienna's choice of words.

"No. Molly's just breaking away. She's doing exactly what teenagers are supposed to do."

"I thought you just said you didn't know anything about being a parent?"

"I interviewed the star of *Nanny 911* once. And I seem to remember a certain incident with the captain of the football team. . . ."

"Shit! Frank Fucking Nelson." I shake my head. "He told me that if I could make out better than Serena Levine he'd take me to the junior prom instead of her."

"And?" Sienna nudges.

"I could and he didn't. What an asshole."

"Right. Every girl needs to date at least one asshole so that when she meets a good guy, she's smart enough to know it."

Thank goodness for Sienna. I can always count on her for a

rational perspective. It's invaluable to have a friend who doesn't freak out over every little thing that happens—not to mention one who remembers the day we sneaked off together to get our ears pierced, and my entire romantic history. "Frank Fucking Nelson, whatever happened to him, anyway?"

"Divorced, alcoholic out-of-work auto mechanic," Sienna says, without missing a beat. "Actually, I hear he's the CEO of a hedge fund."

"Well, at least the out-of-work part is probably true."

"And his knees. The man's a forty-something ex–football player, he probably can't go through an airport security line without setting off an alarm."

I squeeze Sienna's hand. I'd give anything for an alarm to go off in Molly's head right now about Brandon. Or to hear a simple cellphone beep signaling that any of my loved ones is trying to reach me.

I set my phone on vibrate and clutch it in my hand. Sienna points to the room on the other side of the mirror, where the Veronica Agency's clients—aka the Friends of Bill—are helping themselves to cups of coffee and settling into seats around a polished black conference table. Several of the guys are well-toned and others have slightly inflated waistlines, which when worn with an expensive enough business suit tell the world that a man's well-fed and well-heeled. (Ironic that the same waistline on a guy in a sweatshirt with an exposed butt crack casts him into an entirely different social class.) Our clients are mostly average-looking, some above or below, but all of them, every last guy in the room, has one thing in common: Like Bill, our business partner and Sienna's boyfriend, they're all young. Which doesn't go unnoticed by Sienna, either.

"Just look at those guys in there. Do you realize that when they were teething, we were getting braces? And the year we went off to college, they were entering kindergarten," Sienna grumbles. She takes out her mirror and runs a comb through her luxurious hair, which she's wearing an attractive shade darker than she did when she was on camera.

"You do realize Bill not only adores you, he helped us build a whole business around the idea of older women and younger men?"

"Sure, but I always figured I be with somebody thirteen years older, not the other way around. That way I wouldn't have to worry when my looks started to go—the old coot would be too blind to notice."

"You'll always be gorgeous. You're not really worried about your age difference, are you?"

"No, of course not. But I sometimes wish I was with a guy who remembers Watergate. Or water beds. Or when the Water Pik was invented," Sienna says glibly.

Bill calls the meeting to order and I turn up the volume on the control panel of the two-way mirror so we can hear what everybody's saying. For his first order of business, Bill holds up a large silver platter and asks if anyone wants a pastry. Unlike our escorts, who mostly passed on the donuts, every guy takes him up on the offer—except one, whom I recognize as Georgy's date, Gabe.

"My new woman's got me on Atkins," he says with a broad smile, sounding proud that there's a woman in his life who's taking an interest in his health, even if she is on the payroll. Of course, Gabe's the client who brought a French maid's uniform and handcuffs along on the date—he *likes* taking orders.

"Oh c'mon," says a ruddy-faced fellow, reaching for a cannoli. "For what Bill here is charging us you'd better get some free food thrown in with the deal."

"Larry, you're not complaining about the rates already, are you? Quality, gentlemen, comes at a price."

Larry takes a generous bite of the cream-filled treat and, in the bargain, gets a thin dusting of powdered sugar around the edge of his mouth. "Nah, just giving you a hard time," he says with a laugh.

"Speaking of which," says a guy Bill introduced as his graduate school friend, Mike, "it was a hard time. A hard, hard time, if you get my drift. And me *likey!*"

"And me want-to-throw-up-y." I giggle, rolling my eyes.

"You were right, dude, older women are more self-assured," says the cannoli-eater, Larry, who's now moved on to a Danish. Either these guys are going to have to work out their oral fixations in the bedroom or we're going to have to put the lot of them on Atkins.

"Lucy showed me what a woman wants," says Mike.

"Patricia spent a lot of time doing exactly what *I* want," says her date, Matt, the trader who took her to the Literacy Partners benefit. "She looked great, she was comfortable talking to my colleagues, and she even told my boss's wife where to score a discount on an alligator purse. Everyone was very impressed. Me too." Matt whistles. "I haven't had tongue kissing like that . . . Well, never."

And it probably never cost you an extra twelve hundred bucks, I think.

Even Gary, the sports aficionado whom the shy divorcée Rochelle left stranded in a hotel room, has gotten over his initial disappointment. "Thanks for the free ride." He winks at Bill, referring to our cancelling his fee and setting him up for a complimentary evening with Diane, who he describes as "a knockout." A wise decision, because in the long run we'll make more money from a satisfied customer.

Sienna's typing every word into her computer and I'm trying to remember them: self-assured, sophisticated, a knockout, worldly, smart. Bill was right, sexy, adult women are in demand. The Veronica Agency is filling a niche that sounds like it might be even bigger than bamboo flooring. I'm feeling pretty good about being a member of this covetable crowd. Although not every man in the room is enough of a grown-up to appreciate a grown-up woman.

"Yeah, Diane was super, a great gal," Gary says, steepling his fingertips together. "But I was thinking, it might be nice for this stallion to take a tumble with a younger filly, if you get my drift. Got any of those in your stable?"

"Stallion? That idiot thinks he's a stallion? Jackass is more like it," Sienna hisses.

Bill looks sternly around the table at his nerdy Masters of the Universe. "All I've been hearing for twenty minutes is how great these women are. That, gentlemen, is because they're Thoroughbreds."

"I'm with you, man," says Matt, raising his coffee mug.

"Yeah, those twenty-something girls are too insecure and needy. The Veronicas are cultured and confident," agrees Lucy's date, Mike. Then he laughs. "Besides, at their age, they're grateful."

"Grateful? Did that toady little worm actually use the word 'grateful'? He's the one who should be grateful. He can't even get someone to sleep with him unless he pays for it," Sienna fumes, as she takes out her anger on the keys of her laptop.

The guys on the other side of the two-way mirror have no idea that they're being observed with the intensity of Jane Goodall studying her chimpanzees. Like their primate ancestors, I notice that they become more aggressive after feeding—as the meeting winds down they crack a few lewd jokes, slap one another on the back, and poke each other in the ribs. Bill asks the men to fill out questionnaires, and as they leave he takes their requests for future dates. Several minutes later, carrying his suit jacket over his arm and humming, Bill bounds out of the luxurious conference room into our cramped, overlit space.

"I think that went really well," Bill says, leaning in to kiss Sienna who moves her cheek away.

"You do?"

"Yes, look here," he says, spreading out a fistful of question-naires, which he's already tabulated. "Customer satisfaction is over ninety percent. All of the men have signed up for at least three more dates each and at least half of them said they had friends who'd like to become clients, too. And except for that imbecile Gary, no one else wanted to try somebody new— everybody is happy with their match. We're a success!" Bill exclaims, gathering his arms around our shoulders and ignor-ing Sienna's signals that she doesn't necessarily share his ela-tion.

Sienna shoots Bill a stony look and breaks free from his embrace. "I think we have to start being a little more selective about our clientele," she says icily. "Tell that Gary if he doesn't appreciate our services we'd prefer he take his business elsewhere. And that Mike. And that asshole J.D. you set Tru up on a date with."

"J.T. And could everybody stop saying that I went out on a date?"

"Don't be unreasonable, Sienna. This is business. Do you think the dry cleaner loves everyone whose pants they press?" Bill says.

"The dry cleaner doesn't have to get in bed with his cus-tomers, our women do."

"Sienna . . ."

"*Bill!*" Sienna mocks, in a tone that tells me she's asking for trouble. How can my best friend be so levelheaded about my problems and so quick to fly off the handle when it comes to her own? Sure, I wasn't happy about Gary's reaction either, but ten men in the room issued total raves.

Sienna turns her attention back to her computer and vigorously types a few more sentences. Then circling her hand in the air with the baroque flourish of Yo Yo Ma leading a symphony orchestra, she aims her pointer finger at the keyboard and jabs the "send" button.

"How ARE THINGS at the office?" Paige, who of course thinks I'm running a temp agency, asks as she tumbles onto the living room couch. I bite into an apple, producing a crunchy *argh* sound that pretty well describes my mood.

"Fine," I say, sitting down next to her, although I'm rattled by Sienna's outburst this afternoon. Things have been going so smoothly between Bill and Sienna—too smoothly, based on her past romantic experiences—that I can't help worrying that she's making a mountain out of a molehill to put their relationship to some kind of unpassable test. Not to mention the stress she's putting on our business. Still, Molly isn't speaking to me and Peter's off in Hawaii, so I'm in no position to cast stones.

Anxiously I glance at the end table where the answering machine sits. Now that there are cellphones the once essential house phone is about as outdated as a bar of soap in a world of alpha hydroxy. Yet despite that and the fact that no lights are blinking, which already gives me my answer, I can't help asking as casually as I can manage, "Did Daddy call?"

"No, isn't he out of town? He tiptoed into our room before it was even light out the other morning to say that he and Tiffany were going to Hawaii so she could give women at these fancy hotels makeovers and they could sell a ton of BUBB stuff. Lucky Daddy. I wouldn't mind lying around on some beach."

"Well, it's not a vacation," I say archly. At least I hope not. I'm sure Peter's working round the clock with a whole boatload of people, trying to sell Tiffany's cream. Tiffany's probably up to her perfectly turned ankles in mascara and moisturizer; they couldn't possibly have a minute alone.

",Mom," Paige says, fluttering her hand in front of my face, trying to snap me back to attention. "Anything wrong?"

"No. Just wondering if Daddy remembered to bring a sweater," I say distractedly. "It can get cold at night, even in Hawaii." At least I hope he's cold at night in his big, lonely bed without me cuddled next to him. I tuck my feet onto the couch and reach over to rub my toes. Paige wraps my apple core in a napkin and pitches it onto the makeshift crate coffee table. Then she brushes my hand aside and starts massaging my tired soles.

"*Um,* that feels wonderful," I say, closing my eyes and surrendering to her relaxing ministrations. Then the lightbulb goes off. "Okay, what do you want?"

"Mom, that is so, like, jaded. Just because I do something nice why does it have to mean that I want something?"

"Sorry, honey, you're right." I settle back into the pillowy cushions as Paige kneads her fingers across my toes with the perfect amount of pressure. After a few moments she clears her throat.

"So, Mom, I know that you caught Molly making out with Brandon. . . ."

"And you're okay with that?" I ask, startled.

"Well, more okay than you are. At least I didn't go all ballistic or anything when she told me."

"That's very *mature* of you," I say. Call me "mature" and I bristle, but for teenagers, it's a point of pride. Still, what I really mean is: What the heck is going on? If her twin sister was making out with a boy she was dating even the queen of England would show more emotion. "I thought you liked Brandon. Why exactly are you taking this so well?"

"Oh, you know, lots of other fish in the sea and all that," Paige says evasively, and before I have a chance to dig any deeper, Molly walks into the room. Despite my attempts to talk to her before she left for school this morning, Molly barely issued a grunt. But now, she lowers her eyes and sits down next to me.

"I know that I shouldn't have been kissing Brandon in the den. I know I shouldn't even have been seeing him," she says, looking up at Paige, who's seated on the other side of me. Paige stretches her arm across the back of the sofa to reach out for Molly, and I catch them smiling. Then each of them slips a hand into my lap. "I'm sorry, Mom," says Molly, with what sounds like genuine contrition.

"Me too," says Paige. "Neither of us ever should have been dating Brandon, should we, Molly?"

"No, we shouldn't."

"And we agreed, neither one of us is going to date him now, right?" she prompts.

"That's right," says Molly solemnly.

I'm glad, I'm grateful, I'm caught off guard by their united front. What mother wouldn't want to believe that her daughters were throwing over that double-dealing dickhead of a Don Juan and finally getting along? Still, I wasn't born yesterday.

"You're sure?" I ask, swiveling my head back and forth between them. "I know you two must be up to something."

Paige laughs. "Okay, Mol, it's time to come clean. Mom, yes, we do want something. We know that Molly's grounded, but tomorrow is Heather's birthday party. Please, can Molly come? I know we'd have so much fun."

"We'll be home by midnight," Molly pleads, and although she doesn't have to say it, I know what she's thinking. This is the first time since they were in grade school that Paige has invited her to come along with her friends.

"Heather's parents are going to be at the party? You'll be home by midnight? No more fights over Brandon?" I say, making sure we're all on the same page.

Paige leans in for a hug. "Promise. We won't even ask for new outfits. C'mon, Molly, let's go look in the closet. I'll let you borrow that purple Free People T-shirt that you like so much."

A mother whose shit detector was in proper working order might not buy the happy-as-two-peas-in-a-pod sister act, but I'm so ready and willing to believe that peace has been restored to the household that I put any qualms on hold. Maybe the girls really *are* maturing. I know I feel like I've aged a decade in the last couple of days.

Seventeen
❧

Assault and Flattery

EARLY THE NEXT EVENING my apartment looks like the backstage of a tent at Bryant Park during Fashion Week. The girls are getting dressed for Heather's party, I'm trying to pack for Hawaii, and Naomi's looking for something to wear to the Miss Subways reunion. Clothes are strewn everywhere. I navigate around a fuchsia organza blouse and a one-shouldered black-and-white ball gown that are lying on the living room floor, but when I sink down on the couch I accidentally crush a pair of chartreuse chiffon harem pants.

"I'm not so sure anyone would actually want to wear these," I say, fingering the billowy fabric. "But they feel good."

Naomi's standing in front of the full-length mirror in the hallway closet, the one that's slimming. She tugs at the bustline of a sparkly red Bob Mackie dress that looks like it just came off of a sixty-day tour with Dolly Parton. "I know, this looks ridiculous," she says, pulling a black cashmere cardigan on over the getup. "But the reunion's next week and I still haven't got a thing to wear!"

"Don't worry, Grandma, we'll help you tomorrow," Molly says as she and Paige come over to kiss us goodnight. They look adorable in miniskirts and patterned tights—but then again, they'd look adorable in gunnysacks.

"Laurie's mother is driving you home, right?" I say, making them each open their shiny metallic purses to check for cellphones and emergency cab fare.

"Yes, Mom, everything's good," Paige says, swinging her bag's silvery chain. "Although it is a little disturbing to see our mother parading around the apartment in a hot pink bikini."

"It's not hot pink, it's carnation. And it's not a bikini, it's a two-piece suit," I say, pulling the waistband of the bottom up toward my belly button. "And if I do say so myself, it doesn't look half bad."

"It looks good, Mom. Seriously," Molly says, giving me a little kiss as she heads out to the party.

"Have fun," I say. And as the girls slam the door I add under my breath, "But not too much fun."

"It does look good sweetheart, although you could wear something a little sexier," Naomi says, as she heads to the back of the apartment. "Maybe the dress of my dreams is waiting for me in your bedroom closet. Mind if I take a look?"

I walk over to the mirror and study my reflection. I remember the absolute horror of shopping for swimwear in my twenties. Either the underwire in the built-in bras poked into my breasts, or worse, the suit had no support at all. And then there was the inevitable moment when I pinched the flesh at my waist and invoked the Menses Defense—sure that I was either getting my period, having my period, or getting over my period. Now, at an age when you'd think I'd be even more critical of my body, I'm actually more content. If I don't exactly grin at the way I look in the suit, I don't grimace either.

I pick up the rotting apple core that Paige forgot to throw

away last night and my shoes and head for the bedroom to check on Naomi when, naturally, the phone rings. As I grab for the receiver and see Peter's cellphone on the caller ID my favorite nude-colored suede sling-backs fall to the floor and the apple core spins out of the napkin and messily lands on top of them.

"Damn, my shoes, hi, hi," I say, cradling the phone to my ear, holding it—and Peter—as close as I can.

"Tr . . . oooooh . . ." I hear through the staticky connection.

"Peter, sweetheart, is that really you?"

"Ha . . . ha . . ." he says, which I'm guessing means "Hawaii," and not that this whole separation is one big joke. And then, just like that, the line clicks dead.

I'm still standing in the middle of the room fondling the phone when Naomi comes in carrying an armload of magazines.

"Was that Peter?" She smiles, bending down to pick up my apple-splattered shoes. Then she goes into the kitchen and comes back with a paper towel to absorb the stain—a far cry from the Naomi I knew who was so *self*-absorbed that just a few months ago she spilled coffee on the living room carpet and didn't even notice.

"Thanks," I say, finally letting go of the phone and putting the receiver back in the cradle. I look down at my bathing suit and laugh. "He called. That must be good, right? Now if only I could figure out what else I'm going to pack."

"Already done," Naomi says, leading me toward the bedroom and showing me my suitcase, which is sitting by the foot of the bed. She hands me the magazines. "I figure a novel, you'll be so busy with Peter, you wouldn't have time to finish. These are to read on the plane."

"Mom, thank you, you've thought of everything," I say, impressed that Naomi's even tied a gold ribbon around the bag's handle so I'll be able to pick my luggage out from the sea of identical black canvas suitcases on the baggage carousel. The twenty pairs of shoes I insist on taking along never fit into a carry-on.

"There is one more thing," Naomi begins, when the phone rings again.

I listen to the voice at the other end and grab for my coat. "Tell me later. The twins are at the police station. We have to get down there right away."

❧❧❧

"POLICE STATION" AND "the twins" are words I never ever in my life expected to hear together in the same sentence. Not to mention "fight," "they started it," or "the victim wants to press charges."

"It's going to be all right, isn't it? I mean, it's better than their being in the hospital?"

"At least they're not hurt," my mother agrees, although we're both grasping at straws. I look at Naomi and see that she's still wearing the sparkly red Bob Mackie dress. Worse, I realize I have nothing on underneath my coat except my bathing suit—in my race to rescue the Paige and Molly, I was in too much of a hurry to get dressed. I wrap my arms around my chest, protectively. If only the fashion police were my biggest worry.

A few minutes later Naomi and I arrive at the local precinct. Like synchronized swimmers storing up oxygen for an important meet, we each take a deep breath. Then we step into the city-block-sized station to find out how much trouble the girls have gotten themselves into.

My eyes dart around the room trying to find them. The precinct's walls are made out of cinder block painted a grimy gray-green, the fluorescent lighting is enough to make anyone look like a perp, and a large bold-faced clock ticks away precious minutes. Officers in blue uniforms and cuffed suspects wearing everything from ripped T-shirts to Brioni sports jackets file past us, but still no Paige or Molly—where the heck can they be?

Naomi points toward a metal desk where a police officer is sitting in front of an old-fashioned typewriter—the same model IBM Selectric that I used in college to write my papers on Botticelli. There's a pushpin corkboard on the wall next to him but instead of being decorated with pictures of loved ones, it's crowded with mug shots of New York's most wanted criminals.

"Damn!" the officer exclaims as he balls up one set of carbon-paper documents after another and throws them onto the floor in a pile next to his scuffed shoes. "Can you believe the department just spent almost a million dollars on these crappy machines? The NYPD can read license plates from the air but it can't figure out a more modern way to fill out duplicate forms." He takes a swig of coffee from a limp paper cup. "What can I do for you folks? Assault, robbery, arson?"

Which would be the lesser of the evils? I want to blurt. But I know this isn't *Deal or No Deal*. I don't get to pick.

"My grandchildren, Molly and Paige Newman," Naomi says. "We're trying to find them."

"Missing pers—oh, you mean the Twin Hitters?" the officer says, recognizing their names. He points toward the corridor and tells us to take the first left.

Paige is sitting on a wooden bench with her arms crossed defiantly. On the other end of the bench I spy Molly, wearing the—ironic, given the situation—Free People T-shirt that her sister had promised to lend her for Heather's party. The party I gave the girls permission to go to. The party I'm guessing was the site of the melee. Slumped down in between the twins is

Brandon Marsh, who's holding an ice bag against the left side of his face.

Naomi goes over to Molly and I wrap my arm around Paige.

"Are you okay?" I ask, stroking Paige's hair.

"Oh yeah, Mom, never been better. It's Brandon who's suffering," Paige says blithely.

A moment ago I was filled with maternal concern. Now that I see the girls are all right, I let them have it. I release Paige's shoulder and stand up so that I'm glowering over her.

"Stop smirking. What the hell is going on?" I demand. "The officer outside told us you were called the Twin Hitters. *The Twin Hitters?* You and Molly said you were going to a party at Heather's and that her parents were chaperoning. How did the two of you end up here with . . . *him?*"

"We *were* at Heather's," Paige says righteously.

"And her parents were chaperoning. Although they spent the entire night upstairs," Molly admits. She looks at Brandon and starts to giggle. "Whatever happens, Mom, it was worth it."

"I'll tell you what's going to happen. My father is going to be here any minute," Brandon boasts, pulling back the ice bag to reveal his very purple-black eye. "You shitheads are going to be locked up for the rest of your lives."

Heather's parents and a gaggle of agitated teenage girls traipse into the room along with a woman wearing ironed Levi's and a white button-down shirt. We've always tried to give the girls the best of everything—orthodontists, tennis coaches, the top pre-PSAT tutors—but frankly, I never expected to be adding "Denise Rodriguez, social worker" to the list. Everybody starts talking all at once and Denise Rodriguez tugs at a red-and-yellow lanyard around her neck, blowing long and hard on a silver whistle. "One at a time, people. Let's hear it. You first," she says, pointing at Paige.

"Well, Brandon is my lab partner and he liked me but then he took my sister out to lunch even though it didn't really mean anything and we got into this huge competition," Paige says without taking a breath.

"Brandon was dating me first!" a girl in a silvery minidress gripes.

"He liked me best!" complains another, who I recognize as the party giver, Heather.

"When I asked Brandon why he was dating more than one of us he told me that all the other girls were just hamburger and I was the steak," a girl in a pink leopard headband reports.

I can't help thinking that's it been fifty years since we women burned our bras and declared ourselves equal and yet some boys still look at a girl and all they see is a piece of meat.

Paige steps up to the front of the room and shakes her fist in the air. "Girls were not put on this earth to be boy toys!" she shouts to a rally of cheers. Then she turns toward me. "Mom, that same night, right after you caught Brandon kissing Molly, he met me in the back of the school gym and he was kissing me. Except he told me he wasn't dating anyone else anymore and I didn't know he was double-dipping until the next day."

"Yeah, and then we found out that he was making out with everybody else in this room," Heather says petulantly, stomping her stiletto into the police station's gummy linoleum floor.

"Well, not everyone." Heather's mother chuckles uncomfortably.

"I mean all of the young girls." Heather sighs.

"Don't sass your mother," Denise Rodriguez says. "Mrs. Hemmings, where were you when the assault took place?"

"In my bathroom, giving myself a home peel. Big mistake," she says, fingering her lightly blistered cheek. "But Heather said it would be uncool for us to come downstairs."

"Uncool is exactly what parents of teenagers are supposed

to be," Denise Rodriguez says, furiously entering notes into her case file. "Okay, can somebody cut to the chase and tell me how all of this happened?"

Molly steps forward and raises her hand. "We decided to teach Brandon a lesson. When he got to the party we acted all sweet and told him to wait for us in the den. We pretended like it was going to be something sexy. Then we came in and surrounded the little creeper and locked our arms in a circle so he couldn't leave. We told him we'd wised up, that we'd made a pact and nobody was going to date him anymore. Ever again."

"We took back the power!" the girl in the silvery minidress cries.

"It was going really well until Brandon decided he wasn't going to listen anymore and when we wouldn't let him out of the circle, he started shoving himself against our bodies," says Paige. "I mean he purposely shoved his shoulder against Kristin's *boob*. That's when I let him have it and punched him in the eye."

"I socked him, too!" squeals Molly.

"Girls, we applaud your politics, just not your methods. Violence is never the answer. We'll talk about this more at home," I say firmly. "But Ms. Rodriguez, can you tell me how this whole thing ended up at the police station? Kids have fights every day. I don't mean to make light of it, but I'm not sure how it got so blown out of proportion, either."

"My father's the D.A.," the oh-so-full-of-himself Brandon says, jumping up from his chair. "I called the police commissioner's office and told them to come over and arrest everybody. You can't just hit someone from my family and expect to get away with it."

As if on cue, a man with steely blue eyes and a strong jaw swaggers into the room.

I'd never connected him to Brandon before, though he's immediately recognizable from his frequent pictures in the newspaper.

"Sit down!" Colin Marsh grunts to his son. Then he pastes a politician's smile on his face and makes a point to shake each and every one of our hands. "Colin Marsh, Colin Marsh, Colin Marsh," he repeats so we remember who he is when it's time to pull the voting lever.

Heather's mother fawns over Colin Marsh and says that she'd love to throw him a fund-raiser. I'd love to throw him a left hook—the guy's an obsequious phony and while I'd never in a million years admit this to the girls, I get why it was satisfying to deck his son. As the rest of us start yammering again, the no-nonsense Denise Rodriguez pulls the D.A. aside to make her assessment. After a few minutes, two reassuring phrases rise up from across the room. "Think the parents can handle it" and "You don't want this story in the papers, not in an election year."

Colin Marsh stands behind his punk of a progeny and anchors his hands on the boy's shoulders. "Apologize, now, Brandon! I raised you to be a gentleman," he says a little too grandly. As if he's speaking to a phalanx of cameras instead of five adults and a bunch of teenage girls.

The twins and their friends giggle smugly. Until I tell them they have to apologize, too.

Denise Rodriguez issues a strong warning not to get into any more trouble. "We have your names. I know your faces. Next time you won't get off so easily!" she says in a voice that lets everybody know she means business.

I'm bounding down the station house steps to get my family out of there as fast as I can when Colin Marsh, D.A., pushes in front of me and pulls me aside.

"If you ever breathe a word about what happened—about how a group of simpering high school girls made my son look like a sissy—I'll bring you down, Mrs. Newman," he hisses.

"What?" I say, trying to keep my voice steady. Be rational, Tru. Don't panic. Colin Marsh is just being a bully. If the D.A.'s office knew about the Veronica Agency, you'd already be in jail.

"You heard me. There must be something," Colin Marsh blusters. "Everybody has something in their past they don't want people to know about. And believe me, if I make it my business to, I'll find it. Do we understand each other?"

"Just keep your son away from my girls!" I say firmly. Proud that I've stood my ground. And then, before my voice cracks or Colin Marsh can see me shaking, I gather Paige and Molly in my arms and tell Naomi to hail a cab.

Heather's chauffeur pulls up as we step out onto the curb. "Good work, girls!" Heather says, giving the twins a high five. She's about to join her parents in the limo, when Heather turns toward Naomi and looks her up and down. "Love the outfit, Mrs. F!"

"Thanks," Naomi hoots, fingering her sparkly red dress. "You should see what my daughter's wearing."

୬୧ ୭ଞ୨ ୬୧

As soon as we get back home I head toward the bedroom. I want to splash some water on my face. Change out of this ridiculous bathing suit. Call Bill and tell him about Colin Marsh's ominous threat.

Hurriedly, I unbutton my coat and throw it on the sofa. As I race past Molly, she breaks into a giggle. "O-M-G, Mom. Don't tell me you went out without your sash?"

I swivel around and plant my hands on my hips. "I assume you mean the one that says, 'Mother of the Twin Hitters'?

Never again, do you hear me, ladies?" I say angrily. At least I try to say it angrily. Paige and Molly start giggling. Naomi lets out a howl. And in a burst of relief, I start laughing, too.

I put on some jeans and a sweater and we sit down around the kitchen table. While I was dressing the girls made tuna fish sandwiches, and Naomi serves up steaming mugs of hot chocolate. I don't ever remember my mother making her "assimilated chicken soup" when I was a kid, but ever since that pre-dawn heart-to-heart we had about Peter and Nana and how resilience can get you through just about anything, it's become Naomi's signature drink.

"I knew from the beginning that Brandon was a little turd," Naomi says, wagging her finger. "You know, girls, men—even boys—tell you all you need to know about themselves in the first hour. It's just that we women have to listen."

"What do you mean?" asks Molly.

"I mean that Brandon told you he was dating both of you and you even knew he went out with other girls. What, did he have to wear a sign on his forehead?"

"But Grandma, when Brandon took both of our hands that day in the hospital you asked which one of us was going to win him," Molly reminds her.

"That was the old Naomi; she didn't always give good advice. But this is the new Grandma." My mother laughs. "You should pay attention to her, she's very very smart."

"When I met Daddy . . ."

"Oh no," Paige groans.

"Make fun all you want, but when I met Daddy I knew he would be good to me," I say quickly and loudly, so despite the fact that they're screeching like six-year-olds I know they hear me as they run to their room.

"Peter has been good to you. You've been good to each other. For each other. Every marriage has its bumps," says

Naomi. "You'll go to Hawaii tomorrow, you'll straighten everything out. Just one more thing," my mother adds, grinning mischievously and handing me an envelope. "I told you we need a plan. When you get to Hawaii you call this number. I think it'll be a big, big help."

As soon as Naomi leaves, I pull out my cellphone to call Bill. "Colin Marsh doesn't have a thing on us, I promise," he reassures me. "He was just making an idle threat. You're the one who has something over him. Go to Hawaii, straighten out things with your husband. Stop worrying, okay?"

"Okay," I say, as Bill wishes me luck and clicks off the phone. I check my luggage to make sure my name tags are legible. I take Naomi's envelope and stick it in my passport, then I carefully put my passport inside the pocket of my handbag. I know you don't need a passport to go to Hawaii—but at the moment I feel like you can't be too careful. About anything.

Eighteen

❦

A Lei at the Beach

HAVING SURVIVED A SEVENTEEN-HOUR trip, two plane changes, and one rambunctious five-year-old who for the entire last leg of the flight used the back of my seat as a battering ram, I'm grateful to be touching down in Hawaii, even if our jumbo jet does land perilously close to the end of the runway.

"*Wow!*" the five-year-old shrieks with delight as the plane comes to a screeching halt. "Can we do that again?"

I'm as white as a sheet and my matted airplane hair is in serious need of an untangling product that has yet to be invented. Still, I've avoided major tragedy—we didn't crash, I didn't get a blood clot (I popped up and down so many times to pace the aisle I practically could have walked to Hawaii), and despite feeling occasionally homicidal toward him, I didn't kill the boy sitting behind me. Though I did scold his mother.

"You know with those manners he'll never get into Harvard," I'd said primly. Of course for all I know the kid with the Michael Phelps kick is a legacy.

Now that we're no longer in the air and there's no chance that my $150 cellphone will screw up the workings of the $150-million plane, I turn it back on to check my calls. Nothing from Peter, but I'm buoyed by the inspirational messages from Sienna, who tells me, "Kick Tiffany's ass!," and Naomi, who reminds me that "You're a Finklestein, you can do anything you set your mind to. Also, you shouldn't forget to call Jeff Whitman."

Jeff Whitman—that's Naomi's mystery man. I finger the envelope with his contact information, which Naomi stuffed into my purse for safekeeping. "Just call him," Naomi had said when I pressed her for details. "If I say anything more it'll ruin the plan."

The five-year-old, pulling his mother's arm, runs past me as I shuttle off the plane. So few people check their luggage these days that I get my bag in no time and go off in search of a restroom. I readily find the men's room, but it takes me a couple of minutes to realize that the lettering on the door next to it is missing a "W." I reach for the knob and laugh. The first place I'm visiting in Hawaii is the *omen's* room, which I hope is a good sign.

Inside, I splash some water on my face and reach into my makeup bag to pull out an arsenal of three-ounce-tubes—an unexpected plus of the security rules forbidding taking larger bottles of liquids on planes is that I raided department store beauty counters for samples and got all my favorite products for free. Time-arresting, lineless, poreless, flawless potions vie for the chance to save my skin and I dab on some undereye cream, two moisturizers, and a large dollop of sunscreen— eschewing the grander-sounding "70" and "80" for a 30 UV SPF because anything higher offers less than 1 percent more protection and needs to be applied about ten times more frequently. Finally ready, I put on my tortoise-framed sunglasses and step outside into the beautiful sunshine where, just as I expected from all of pictures I've ever seen, dozens of Hawaiian greeters are waiting to bestow flowery leis on new arrivees. Fortified by the festive atmosphere, I line up behind a group of fellow tourists.

"Nice custom, isn't it?" I say pleasantly to a balding, sixty-something man who's already changed into a Hawaiian shirt. I'm so used to the luxury of casual conversation—between my family and Sienna there's always someone around to exchange mindless banter with—that after my long solo flight I'm chat-deprived. "You know the Hawaiians say 'aloha' for 'hello' and 'goodbye.' Just like 'shalom.' "

Before he has a chance to even open his mouth, the woman in a bright blue flowered muumuu standing next to him spins around.

" 'Shalom,' is it? Stop hitting on my Harry!"

I point to my wedding ring to assure her she has nothing to worry about. "I was just making conversation. I had a fight with my husband and I came to Hawaii to make sure his beautiful lady boss isn't putting the moves on him."

"Well, don't you go thinking you can replace your husband with mine," she warns, still suspicious.

Harry leans in to whisper something in her ear. "Oh Harry!" She blushes. Then she turns to me. "Sorry, honey, it's just that a wife has to keep an eye on her man. Not that my Harry would ever stray on his own, but look at that John Edwards fellow. That little homewrecker came along and seduced him, then she had his baby! How dare she say that to a married man, 'You're so hot!' "

Unless "the little homewrecker" incanted her spell while casting a fishing line onto the zipper of Edwards's pants, I don't think she deserves all the blame. Still, I know what Harry's wife means about the lure of temptation. Particularly five-foot-six, creamy-skinned, blond-bombshell temptation. Which is after all why I'm here.

"I'm Elaine," says Harry's wife. "And shalom to you, too. My Jewish grandmother told me it also means 'peace.' " Midwest Elaine has a Jewish grandmother? You just never know about people, I laugh to myself. Or, as it turns out, customs.

Harry and Elaine step up to get their leis and the greeter drapes a pretty strand of flowers around each of their necks.

"I'd like the double row of orchids," I say, pointing to a luscious white-and-purple necklace.

A look of dismay crosses the greeter's face as he scans a list of names. "No, no Tru Newman," he says. "Sorry, lady."

"That's okay, a single strand of carnations and shells looks fine," I say, downgrading my expectations. But still no dice.

Harry reaches into his wallet and hands the greeter his credit card. The flowers, it turns out, aren't free. I wonder what other surprises await me in Hawaii. Now that I'm within spitting—or hopefully kissing—distance of Peter, I cross my fingers and say a little prayer that he's as happy to see me as I know I will be to see him. What husband wouldn't be touched that his wife flew 5,000 miles to surprise him? I won't even let myself consider an answer like "A husband who's still angry."

Elaine smiles and adjusts my lei so that, island-style, the fragrant flowers are equidistant front and back. "Welcome to Hawaii," my new friends say, as I get into a taxi. "Go get your fella."

It's not until I'm in the cab careening toward the hotel that my stomach starts doing cartwheels. We barrel past a skyline of skyscrapers that might lead me to believe I was still in New York if it wasn't for the idyllic stretch of sandy beach and the emerald ocean that seemed fashioned by a different creator than the one who made Coney Island. Dramatic peaks rise out of a lush mountainside and the driver points out Diamond Head off in the distance. "The world's most famous volcanic crater," he says proudly.

No, it's not, I think, clutching my stomach, which is churning 2,000 rpms with the intensity of a high-powered washing machine. Mercifully, just as I'm considering asking the driver to pull over, we arrive at the hotel. I pull my luggage up the steps and stumble into the lobby, where the very first thing I bump into is Tiffany Glass. A life-sized cutout of Tiffany, anyway, holding a BUBB compact in one hand and powdering her cheek with the other. She's wearing a bikini and a bubble coming out of her head invites customers to sign up for free consultations. "Bubblehead," I mutter, slapping past the sign and smack into a concierge. My luggage goes skating across the lobby and the entire contents of my purse empty onto the marble floor. I'm bending over to pick up a good luck tiger's-eye charm and a tube of Frizz-Ease (which I'd hoped would tame my hair in the tropical humidity) when I feel my knees buckle.

"Are you all right, ma'am?" the concierge asks, holding out his hand to steady me.

"I'm Tru Newman, Peter, my husband, his room . . ." The lobby whirs around me. Then suddenly I feel another sharp cramp in my stomach as I faint to the floor and land on top of my suitcase.

❧

"FLU," SAYS A MAN whom I can only hope is a doctor. He's wearing shorts, sandals, and a red-striped polo shirt, but he does have a stethoscope and he seems to be writing a prescription. "In twenty-four hours you'll feel like new. Or at least as good as your old self." He chuckles.

"Oh thank goodness, darling, I was so worried," Peter says, rushing across the bedroom to take my hand. Except that as he approaches my bedside I realize that the tall, silver-haired, deeply tanned man isn't Peter.

"Who, what . . . ?"

"Confusion, perfectly normal with her fever," the sandal wearer says as he walks toward the door. "I'll be on the golf course if you need anything." The second stranger thanks him for coming and promises that I'll get plenty of rest and fluids.

I struggle to sit up and take in the scene. The room, which is about four times the size of my bedroom at home, is decorated in soothing shades of cream and blue, and through the floor-to-ceiling-windows I see an oversized lanai and a stretch of ocean dotted by white sails. But who's the mystery man and how did I get here? Images from an endless parade of movies-of-the-week swirl before my eyes—movies in which an unsuspecting heroine puts down a soda can at a frat party and damn if before you can say "Diet Pepsi," she isn't immediately drugged and date raped. Still, I don't think that any of those heroines were tucked into a cozy carved cherrywood bed or attended to by a guy solicitously pouring her a tall glass of Gatorade.

"You need your rest now," says the attractive-as-Harrison-Ford fellow, urging me to lie back on the pillows that he's freshly plumped. "By the way, I'm Jeff Whitman."

"Jeff Whitman. Naomi's Jeff Whitman?" I say with a start.

"The very same."

"But how?"

"The concierge took you to your husband's room, but Peter's away until tomorrow, working on another island. Then the concierge saw the envelope in your purse that had my name and number on it so he phoned me. Get some rest, Tru," Jeff says, patting my hand. "We'll talk about it more in the morning."

"Okay, Jeff Whitman, I think I'll get some sleep now," I say, sinking into the pillows as instructed, way too tired to resist. "By the way, how do you know my mother?"

"Ah Naomi." Jeff Whitman sighs wistfully as he drapes the top sheet over me and turns down the bedside light. "She was my first love."

❧❧❧

IN THE MORNING, I awaken to a stream of bright sunshine pouring through the window and Jeff Whitman asleep, his six-foot frame sprawled awkwardly over the rattan chair just a few feet away from my bed. The doctor was right; except for the unsteady-on-your-feet feeling of having been in bed for almost twenty-four hours, I'm feeling much better. I'm wrapped in a hotel robe that I remember stumbling into sometime in the middle of the night, but now, I slip out of bed to find something more appropriate to wear. I check my suitcase, which is empty. Guessing that Jeff or someone from the hotel has helpfully unpacked for me, I fling open the closet looking for a sundress or maybe a pair of shorts—but all I see are the purple body-hugging knockoff Versace cocktail dress I wore to Lincoln Center, my tightest white jeans, and assorted rainbow-colored miniskirts and a see-through leopard-print blouse, which I've never laid eyes on before and that still have tags on them. The loose hoodie and sweatpants I wore on the plane are nowhere to be found, and the drawers are filled with sexy lingerie and only my skimpiest bathing suits. A quick check of the shoe tree tells me that yup, I have the requisite twenty pairs, but there's not a sneaker or a flip-flop in sight.

"That's what I get for letting my mother pack." I laugh,

pulling out a stretchy baby-sized tee and a bright orange mini, wondering how I'm going to get through the next few days dressed as Charo.

Jeff Whitman lets out a sigh, and I see him flopping around trying to find a way to make himself comfortable in the chair, which is about two sizes too small for his body.

"Jeff," I say gently, shaking his arm. "I'm going to take a shower. Why don't you move to the bed, you'll be more comfy."

Half-asleep, Jeff thanks me and takes me up on my offer. I've just started running the water when I hear the door swing open and the thump of a bag landing on the polished stone floor.

"Peter!" I say, running out to greet my husband. And then before he has a chance to think or react or know what hit him, I pull him toward me and kiss him like there's no tomorrow.

"Peter, I've missed you, I love you, I don't care that you didn't tell me about your job, and I hope you can forgive me for not telling you about mine. I want to, I will, I'm going to tell you everything. No more secrets, just like you said. But I'm not going to let the last few months wreck twenty years," I say determinedly, stepping back and finally coming up for air.

Peter reaches for me and runs his hands across my body, as if he's reacquainting himself with a familiar landscape, or he just wants to make sure that I'm really here in the flesh.

"I love you too, Tru," he says. "I've missed you like crazy. All this fighting—I've been trying to make sense of it."

"Maybe it's because we're in the adolescence of our marriage."

Peter looks at me quizzically.

"Oh, I just read that on the plane in one of Naomi's magazines. How somewhere around the midpoint of a long marriage, people push and poke at each other, testing, just like a teenager does with his parents."

"But teenagers are getting ready to leave," says Peter, wrapping his arms around me even more tightly. "And I'm not going anywhere. Not if you'll have me."

"I'll have you and have you and have you," I laugh, reaching up for Peter's lips.

We still have a lot of things left to say, but we've said the most important. I let the robe slip off my shoulders and Peter lifts me in his arms with the eagerness of a groom. We're kissing and cooing when my handsome husband bends over the side of the bed to set me down and we hear a *thwack*.

"Oooh," Jeff Whitman moans as I hit him like a sack of potatoes. I quickly pull the sheet around my body to protect whatever modicum of modesty I have left. Jeff instantly recoups his savoir faire and plants a big smile on his face. Then, as he's sitting cozily next to me in bed, I feel his arm reaching around my shoulder.

"Stop that," I say, lightly smacking his fingers.

"What's going on? Who is this man?" Peter demands as hurt, confusion, and anger flash across his face.

Jeff Whitman, on the other hand, looks merely amused. "I was just going to ask the same question, darling. Who is this man? Is this *the husband?*" Jeff asks in a tone that suggests that whoever "this man" is he's no more an important figure in my life than the toll taker I see from time to time on my drive up to Woodbury Commons.

Jeff swings his legs over the side of the bed and faces off with Peter.

"Peter, sweetheart, there's a simple explanation," I say.

"That's right," says Jeff Whitman, reaching for my hand. "I'm in love with your wife."

"I thought you were in love with my mother!" I protest.

"That was then, this is now. Peter, I'm in love with your wife."

"What the fuck?" mutters Peter.

"Jeff, are you crazy? You sound just like Faye Dunaway in *Chinatown.* Your mother, your wife. Are you going to make me slap you?" I ask, remembering how Jack Nicholson got Faye's character in the movie to make up her mind. Then I burst out laughing at the absurdity of the whole scene.

Peter takes a step closer to Jeff to try to get to the bottom of things. He fastens his hand under Jeff's chin and pivots it from side to side. "He does look a little old for you."

"I am neither too young nor too old," Jeff exclaims. "I was in love with the mother and now I am in love with the daughter. It is a perfectly natural situation."

"Perfectly natural if you're French," Peter says.

"I am half-French," Jeff parries.

"Gentlemen, please. This isn't about your heritage, it's about my future. Peter, I love you. I came out here to make up, I got the flu, the concierge let me into your room, and he found a piece of paper with Jeff's name and phone number on it in my purse. Naomi masterminded this whole fiasco. My guess is she wanted to make you jealous. Help me out here, Jeff. Am I on the right track?"

"Yes, my darling, you're absolutely correct! My job was to bring you two back together, and I can see that I've done that," Jeff says, missing the point that this half-baked scheme might just as easily have wrecked everything. He leans in to kiss me on both cheeks, "the French way." Then he pats Peter on the back and hangs the DO NOT DISTURB sign on the doorknob as he makes his exit. "Ah, *amour.* I envy you two lovebirds the making up. You are about to have the most wonderful, wonderful sex."

JEFF MIGHT NOT have had the right idea about how to bring us back together, but he was 110 percent on the money about makeup sex. Peter and I spend the next few hours in bed kissing and caressing, teasing and pleasing each other with an intensity that makes me understand what people mean when they say that the earth moved or "I felt liked we merged into one person"—empty-sounding clichés until they happen to you. Despite the air-conditioning and the whirring overhead fan, Peter and I are drenched in a pleasant shared sweat that makes our smells and our bodies indistinguishable from each other's.

"I can't move." Peter chuckles as he strokes my salty skin.

"I think we're going to have to." I nibble at the tip of his finger. "I'm starving."

"Oh, Mrs. Newman," Peter sighs, turning to face me and pretending to feed me his entire hand. "You are so *sexy* when you're hungry."

"And you're so corny," I say with a giggle.

"I know, just one of my many lovable qualities." Peter pauses. "I do still have some lovable qualities, right? Tell me I haven't ruined things completely, it must mean something that you're here?"

I look at my husband, really look at him. How could he ever imagine that I'd want to be anywhere but with him? If anyone had asked me six months ago which one of us was the vulnerable one, I would have had to say me. Still, I've changed in these last few months; I've had to. The old Tru wouldn't have had the nerve to come down here after Peter or to start the Veronica Agency, but after everything that's happened I've learned you have to fight to keep the things that are important. And truth be told, I was probably never the hothouse flower that either of us made me out to be. Just as Peter is more, much more, than the I'll-take-care-of-everything Wall Street banker. Molly could see that her father was the kind of man a girl should marry—even if she was momentarily sidetracked by that smarmy Brandon. And like daughter, like mother.

"Sweetheart, how can you even think you have to ask?" I say, leaning in to kiss him.

"We can live in SoHo or eat peas out of a can," Peter says, remembering our disastrous dinner at the Hudson Cafeteria when I accused him of not letting me make decisions. "I want us to make a fresh start."

"I like our home just fine," I say. "I'm just grateful that we're going to be able to stay there."

"Me too," says Peter, relieved by my reassurances that I'm in this for the long run. Marriage, mortgage, mistakes, and—knock wood—many more happy years together. He playfully pats my backside. "Okay, you, let's get that lunch. Unless," he says, in the spirit of not forcing me to do anything I don't want to, "you'd rather stay here."

"No, I'm famished," I say. "But if we're going to make a fresh start, there's something I need to talk to you about."

"About your business, the one you started with Sienna, and that woman we ran into . . . what was her name?"

"Georgy."

"Right," says Peter, standing up to put on a pair of khaki shorts that I swear he's had since college. Then he pulls on a blue oxford shirt that's the same color as his eyes. "What an idiot I was to be so upset because you hadn't told me about it. But don't worry, sweetheart, Paige and Molly explained every-thing."

"They did?" I ask, alarmed.

"They said you'd opened a temp agency but you didn't want to tell me about it until you were sure it would be a success. It was the morning I went into their room to kiss them goodbye before Tiffany and I left for Hawaii. Shit, Tiffany!" Peter cries, echoing the first word that comes to my mind when I think of his vixenish boss. He looks at his watch and scowls. "Tru, sweetheart, I'm sorry, Tiffany's waiting, I was supposed to be at a meeting on the beach half an hour ago, it's with the head cosmetics buyer for the largest department store chain in Hawaii. I'll make it up to you, I'll . . . come with me!" he says, pulling me toward the door.

I look down at my robe and tell Peter to go ahead. "I'll be down in a minute. I just have to get dressed. And by the way," I call after him as he's hurrying off to his appointment, "it's not exactly a temp agency. Sienna and Bill and I are running an escort service. For high-class courtesans. And they're all over forty."

Peter spins around and his jaw drops open. "What the hell? No wonder you didn't want to tell me where you were sneaking off to, I . . . I have to *go,* is what I have to do," Peter says, stabbing a finger at his Timex. "Besides, I wouldn't have a clue what to say to you now, anyway."

⊱✦⊰

TWENTY MINUTES LATER I've summoned my courage to stuff myself into one of Naomi's postage-sized outfits—and to face Peter. As if there aren't enough crazy things going on at the moment, when Peter had said that their meeting was at the beach he neglected to add that we wouldn't be sitting around a table, we'd each be sitting *on* one. Who else but Tiffany Glass would do business with a big-shot client while the group of us has massages?

"Why, Tru, how sweet to see you. Peter said you were here. The little wife coming down to check up on her husband?" Tiffany squawks as she rolls over on her massage table, which is lined up in tandem with three others. The sky is a cloudless blue, yellow trumpet-shaped hibiscus dot the screened-off-for-privacy beach area, and the pink sand beneath my feet is as fine as powdered sugar. The only sour note is the tiki torches—a little touristy and frankly they remind me of *Survivor*. I only hope I'm not voted off the island.

Peter emerges from a thatched-roof hut with a sheet wrapped around him. He looks at me searchingly. I can't tell if he's just surprised and confused or really angry. Peter grips his hand firmly around mine and pulls me toward Tiffany. "Tru and I are going to go down the beach a little ways. Give us ten minutes," he says.

We walk at a clipped pace, past languid sunbathers and a group of children building sandcastles with the intensity of future I.M. Pei's. "They remind me of Paige and Molly," I say, conjuring up memories of our family in calmer times.

Peter nods. Then he kicks the sand. "I'm trying to understand, Tru. Really. But if we're talking about Paige and Molly . . . isn't what you're doing illegal? Couldn't you get into a lot of trouble?"

"Bill's set up the business so that no one will know what we're up to. We're incorporated as a temporary help agency and we even pay our taxes," I say, repeating the line I always tell myself when I wonder if we're doing anything wrong. I just pray that Bill is right and that that miserable S.O.B. of a D.A. Colin Marsh isn't onto us. Still, right now I have more immediate worries.

"Do you hate me?" I ask haltingly.

"I could never hate you. It's just that . . . an escort agency?" Peter pauses. "The night I ran into you at Lincoln Center, when you said you were on a date . . ."

"Oh no. No! I *run* the agency. That night? Bill's friend just needed someone to go with him to a party, to impress his boss. No sex, no touching, nada, zip, nothing, no physical contact at all. And it was only that one night, usually I never even meet the Johns."

"The Johns?" Peter repeats.

"The men. The very nice men, who are all Bill's friends, whom we set the women up with. And I got five thousand dollars for just being charming," I say with a hint of pride. "Well, I would have, if I had stuck around."

Peter stands there silently for what seems like an eternity.

"I should have told you," I say, reaching out for his hand.

"I need to figure out how I feel about all this," Peter says, squeezing my fingers, and then letting them go.

A well-built man who I recognize as one of the masseurs comes up behind us and puts his arms around our shoulders. "Feel, *schmeal*. No time for talk. Time for Lomi Lomi."

Peter seems relieved for the interruption.

"We'll talk later," Peter says hastily, walking a few paces ahead of me. Then, wordlessly, the masseur ushers us back to the massage area and I duck into the thatched hut to change out of my clothes.

✣✣✣

I CLIMB ONTO the massage table a few minutes later feeling vulnerable, and it's not just because I'm naked under a flimsy sheet. When I reach out to touch Peter, he turns away. Peter's table is sandwiched between mine and Tiffany's. And I see, with a start, that while I was undressing, their big deal client took the spot on the other side of Tiffany. Their big deal client, who's "the head of the largest chain of department stores in Hawaii"—who also just happens to be none other than the wily Jeff Whitman.

"Ah, the Newmans, such a lovely couple," Jeff Whitman tells Tiffany. "I met them earlier and we spent the most delightful time together. I feel like they're practically family."

"Is this for real? Or is it another one of Naomi's crazy schemes?" I whisper to Peter.

"I don't know. I don't know what to believe anymore," he says.

The head masseur steps forward to swing a brass mallet against a flat metal gong, producing a roaring *boom* that sounds like waves crashing against the shore. "I am Kawikani, the Strong One. We start now," he says.

"And I am Alana," says my masseur, "Hawaiian for 'awakening.' Or Alan."

Alana rests his hands on the small of my back. Kawikani stretches his arms toward the heavens to offer a prayer. "Renew, revive, revitalize," he says, sounding like a spokesperson for Lancôme.

Tiffany starts giggling, but Alana shakes his head. "Take seriously. The Lomi Lomi is not just to heal physical pain. It is to heal the heart, to bring mental and spiritual resolution. Whatever is blocked, let it out, get rid of it, go with the flow."

Alana motions for Kawikani to come over and the two of them spend a few moments whispering.

"Okay, for this group, we give them the tea, too," agrees Kawikani, who returns with a tray and four steaming cups. Obediently, we each take a sip.

I settle back onto the cushioned table and close my eyes. Alana hums softly, telling me, "Take deep breaths and enjoy the rhythmic sensations." Given the tension between me and Peter, it's going to take more than some crazy Hawaiian massage to make me unwind, but as instructed I close my eyes. Alana's hands move over me like gentle waves and I feel a small jolt of energy surge through my body. I feel deeply relaxed, yet energized at the same time. My back muscles are about a thousand times looser. And, strangely, so is my tongue. I haven't felt this uninhibitedly talkative since the dentist gave me a shot of Sodium Pentothal—and I'm not the only one.

"Alana, your hands are so strong and powerful!" I squeal in stream-of-consciousness admiration.

"I love a man with strong hands. Peter has strong hands," Tiffany purrs.

"I do, don't I?" says Peter. He spreads his fingers apart and flexes them into a fist.

"Um," says Tiffany. "Your hands are big, but Kawikani's are bigger. Jeff, what kind of hands do you have, are they huge?"

"Naomi used to say they were so large that I could hold the whole world right in my palm."

"Naomi has long fingers, perfectly shaped. She posed for a magazine ad once," I say, recalling a moment of my mother's faded glory. "Her index finger was polished a deep shade of red. And she was pointing to a toilet seat in the *Ladies' Home Journal.*"

"That's why I love her," says Jeff dreamily.

"Tru grew up with a mother who took more pleasure out of pointing to toilet seats than raising her daughter. But that didn't stop my honey from becoming a great wife and mother," Peter says. "That's why I love *Tru.*"

"You do?"

"Uh-huh," says Peter, who's unflexed his fist and now is staring at his palm.

"He loves me." I giggle. "Because I'm a wife and mother . . ."

"And a businesswoman. A businesswoman with a stable of forty-year-old hookers." Peter laughs, pressing his outstretched fingers against his face, as if he's trying to locate his nose.

"Hookers." Tiffany giggles. "I've always wanted to learn how to give good head. Do the hookers give good head? Do they use BUBB?"

"BUBB-de-BUBB-BUBB," Peter sings. "I didn't know from Adam but I'm married to a madam."

"And you're okay with that?" I ask.

"I'm okay, you're okay, we're okay," Peter croons. "O-kaay!"

For a moment I have to wonder if Peter's talking from the tea. Or the massage. Or his true feelings. Then he wraps his sheet around his torso—his torso that is brown as a berry from having already been several days in the sun—and comes over to sit down next to me on the edge of my massage table.

"I'm not as zonked out of my mind as I may seem. Well, maybe not *quite* as zonked out of my mind as I seem. I think your business choice is . . . unusual, honey. And I'm having a little trouble picturing you, you know," he says sotto voce, "running *a call girl operation*."

"I would have said the same thing. But it's not much different from running a benefit committee. You have to be organized and diplomatic. And you have to be sure you make your nut."

"Your nut?" Peter laughs.

"Your number, your net, the figure that's going to put you in the black. Though, frankly, I prefer thinking of it as being in the pink. Pink is a much more cheerful victory color."

"You're the nut," Peter says, bending over to kiss me. "I love you, Tru. I can't say that I wouldn't have liked it better if you'd opened a catering business. . . ."

"Not really an option. Remember me? I'm the wife who doesn't know a carving knife from a broccoli spear."

"Good point. And if running an escort agency makes you

happy, I want to be supportive. God knows you've put up with my crazy hours and everything else about my work for all these years," Peter says, pointing toward Tiffany.

"You, sir, are very, very nice." I say reaching up to wrap my arms around his neck to press my lips against my husband's.

"Nice, who's nice?" Tiffany says, propping herself up on her elbow. "Jeff is nice."

"Yes," I say with a laugh. "Jeff is nice."

Jeff looks over at us and winks. "Tiffany, what do you say you and I go find ourselves a quiet place to talk? You can tell me all about your makeup and I'll show you around the island. You two skedaddle." Jeff waves his hand in our direction—his strong, large, he's-got-the-whole-world-in-it hand, which he's got Tiffany eating out of.

"Yes, you two skedaddle," says Tiffany. "Peter, you can go home to New York now. I'll see you next week when I get back. I'm going to stay in Hawaii and get to know Jeffy better. I always had a thing for Harrison Ford, and Jeffy, you do look a lot like Indiana Jones."

And just like that, Tiffany switches her affections from my husband to my mother's ex-boyfriend, who's old enough to be her father.

"Who would have guessed that Ms. Glass was so fickle?" I laugh as I slide off the massage table and Peter enfolds his sheet around us both in a cozy cocoon.

"Tiffany's got a good head on her shoulders; she knows when something's a lost cause."

"You're not a lost cause," I tease.

"I am romantically as far as Tiffany's concerned. I always have been. You know that, don't you, sweetheart?"

I nod. "And I'm not sure that girl's going to have any more luck with Jeffy-poo. If he's a cosmetics buyer then I'm Mahatma Gandhi."

"You do have pretty good peacemaking skills," Peter says with a kiss. We move forward under our shared toga, feeling as young and carefree as a couple of preschoolers giggling themselves silly under a tent.

"Kawikani, Alana, thank you. I wasn't sure about the Lomi Lomi, but you've made me a believer." We say goodbye and Peter and I start to walk down the sun-kissed beach toward a woman in a grass skirt who's giving a hula demonstration.

"Yes, Lomi Lomi very good, ancient Hawaiian tradition," Alana says as he packs up his equipment. "But to make massage work even better," he calls out as I turn around to wave one more goodbye, "always drink the tea." Then he laughs and raises the cup to his lips.

Nineteen

❦

Dog Day Afternoon

DESPITE TIFFANY'S HAVING SAID that Peter was free to go back to New York, we stay in Hawaii for three more days on a mini-vacation. Once upon a time if I'd called to tell the girls we weren't coming home I'd have had to promise to bring them back a present, but from the sound of their voices, I get the feeling that they'd be willing to bribe us to stay away. Naomi says not to worry, "Everything's going swimmingly." But just as I'm about to say goodbye, Molly gets on the line.

"We have a surprise for you, Mom," she says mysteriously.

"Don't tell!" says Paige, grabbing the phone from her sister as I hear some sort of tumult in the background and the girls hurriedly hang up.

For the next couple of days Peter and I make a game out of guessing what the twins are up to—agreeing that it's probably nothing as shocking as them having gotten body piercings or that Paige has cleaned up her side of their room. We enjoy exploring the island—hiking up twisty trails to Diamond Head;

going snorkeling at the very same beach where Elvis Presley filmed *Blue Hawaii*; and swimming with dolphins, who, our guide tells us, shed their skin nine times faster than humans. "They must save a fortune on exfoliants," I quip. With all of our time spent sightseeing—or closeted in our room making love—we only run into Tiffany and Jeff once, when we ride past them in our golf cart and exchange hurried hellos.

"Jeff looks a little worse for the wear," I say as we wave and I notice that his tan—and his patience—seems to be waning. Tiffany jerks Jeff's arm around her waist while he tries to pull it away.

"We owe that man a debt of gratitude and a box of cigars," Peter says.

"Havana cigars." For his term of service in diverting Tiffany's attention Jeff deserves only the very best.

On our last night we're walking down the beach with my friends from the plane, Harry and Elaine, when a young couple invites us to join their seaside wedding celebration. The bride is simply beautiful in a turquoise and deep blue tie-dyed sarong with a pale lavender orchid pinned in her hair at the nape of her neck, and the groom has a grin on his face as wide as the Pacific Ocean, which he just happens to be standing in front of. Dinner is a luau of roast suckling pig wrapped in banana leaves and, afterward, we break out into a spontaneous chorus of "Here Comes the Bride." As the young couple walks toward the ocean to pose for photos, the bottoms of their sandals leave an imprint in the sand filled with promise—*Just Married*.

Peter pulls me toward him and I cuddle my head in the crook of his arm. "I feel like I'm surrounded by Marriage Past and Future," I say, pointing to the radiant newlyweds and then to our friends Harry and Elaine, who, having settled the inevitable differences that are sure to come up throughout an enduring union, seem happy and comfortable. "You and I are going to get to be an old married couple, too," Peter says, hugging my shoulder.

"That we will." And then I look up into his deep blue eyes to make him a promise. "I'll always love you. And I swear that even in twenty years, even if we come back to Hawaii, I'll never wear a muumuu."

OUTSIDE OUR APARTMENT Peter fixes one last vacation kiss on my lips. On the other side of the door I hear loud music and the cheerful commotion that tells me the girls are at home. Peter picks up our bags and we walk inside.

"Hello, we're home," I sing, when out of nowhere, a brown-and-white furball lurches through our legs and out the open door.

"Brandon, you get back here!" Molly screams as the twins careen past us to catch the puppy flying down the hall. The forbidden puppy that's obviously our welcome-home surprise.

"Molly and Paige, *you* get back here!" I shout, racing after them. The elevator door opens and my ninety-six-year-old neighbor, Mrs. Pinchot—who's survived the Depression, World War II, and the closing of Alexander's, her favorite department store—steps out and surveys the scene. Mrs. Pinchot pulls back her shoulders and uses her still-solid body to block the puppy from making his way into the elevator and out of the apartment building.

"Let him go," I cry. "He looks resourceful, he'll find a new family in no time." But Mrs. Pinchot picks up the puppy and hands him back to the girls.

"Having a pet teaches children responsibility," Mrs. Pinchot says when I protest keeping the dog I've always been adamantly opposed to getting. "You'll see, dear, soon you won't be able to imagine your lives before Brandon was part of the family."

Peter rolls his eyes, but I know he's almost as eager as the girls to keep the pooch.

Naomi comes out carrying a bowl of water for Brandon, which she sets down on the oriental carpet. "The girls missed you. I just had to let them get the dog."

Paige makes the ultimate argument. "Mom, look at you. You're wearing white jeans. How much more work do you think it is to take care of a puppy?"

As if he has a sixth sense that I'm the one he has to win over, the puppy sits at my feet and eagerly wags his tail. I bend down to pet him, knowing that I'm going to have to give in. "But did you have to name him Brandon?"

"Absolutely," Molly says, tossing a rubber ball. "After all, the real Brandon's a dog. Thanks, Mom, you're the best," she cries, not even waiting for my official answer, as the girls and Brandon scamper off toward the library where the dog is already making himself at home.

Naomi settles down next to me on the couch. "I shouldn't have let them get the puppy without your permission. I'll never do it again," she says with an unmistakable sparkle in her eye—because we both know that she's only promising not to turn my house into a kennel, and not to never do anything else against my wishes ever again. Still, asking Naomi not to meddle would be like asking Barbra Streisand to stop over-enunciating. And besides, at this point life would be positively boring if my mother didn't mix in.

The six-hour time difference between New York and Hawaii is catching up to me. Peter volunteers to go into the kitchen to fix some coffee and several minutes later he comes back with a freshly brewed pot. He sits down next to us and tosses some newspapers and magazines onto the floor so he can put his feet up on the new coffee table that Naomi's bought in our absence.

"A little present," Naomi says dismissively, "to thank you for all you've done."

"That was very nice of you. I even like it." I take a sip of coffee and balance the cup on my knees. "So, Mom. Tell us about this Jeff Whitman."

Naomi blushes. Then she busies herself rearranging packets of Splenda into a diamond pattern.

"Mom?" I coax, putting my hand over hers to get her to stop fidgeting.

"We were both sixteen and his family moved into the apartment next to Nana and me. I was his first love."

"You mean you were each other's first love?"

Naomi clears her throat. "Well, we never really went out on a date together. Nana forbade it. She said Jeff was *traif*."

"*Traif*? You mean like shellfish or pork?" Peter says, translating the Yiddish word for forbidden food.

"Jeff wasn't Jewish. He was the ultimate forbidden food."

I put my cup on the table and clap my hands together. "Mom! That is so *Romeo and Juliet*! Didn't Nana's forbidding it just make you want to sneak off with him more?"

"It wasn't like today, it was a different time." Naomi sighs. "But that Jeff, he wrote me beautiful love letters. He'd wait on the corner for hours just for the chance to say hello. He sent five hundred votes for me to the Miss Subways contest—he went all over the city to mail them from different postboxes so the judges wouldn't think anything fishy was going on. Wasn't that sweet? He even went to Staten Island."

"On the ferry?" I ask, and Naomi nods. "That's love."

"Maybe I was in love with him, too," Naomi says thoughtfully. "What girl wouldn't be, a boy so beautiful who loved you so much? But I swear, I never so much as kissed him."

"And you kept in touch with him all this time?"

"For years I didn't know what had happened to him. But when your father died, he read about it in the paper. . . ."

"And he got in touch with you!" I exclaim.

"By then Jeff had become a big real-estate developer. He was divorced and living in Hawaii. He wanted to come to New York to see me but I wouldn't let him."

"Why not?" Peter asks, as intrigued as I am by my mother's romantic history.

Naomi places her hands squarely on her knees. "I want Jeff to remember me the way I was, a flawless sixteen-year-old."

"Oh Mom, no! So you're not flawless. Big deal! You're still beautiful. And you probably weren't flawless even back then—what teenage girl doesn't have the occasional outbreak of acne?"

Naomi pretends to ignore me. She stands up and starts clearing the debris of our coffee klatch off the new table.

"Mom, you have to let him come here. Jeff still idolizes you. You should see the look on his face when he talks about you. . . ."

"Good! I want him to keep getting that look on his face, to picture me just the way I was. Enough now about Jeff Whitman," Naomi says, declaring this particular conversation over. "Tell me about your trip."

I can't believe that my cocky, confident, take-on-the-world mother is frightened of seeing an old boyfriend, especially one who still adores her. But I know that arguing with her right now won't do any good.

"The trip was great, we saw sea turtles, I learned to do the hula, and we ate so much pineapple I'm thinking of changing my middle name to Dole."

"That's nice, sweetheart," Naomi says, bending over to kiss each of us on the foreheads. She picks up the tray and heads toward the kitchen. "You've always been my favorite son-in-law," she calls back to Peter.

"Your only son-in-law, now and forever," Peter says with a laugh.

"That is so sad about Jeff," I say, and then I let out a yawn. "I may have to go into the bedroom to take a little nap."

"I'll go with you," Peter says. But instead, I settle my head on his shoulder, and we stay rooted on the couch, too tired and comfy to move.

I'm starting to doze off when I hear Paige holler across the apartment for Brandon to "come back!" I snap open my eyes just in time to see the pumped-up pooch scurrying over the carpet, underneath the couch, and out the other side to where we're sitting. Before we can stop him, Brandon finds the pile of newspapers that Peter had strewn on the floor, squats down, and takes a large dump.

Molly and Paige come running in, full of apologies. "At least he's paper trained," Paige says.

"Take that dog out immediately!" Peter tells the twins. "Before he gets used to going in the house."

I shake my head and laugh. "I can't wait to see what our new dog does next. This is just the beginning of our troubles."

Peter bends down to carefully fold over the soiled newspaper so he can carry it into the kitchen and wrap it up in a plastic bag.

"Fuck it, what did you say about the beginning of all of our troubles? Take a look at this!" Peter says, sliding the front page of the *New York Post* out from underneath the shit.

He holds the paper in front of me, and in disbelief I stare at
the two-inch headline.

MADAME XXX

See Page Six to find out:

Who's Running New York's Newest

Call-Girl Operation?

THANK GOODNESS THE story in the *Post* is a blind item and the
columnist doesn't know who's behind the business yet. But
he's on the case and promises to crack it this week, and he's already got an alarming number of details: "A once famous TV
personality . . . Forty-year-old call girls . . . One of the hookers
has even put her John on a diet . . ."

Frantically, Peter and I hop in a cab and go racing down to
the Veronica Agency offices. Which, he's surprised to discover, are in the same office building as BUBB's new warehouse space.

"How do you run a fancy call-girl operation out of the same
building we use for storage space? And how come I never ran
into you?" Peter wants to know. We step inside the lobby and
ring for the elevator—which comes swiftly now that Peter's
contractors aren't hogging it.

"We almost ran into each other, the night you were checking on the construction and you slipped a note under the
door of your neighbors who were complaining about the
noise?"

"That was you?"

I wince, remembering that awful night. Running into
Georgy. And that huge blowup with Peter at the Hudson
Cafeteria. "We picked this building for its low profile. Can't
be too careful."

"You should have told Sienna that," Peter says, as we step out of the elevator and go into my office.

"I'm a *reporter*; it was perfectly natural for me to write the blog. Besides, it's done now. Can you stop telling me how I've made a mess of everything and help figure out how to make it right?" Sienna wails.

"Hello," I say.

"How could you do it? What were you thinking? Were you purposely trying to sabotage everything?" Bills asks in a tense, controlled voice.

"Um, hi?" I try again.

Sienna hunkers down in her chair and defiantly crosses her arms in front of her chest.

"Oh *damn it!*" I finally yell to get their attention since neither of my partners will stop arguing long enough to acknowledge that Peter and I are in the room.

Sienna glares at Bill and then looks over at us. "Glad you two are back together. Looks like you got some sun."

Peter walks up to his tax attorney and lets him have it. "How could you get the girls mixed up in something like this?" he rails to Bill.

"Talk about your chauvinists," Sienna mutters.

"The Veronica Agency was my idea. I'm the one who thought of it, I'm the one it means the most to, and I'm the one who's going to figure a way out of this mess," I say with a bravado that borders on the ridiculous. Because really I have no idea what we're going to do.

"I'm sorry, honey, and you too, Bill," Peter says, stuffing his hands in his pockets. "I'm just upset."

"Who isn't?" asks Bill. "We're in a pickle."

"We're in a *pickle*?" Sienna says.

"Okay, we're up shit's creek. Do you like the sound of that any better?"

"Bill," Sienna says formally. "I am sorry if you think I put the company in jeopardy. That was never my intention."

Normally, the easygoing Bill I know would accept Sienna's grudging apology, but not this time. This time Sienna's pushed him too far. "People judge you by your actions, not your intentions. And yours were pretty reckless," he says frostily.

Sienna walks across the room and opens and closes the refrigerator door. Peter stretches his hands over his head and Bill paces circles around the office. Me, I'm pushing my elbows up and down on the armrests of the chair—if nothing else, the calamity is providing our daily dose of exercise.

I try to convince myself that things aren't as bad as they seem—after all, Sienna's said a zillion times that nobody reads the newspapers anymore. Still, ever since the story broke this morning Sienna's Madame XXX site has gotten so much traffic that it's already crashed twice. (Crashing being the Internet equivalent of people being trampled to death at a sale in a department store. On the one hand, a disaster. On the other, proof positive that the public wants what you're selling.) I glance nervously over at the phones which are flashing like Vegas slot machines. "Maybe we better listen to some of these voicemails," I say, stabbing the message button.

The first is from Lucy, who wants to know if she should lie low or go to work tonight. Georgy—not realizing that Sienna has purposely changed the details in her blog—wants to set the record straight: She put Gabe on the Atkins Diet, not Jenny Craig. She would never recommend that anyone eat prepackaged food. Several of Bill's client-friends say they've left messages on Bill's cell but he hasn't returned their calls. Matt, the trader who took Patricia to the Literacy Partners benefit, is alarmed that someone might connect him to the agency. Gary—the stallion who wanted to try a younger filly—is nominating Clive Owen to play him in the movie. "How about

Flicka?" I mutter, punching the delete button. Dozens of messages later my head is spinning and I wearily sink into my chair. Peter comes over to massage my shoulders. Across the room I see Bill on his Palm Pilot finally getting back to people and Sienna typing on her computer —more of the same damned thing, I'm guessing, that got us into all this trouble in the first place. "Holy shit, what are you doing now?" Bill says as he drops his phone midsentence and goes over to see what she's up to. Just as I'm walking over there myself, the office phone issues one last, loud blaring bleep.

"Get back to me immediately, as soon as you can," howls Patricia, the money manager and former college working girl. "I just had a meeting with the reporter from the *New York Post*."

I call Patricia and arrange to see her right away in a coffee shop down the street. Peter wants to come with me, but I tell him no. "Paige has a soccer game; you better get over there. Besides, I'm a big girl now. This is something I have to take care of myself."

"Okay," Peter says, reluctantly. "Just promise you'll call if you need me. And let me know what's going on."

"Ditto, I want to know every time Paige scores a goal. Text me, okay?" I'm glad not to be just a soccer mom anymore—but I'm sad not to be a mom who's free to go see her daughter's soccer game. Especially today. Sienna agrees to stay behind at the office to begin destroying any incriminating evidence. And Bill's off to see a friend who's a criminal attorney. "Just to be on the safe side," he assures us.

⚜

WHEN I GET BACK to the office an hour later, Sienna's packing. She drags a cellophane tape dispenser across a large cardboard box to seal it closed. Then she stands up and wipes her hand across her brow. "How did it go?" she asks, anxiously.

"Well, the guy at the *Post* knew all about how Patricia paid her way through that pricey Ivy League college. And how even after she became a money manager, she still enjoyed turning a trick. He threatened to expose the whole story unless she told him who was behind the blog."

"She didn't, did she?"

"No, she didn't. She slept with him instead. And then she asked me for ten thousand dollars. All things considered, I think we got off easy." I pick up a client file and start grinding it through the shredder.

"So who's that creepy little journalist going to pin as the madam?"

"That's the funny part. After Patricia slept with him the guy from the *Post* admitted that he'd had calls from a half dozen people. *Asking* to be named! One of the Housewives of New Jersey even offered him a bribe. She said if viewers thought she was Madame XXX, Bravo might even give her her own show."

"Sounds like we dodged a bullet," Sienna says, sounding relieved.

"I guess. But we were just getting started." I sigh, running my finger across my desk, already feeling nostalgic for the business.

Sienna shoots me a withering look. She cuts off a piece of bubble wrap from a large roll and begins winding it around the bust of Mozart that she brought in to lend the office a touch of class. "We came dangerously close to being in a huge amount of trouble," she says, as if I'm the one who got us into this mess.

"In trouble because you had to write about it, Miss-I'm-a-Journalist-and-Who-Cares-What-Happens-to-My-Business-Partners? If it weren't for you we could have been something *great!*"

Sienna grips her fingers more tightly around Mozart's neck. "A great call-girl operation?" she snarls.

"There's nothing wrong with call girls. Besides, our ladies are 'courtesans.' "

"Hookers, call girls, courtesans—is that what you want Paige or Molly to be?" Sienna bangs the Mozart bust so hard against the desk that despite the wrapping, it bounces onto the floor and splits open.

I shift my weight from side to side and try to control my anger. I came back with good news, the *New York Post* isn't going to out us, yet here we are fighting—all of my frustration over Sienna's blog and Sienna's resentment about her back-room role in the business are like sparks igniting a wildfire. And Sienna's question hits a nerve, a raw one. It's not like I haven't thought about it myself. As desperate as I was to get money—and as much fun as I've had running the business—everything boils down to one simple question: Would I choose this life for my daughters?

"If being a call girl is a choice a woman makes of her own free will, then I have no moral objections," I say righteously. "It's a good way to earn money and Patricia and Lucy seem to enjoy the work. And I shudder to think what we'd be wearing if Coco Chanel hadn't had a sugar daddy. Can you imagine life without the little black dress?"

"No, I can't. But Paige and Molly, is this the life you want for the girls?" Sienna asks again.

I kick the toe of my shoe against the side of a box and avoid looking Sienna in the eye. "I've always thought that Molly would be a great teacher or that she'd go off to some third world country to save the planet. And with that quick tongue of hers Paige would be a natural for public relations."

"Or a great telemarketer. That girl could sell solar panels to the coal company," Sienna says, coming over to stand next to me.

"Or a talk show host or a restaurant hostess or a stay-at-home mom or a working mom or . . ." My voice trails off and I take a deep breath. "I want the girls to do whatever makes them happy. But no, I'm hoping they pursue a different direction."

Sienna reaches out to squeeze my hand. "Me too," she says.

"I don't want the girls to go out on dates for money. I want them to know the thrill of possibility. Remember the commercial that used to be on TV when we were kids for that breath freshener?"

"Certs?" Sienna smiles. "The one where the girl pops the mint into her mouth, walks around the corner, and bumps into a gorgeous guy?"

"I want Paige and Molly to feel that life can be like a Certs commercial. When they go out on a date I want them to know that they could end up meeting the love of their life."

I feel my eyes well up with tears. Sienna encircles her arms around me and when she presses the piece of bubble wrap she's still holding against my back we hear a crackly *pop*.

"That is such a satisfying sound!" Sienna says.

"Here, give me some of that stuff," I say, snatching a piece of the plastic and punching away at the bubbles. Which, Sienna's right, is very satisfying. "I'm not sorry we started the business. I feel like I learned a lot. And I'll never buy another artichoke."

"Neither will I." Sienna laughs. "But I also found out I'm not a very good team player. I need to tell you I'm sorry, Tru. I really thought I could keep the blog anonymous, but I never should have done something so irresponsible."

"It's okay, I forgive you," I say, popping one final plastic bubble and telling Sienna to wipe the stricken look off her face. "We were probably lucky to get out when we did. There was no love lost between me and the D.A. I've been jumpy ever since Colin Marsh made that threat. And if nothing else, at least I found out that I like working."

"Well, that's a switch."

"I'm glad I got to stay home all those years when the girls were younger. But now I'm ready to start Act Two. Although I haven't a clue about what to do next."

"Something will come to you," Sienna says.

"What about you?"

"Not sure. I got an email on the site this morning from an agent who thinks I might be able to turn the blog into a book. Nothing definite. But maybe Madame XXX will bring me better luck in business than it has in love, since it seems to have totally destroyed my relationship with Bill. Oh well," Sienna says, picking up a box and carrying it across the room to a stack of others. *"Que será, será."*

"Whatever will be, will be? Is that all you can say about the only man I've ever seen you truly in love with?"

"Bill's too young. Besides, he's furious with me."

"Forget about your age. Find a way to make Bill unfurious. A good man is as hard to find these days as a Javan Rhino. There are only about fifty of them left in the whole entire world. I can't believe you're not going to fight for him."

"I said I was sorry and he refused to accept my apology," Sienna says briskly.

"That was in the heat of the moment—not to mention it was a pretty lame apology. I'm sure Bill would forgive you if tried again."

Sienna shakes her head. "Here," she says, changing the subject and tossing me a marker. "Before you dream up your next project and become a titan of industry, think I could get you to do some manual labor?"

I'm just uncapping the Sharpie to start labeling boxes when my cellphone beeps. "Paige just scored a goal!" I say with a whoop.

Twenty

The World
According to Cher

MOLLY HAULS A BLUE-and-white-striped golf umbrella out of a gigantic tote bag and positions it over her grandmother's head.

"Do you have an ark in there?" Naomi frets. "This rain is coming down in buckets."

"Relax, Grandma, I've got you covered." Molly smiles.

Paige, who's standing under the awning next to her sister while we wait for the downpour to stop long enough for all of us to dash across the street without being drowned, jams her hand into Molly's bag to see what other emergency supplies her twin sister has brought along. She pulls out a tweezers, a curling iron, and the same brand of double-sided tape that Jennifer Lopez used to keep her Oscar dress in place—the dress that plunged in an open V down to her navel.

"Impressive. Looks like Molly has thought of everything." Paige whistles, ripping off a strip of tape and unzipping her slicker to stick it between her skimpy mini and the very upper-most part of her thigh.

"What, they charged you for this dress by the inch, and you

couldn't afford something longer?" Naomi complains. She squeezes Paige's hand and apologizes. "Sorry, *bubbala,* I'm just nervous about the reunions—I mean the Miss Subways reunion," Naomi quickly says. She reaches into her own bag— a small beaded clutch shaped like an old-fashioned subway token that the girls found at Target to celebrate the occasion— to retrieve a pretty pearl-encrusted comb, which she sticks into her hair at the side of her chignon. Then she pulls the comb back out again.

"You look beautiful, Mom," I say.

"Thank you, you girls look beautiful, too." Naomi sighs, stuffs the comb back into her purse, and fidgets with the clasp. "I'm sorry I made you go to so much effort. Maybe we should all just go home now?"

"Not after I found a parking space." Peter laughs, ducking under the awning to join us. Like a wet Labrador who's just escaped from the bathtub, he shakes his head and water goes flying everywhere.

"Ew!" Paige shrieks. She grabs the copy of *Town & Country* that Peter had been holding over his head but as she starts rolling it up to swat him, I snatch it out of her hand.

"Let me see that," I say, recognizing the picture on the society page of my very own former employee Georgy, looking lovely in a jade necklace and a chiffon lavender gown. I'm glad to see that she's still working, although I hope she's charging this particular client a mountain of money—she's on the arm of the sleazy Colin Marsh. Colin Marsh, the power-abusing D.A. who threatened to dig up dirt on me if I dared breathe a word about his double-dealing two-timing son. Ha, let's see what he can do to me now that I know he's dating a call girl!

"Molly," I say sweetly, "you know that essay that you're supposed to write for English class called 'The Most Courageous Thing I Ever Did'? It was stupid of me to tell you not to write about Brandon. In fact, why don't you enter it in the national competition?"

"Thanks, Mom, I'll think about it. But right now it's Grandma who has to be brave. C'mon, Grandma, let's show them what the Finklestein women are made of! Then, before Naomi has a chance to protest, Molly takes her grandmother's hand and tugs her toward the celebration.

⊱⊰⊱⊰⊱⊰

WHEN NAOMI FIRST told me about the reunion I didn't understand why it was being held in a diner—even a hip, retrofitted 1950s theater district favorite—until she explained that the owner of Ellen's Stardust was a former Miss Subways herself. Inside the front vestibule guests are shedding trench coats and stowing umbrellas. And then there are those who are balancing themselves on one leg to slip out of rain boots into more elegant footwear. "They look like a bunch of flamingos at a designer shoe sale." Molly giggles.

About fifty of the former Miss Subways winners are expected here this evening, and although they range in age from their fifties to a now-ninety-year-old who was crowned in 1941, a quick look across the room reveals that the only silver fox in the bunch is a real fur one. In a sea of blondes, brunettes, and redheads and by the dint of soft lighting, Botox, and sheer will, it's hard to distinguish the septuagenarians from their offspring. The diner is playfully decorated with a drive-in movie theater screen and a choo-choo train that whistles its way around the mezzanine. The walls are filled with framed posters of the former Miss Subways. I give Naomi a nudge and, with Peter and the girls trailing behind us, I push her toward the center of the room. Within seconds, she's surrounded by a circle of women.

"Naomi Finklestein, it's good to see you!" a big-haired

blonde gushes. She hugs my mother, then runs her hand down the hips of the scoop-neck cocktail dress the girls picked out for Naomi to wear. "No girdle," the blonde reports approvingly. "As I live and breathe, you look fabulous!"

"I hope you should live and breathe—we should all live and breathe for the next one hundred years! Or at least the next fifty!" a redhead jokes.

With obvious relish, the women banter about their conquests—remembering the smitten fellows who proffered orchids, diamond rings, and the one who sent a proposal hidden inside a three-foot-wide lemon pie. "Can you imagine how much weight the girl who married him must have gained!" The big-haired blonde giggles. Naomi's laughing, too, and despite my mother's worrying—over coming or not coming, what she was going to wear, and even how her pelvis might measure up—within moments she's clearly feeling at ease in this sorority of former beauty queens.

As I listen to their stories I realize that while none of them became the next Doris Day, Naomi was right. They're an accomplished group of women, including a supreme court appellate judge, a former FBI agent, a woman who worked with the Red Cross after 9/11, and of course Ellen Hart Strum, the owner of the nostalgia-filled diner. When a svelte brunette who's a senior dancer with the Nets asks what Naomi's been up to, I hold my breath. After all, this is the question she's been dreading. Still without missing a beat, my mother points to me and the girls. "These are my proudest accomplishments." Naomi beams, and from the easy, infectious smile on her face—the one that for all those years I had so much trouble coaxing from her—I know that she means it.

Molly guides me over to the wall of posters. "Says here that three decades before Vanessa Williams was crowned Miss America there was an African-American Miss Subways. And look, there's Grandma! 'Beautiful Naomi Finklestein has appeared in school plays and plans to pursue a career in modeling. She is also devoted to children and helping make the world a kinder, gentler place,' " Molly reads aloud. I always thought that last part was a lot of malarkey. But now it has the ring of truth.

"Check this out," says Paige, looking at a photo of the Keehlers, the only pair of twins to reign simultaneously. "This says they were 'as identical as two cigarettes in a pack.' Nobody could ever say that about us," my blond, straight-haired daughter says, pointing to her sister's curly brown locks.

"Thank goodness," Molly teases. "I wouldn't want to grow up in Manhattan looking like a California surfer girl."

"And I wouldn't want to be a slave to detangler."

"And I wouldn't change either of you for the world," I say, drawing the girls in for a hug.

"Okay, Mom," Paige says, moving a step away from my clutches. "We know, we should 'celebrate our uniqueness!' Yikes, you said that so many times when we were growing up I used to think it was like the state motto."

"It's the Newman motto." Peter laughs as he brings me a Perrier. "Whether it's about looks or personalities. Or," he says, with a wink, "career choices."

"O-M-G, you guys are so weird," Paige says. "But now that we're talking about careers, you never really explained why you and Sienna closed your temporary help agency. Did it go bust?"

"Not exactly. Let's just say that it was a learning experience. A chance to get my feet wet. And I'm looking around for something else to sink my teeth into."

"Mom, could you use a few more clichés?" Molly, my budding writer, asks.

"Okay. Whatever. One day we'll get it out of you," Paige wheedles. Although I know they never will.

I take a sip of water and hand it back to Peter. The ice-filled glasses at these parties are always too cold to stand around holding, although Peter's happy to be of service—just another of about a thousand reasons I can think of these days that I'm grateful for my husband. A waiter wheels out a four-foot-high chocolate fountain and Molly gasps. "That must be the Magic Mountain. I think I saw it once in a Disney movie." Paige takes her sister's hand and the two of them walk off trancelike toward the cascading tiers of velvety liquid.

"Bring me back a strawberry, dripping in chocolate," Sienna calls after the girls as she joins me and Peter.

"Oh no, no, no, no, no! I know you're not on television anymore, but you never know, somebody might let you be a newscaster again. Just in case, you should stay in shape," coos Tiffany Glass, who's followed Sienna over to our little group. Tiffany's wearing one of her trademark body-hugging dresses and she's arm in arm with the "plus one" that Naomi invited her to bring along to the reunion. The "plus one" I so helpfully introduced Tiffany to—our old Veronica Agency client Gary, the sexist stallion.

"I just signed a book contract. My figure can go to hell; nobody cares what an author looks like." Sienna laughs. Tiffany dispatches Gary to get her a drink. Then emotionally she clasps my hand between hers.

"Tru, thank you again for Gary. I have to tell you, after striking out with Peter and Jeff Whitman I was starting to wonder if I'd ever trap, er, I mean, *attract* a man again. But Gary calls me his treasure."

"He also calls her his cheap date," Sienna whispers, as Tiffany leaves to go congratulate Naomi. "Gary must still be pinching himself that a woman will sleep with him and he doesn't have to pay for it."

"Tiffany's not so bad." Although what I probably mean is that I'm finally secure enough about Peter—and myself—that I don't see her as a threat. Especially now that Tiffany's made Peter head of all U.S. operations. *And* she's moving to Hong Kong to develop BUBB's Asian markets.

The overhead lights blink on and off and a sonorous voice over the loudspeaker summons the former Miss Subways. "It's tiara time, ladies. Please join us in the backstage area to don your sashes and for hair and makeup touch-ups." Naomi sweeps past us in her glittery dress and Sienna asks if she needs any help.

"I'm pretty good with a hot roller," my best friend volunteers.

"No, stay here!" I say, pulling Sienna back to my side. "Paige and Molly should go with their grandmother. It's important for the girls to see how much work it is to be a beauty queen."

"So they give up their dreams of becoming Miss America and decide to go to college and become brain surgeons?"

"Something like that. I pause. And because Bill is going to be here any moment and I want you two to make up."

"Whoa," says Paige, who's finally come back with those chocolate-covered strawberries. "Good one, Mom. Can't we stick around and see what happens?" I raise an eyebrow and reluctantly the girls go backstage. Sienna smoothes her hands across the bodice of her ruched dress.

"I suppose if Bill's finally decided to apologize, I'll let him." Sienna sniffs. "After I make him grovel."

"Bill doesn't exactly know that you'll be here," I admit. "He thinks he's meeting me at the diner for a cup of coffee and to go over the Veronica Agency's dissolution agreement. You're both so pigheaded. I figured the only way I could get you two back together was if I ambushed you."

Peter laughs. "My wife, the matchmaker."

"Your wife the crazy woman! Listen, you two. I'm willing to buy wildly expensive perfume, hobble myself in five-inch heels, and freeze my ass off in a backless dress and bare legs at some fancy over-air-conditioned restaurant. But I draw the line at ambushing Bill—or any man—into falling in love with me."

"He's already in love," Peter says.

"And you are, too. It's just that one of you has to be willing to make the first move." I look up and spot Bill at the entrance to the diner. "Be nice when you see him. Remember the Javan Rhino."

"The what?" Peter asks.

"Tru has some idea that you and Bill are the last two good men left on earth."

"Two of the last fifty," I chirp.

"Is that better than one in a million?" Peter asks.

"Meet me in bed in a couple of hours and we'll do the math," I say with a wink.

Minutes later, I've explained the situation and literally had to drag Bill across the room. He stands stiffly in front of Sienna and pretends to look past her. "I want to state for the record that I had no idea you were going to be here."

"Believe me, I wouldn't have been here either if I knew you were coming," Sienna snaps. Her eyes narrow and Bill mimics her *High Noon* stance.

"Good. Important to get the dialogue going," I say perkily. Then, before I can coax another word out of either one of them, a buzz ricochets through the room like a small jolt of electricity. I look around to see what's causing the commotion.

"I heard that the blond mom from *Gossip Girl* might stop by," a woman in front of me squeals.

The woman next to her stands up on her tiptoes to get a better look. "No, this woman's got dark hair. Lots of it. . . . Oh-my-god, it's Cher!"

"Cher? Are you sure?"

"I'm sure it's Cher," the woman, who's now jumping up and down for a premium view, reports. "She's wearing skin-tight leather jeans and a bitchin' leather jacket that has no right to look so good on her!"

"I thought that after forty we were supposed to stop dressing like our daughters," a woman next to her nitpicks.

"Hell, if you look like that you can dress like a kindergartner!" the first woman cries.

As people repeat the superstar's name a chant goes through the diner that could be straight out of a socialist rally: "Cher, Cher, Cher, *share!*" the audience sings. The orchestra plays "I Got You Babe" and people pull out their cellphones to snap photos. Cher smiles and graciously signs a few autographs. She makes her way through the throng and hesitates, before climbing onto a platform at the front of the restaurant. "I nearly didn't make it up here in these boots!" Cher whoops, tapping the tops of her thigh-high stilettos. "But ladies and gentlemen, tonight isn't about me. I'm here, like all of you, to celebrate a national treasure. The superlative Miss Subways! So please join me in welcoming them now!" Cher punches her fist in the air and the crowd roars. As she walks toward the edge of the stage to make her exit, a man steps out of the shadows and extends his arm to help her down.

"Jeff Whitman!" Peter hoots, pulling me in for a hug. "Honey, I have to hand it to you. First you get Bill to show up. Now Naomi's old boyfriend. With Cher, no less! How in the world did you get them here?"

"I had nothing to do with it."

Sienna looks at me skeptically.

"What, you think I wouldn't take credit for this if I could? I'm as much in the dark about this as all of you."

I'm just starting to push through the crowd toward Jeff Whitman to find out what the heck is going on, when the overhead lights dim—and we're really in the dark. A spotlight beams on to follow a suave-looking man in top hat and tails onto the stage, and there's a clamor of plates as the waitstaff— all aspiring actors and actresses—abandon their trays to join the emcee. The audience is stilled as the orchestra leader raises his baton. Then the band starts playing and the singers break into a chorus of *The Most Beautiful Girl in the World*—adding an "s" after the noun so that none of the women feel excluded. With a follow spot guiding their way, the beauty queens in their tiaras and blue satin sashes swan gracefully around the restaurant. Friends and relatives shout out enthusiastic congratulations.

Molly, who's devouring a last bite of chocolate-covered strawberry, comes over to stand next to me. "Look, they're doing the Miss America wave! You know, where they just turn their wrist back and forth in a single motion so they don't exert too much pressure on their elbows."

"Love the tiaras," says Paige, clapping. "I wonder if Grandma will lend me hers to wear with her *amaazing* harem pants."

As Naomi sashays by I pat her lightly on the shoulder. "I'm proud of you, Mom," I say.

"Me too," says a man coming up behind her. Despite the roar of the music and applause and the general din of excitement, I know that my mother heard the clear baritone greeting. And I know that because she ducks down, huddles toward the glamour girl in front of her, and tries to keep walking.

"Mom, it's Jeff," I say as I gently guide her out of line. "Jeff Whitman, the man who fell in love with you when the two of you were just teenagers. The man you arranged to have help me in Hawaii. The man who's been waiting for five decades to hear your voice again."

"I know who it is, damn it! I'm not senile," my mother snips.

"That's the Naomi I remember!" Jeff laughs. "The dulcet vocal tones, the gorgeous face! I've been watching you from across the room, my darling. You're still as beautiful as ever."

"And you're still as charming! How are you doing?" Peter says, patting Jeff on the back.

"I'm good, I'm good. And everyone, this is Cher," Jeff says, as if the beauteous Oscar, Grammy, and every other kind of award winner—who's got her arm draped arm around Jeff's shoulder—needs introducing.

"Nice to see you again," Naomi says politely to Cher.

"Mom, you *know* Cher?"

"Of course, who doesn't know Cher? I enjoyed that *Moonstruck*, good work. And I liked how you cast a spell on Jack Nicholson in *The Witches of Eastwick*."

Out of an oeuvre that includes dozens of roles as independent, headstrong women, my mother managed to pick the one Cher movie where she uses magic to get what she wants. I guess I come by my superstitions honestly.

"Thanks. That movie was fun, but I don't really believe in all that hocus-pocus. We make our own luck," Cher purrs, casting a lascivious gaze on Jeff and fingering his collar. "And I hear you and Jeff were . . . childhood friends?"

"Yes, something like that," my mother says, evasively.

Molly leans her head toward mine. "I have to hand it to you, Mom," she whispers. "Getting Grandma's old boyfriend *and* a celebrity to show up at the reunion. Wow!"

"But I told you, I had nothing to do with it!"

"Tru's right. I invited Jeff to come," Naomi says, straightening her sash. "But now I've changed my mind. I'm sorry you had to drive from the airport through all that horrible Midtown tunnel traffic. But I'm glad you have another woman friend to keep you company," Naomi says as if the iconic pop star is just "another woman friend." And Naomi didn't have something more in mind than a three-minute hello when she hauled Jeff here from Hawaii.

"Naomi?" Jeff pleads.

"The man flew five thousand miles, Mom. The least you can do is say a civil hello."

"A civil hello," Naomi parrots.

"Mom, turn around."

"No," Naomi barks. She straightens her shoulders and turns around. Then she follows the spotlight through the darkened room as if it's the North Star to make her way back to the line of Miss Subways.

"I'm sorry, Jeff. You know how stubborn my mother is," I apologize.

"Me too, Jeff. Do you think I laid it on a little too thick?" Cher asks. She turns toward us. "Jeff used to be my manager, back in the day. He's the one who convinced me to record my comeback record, *Believe*. I'd do *anything* for him! Although I told him all along I didn't think this was a very good plan. Send a woman a Ferrari and tell her you love her. That's what always works with me."

"Jeff, you have to stop trying to make people jealous!" Peter chuckles.

"But it worked for you and Tru. Look at how happy the two of you are! I'd like to think I can take just a little credit for your reconciliation." And I'd like to think I can take just a little credit for world peace. Which I suppose I can since Peter and I have stopped fighting. Though our détente was despite Jeff, not because of him.

"This isn't about Grandma being jealous," Paige says. She cranes her head to spot her grandmother in the pageant line and as the Miss Finbwaya make another circle around the room past us, Paige pulls Naomi out of the procession. For the second time in practically as many minutes.

"What is it with you people?" Naomi yelps.

"Sorry, Grandma. *Glam-ma*. It's just that this is so romantic." Paige tries tugging Naomi's hand toward Jeff's, but Naomi wiggles free of her clutches.

"Paige, stop it, everybody stop it! This man is a stranger, I don't know what I was thinking telling him he could come here! I haven't seen him in a hundred years. I don't know anything about him!"

A Cheshire cat smile crosses Paige's face, as if she's the older, wiser family member, instead of Naomi. "But Grandma, you know *everything* about him. You said that men tell women all we need to know about them in the first hour. It's just that we women have to listen," Paige says smugly. "Listen to your heart, Grandma. Don't be like Newland Archer."

"Newland Archer?" I say bumping into Peter and nearly spilling my drink.

"Don't be so shocked, Mom, I watch old movies. Newland Archer, from *The Age of Innocence*? He was in love with Michelle Pfeiffer for his whole life. But when they were old and he had a chance to see her, he didn't. He was afraid the reality wouldn't be as good as their memories. Don't be afraid, Grandma."

"You have a smart granddaughter," says Jeff.

Naomi smiles. "You're a chip off the old block, *bubbala*," she says, leaning in to give Paige a hug. Then she beckons for Molly and me to join them. "I have two gorgeous, smart granddaughters. And a very gorgeous smart daughter," she says squeezing my shoulder. Then my mother steps forward and plants a kiss on Jeff Whitman's cheek. "The Finklestein women aren't afraid of anything!" Naomi says boldly. "Now, does anybody mind if I enjoy the next few minutes parading around this damned restaurant?"

Jeff taps his finger on the spot of the kiss that he's been waiting for for fifty years. "But Naomi, does this mean . . ."

"It means that we'll talk, I'm not promising anything," Naomi says with a grin. A grin that despite her words seems to be *filled* with promise.

"Your mother's a spitfire." Jeff laughs. "And she's still a stunning woman."

"That she is," I agree. But she's also a great deal more. So much of not only Naomi's life but mine was shaped by the fact that she was beautiful. It's ironic that at an age when her natural beauty is fading, Naomi's inner beauty is taking root. Maybe the Bikram yoga sweat away all of her demons. Or maybe my mother's heart attack is responsible for her change of heart—if something like that can't shake you into letting go of past disappointments and making the most of the years ahead, what can? And from the looks of it, Naomi's going to make the very most of these upcoming years.

Peter comes over to stand behind me with his hands resting comfortably on my shoulders. He juts his chin in the direction of Sienna and Bill. Bill, who's standing awkwardly with hands stuffed in his pockets, is stealing glances at Sienna. And Sienna, who's fiddling with the neckline of her off-the-shoulder dress, is looking back. It's just that their eyes never meet. "One down, two to go. Think you can sprinkle some fairy dust over them?" my husband asks.

Determinedly, I walk over to face my two best friends.

"Okay, now what about you two?" I scold. "I know that neither one of you has ever been in a long-term relationship before so you're fairly lame about what you need to do to get back together. But let's do this, people!" I say in a take-charge tone. One of the things about running the agency is that it taught me that you can get a lot more accomplished if you tell people exactly what you want them to do. "On the count of one, two, three . . ."

My efforts are met with the sounds of silence. "Again!" I say even more forcefully. "One, two, three . . ."

"I'm sorry," Sienna says, so softly that I practically have to read her lips to be sure of her words.

"I'm sorry," Bill tells his shoes.

"Geez, you guys!" Molly says.

"Bill," I say, planting myself nose-to-nose with my ex-partner. "Sienna loves you, she wants you, she needs you. And I know that you want her, too. She's strong-willed and passionate; I know that can make her hard to live with. But that's probably what makes her hard to live without, too."

Sienna takes a step closer to Bill. "Can't live with me, can't live without me. Quite a dilemma, huh?"

Bill shakes his head. "Not so bad." He reaches for Sienna's hands and gently kisses her fingertips. "At least we never want to kill each other."

"Well, sometimes I want to kill you, when you toss your jacket over the living room chair, or . . ."

"Ssh," Bill says, wrapping his arms around her.

"And I want to kill you when you say 'Ssh,'" Sienna starts to say, and then she laughs. "Bill, I love you."

"I love you too, Sienna. I've never said that to any other woman."

"And I've never told another man that I want us to spend

our whole lives together. I've never been willing to share my heart with anyone. . . ."

"Or your bathroom," I note.

"Hmm, the bathroom . . ." Sienna smiles. "Why don't we start with my letting Bill leave a dish in the sink every now and then, and see where we go from there."

Bill gathers Sienna in his arms and pulls her close for a kiss. "Sienna, you're my, you're my everything!" Bill says, unable to find a word large or important enough to encompass everything that he's feeling.

"And you're my Javan Rhino." Sienna giggles.

"She'll explain later," Peter leans in toward Bill to whisper. "Trust me, it's a good thing."

⁓⁓⁓

PETER ENCIRCLES ME in his arms. "You really are pretty good at this matchmaking stuff."

"I am, aren't I?" I say contentedly, snuggling against Peter. Then excitedly, I turn around. "Don't think this is crazy, listen to the whole idea . . . but what if I started a matchmaking business? A real matchmaking business, pairing people together to help them find *love*," I say, making an important distinction between this new idea and my last venture.

"You know, you really don't have to work anymore; *BUBB* is starting to pull in the big bucks and . . ." Peter pauses and shakes his head. "I think that would be a swell idea, honey. And I think you'd be good at it. I even have the perfect name, *Tru Love!* I guess if we can't open a diner just to call it 'Tru Grits,' this is the next best thing."

"Tru Love," I say, rolling the words around in my mouth. "It's destiny! Finally, I understand why the universe allowed Naomi to name me Truman."

"Are you and Daddy making word plays with your name again?" Molly says, as she and Paige walk over and catch the last part of our conversation. "I thought you were going to come up with a perfume and name it 'Tru Romance'?"

"That was just a pipe dream." I laugh. "But I think I can really do this. I can't give people romance in a bottle. But I can help introduce them to the love of their lives."

"Oh groan, Mom. Just promise you won't have a teenage division, okay?" Paige teases.

"I promise." I laugh. "Besides, your dad and I aren't planning on letting you date again until you're thirty-six."

"How about thirty-two?" Molly smiles.

"We'll talk."

"Tru, that could be perfect!" Sienna yelps. And then realizing what she's said, she backtracks. "I mean it could be very, very good."

Cher cocks an eyebrow.

"My mom has this thing about not tempting the fates. If you say something's perfect, it's sure to go to shit," Paige explains. "I mean, it will turn bad."

"Perfect. Very, very good. Ladies, I told you, we make our own luck! I'm living proof!" Cher hoots. "My career's been up and down more times than Kirstie Alley's weight. But at the end of the day I've sold more than one hundred million records. I'm the oldest artist to have ever had a hit record in the Hot One Hundred. And I've never been happier. If you really want something you can figure out how to make it happen. And oops," Cher says, looking at her watch and blowing us all air kisses. "What I need to make happen right now is not missing my plane." She loops her arm through Jeff's. "Tell Naomi I'll sing at the wedding. Hell, I'll sing at your wedding, too," she says, waving toward Sienna. Jeff helps Cher make her way

past her adoring fans and then he finds Naomi. From a few feet away I see him gazing at my mother with that goofy, cockeyed look of a man who wonders how he got so lucky.

"If Naomi's ever worried about staying young, all she has to do is catch her reflection in Jell's eyes," I say.

Peter smiles and turns my head toward his. "You could say the same. We didn't meet when we were sixteen, but you were my first love, too," he murmurs. "Looks like a happy ending."

"More like a new beginning, for everybody," I say, leaning into Peter's body and interlacing my fingers with his. "I'm glad they're getting a second chance."

"I'm glad we're getting a second chance," Peter says, kissing me, and discreetly moving his lips down my bare shoulder.

A tingle goes through my body, the familiar yet new tingle that pleasures me, comforts me, and still surprises me after all of these years. "Hey, mister, when we get home there's been something I've been meaning to show you," I say, remembering the musical toy I bought all those weeks ago on my shopping expedition with the girls from the Veronica Agency. "Think you can dig up a recording of The William Tell Overture?"

Across the room, in a corner, Bill and Sienna are can't take their eyes—or their hands—off each other. Over by the chocolate fountain, Paige is sweet-talking a waiter into giving her extra strawberries and Molly seems to be flirting with a cute boy I'm guessing is somebody's grandson. There's another raucous round of hooting and clapping as the Miss Subways take a final bow. Then, just as the band is reaching a last crescendo, I hear the unmistakable crash of thunder.

"Rain is lucky, at least at a wedding," I say, looking up at Peter. "The last time I tried to convince myself that bad weather was a good omen was the night of the global warming benefit. And we all know how that turned out."

"Not so badly," Peter says, wrapping his arms around me.

"If you really want something you can make it happen." I laugh, repeating Cher's words, which I've vowed to make my new motto. We make our own choices. We chart our own course. We make our own fate. Then, just as Peter's about to kiss me, I finger the turquoise scarab necklace that Sienna gave me the night of that other, fateful party. Because I'd have to be a complete idiot not to realize that right now, at this very moment, I'm the luckiest girl in the world.

Acknowledgments

❦

I'M GRATEFUL TO MY most intelligent, lovely, and loyal agent, Jane Gelfman, whose encouragement keeps me going. To the smart and savvy Jill Schwartzman, an author couldn't ask for a better editor—throughout every aspect of publication, Jill helped come up with *The Best Laid Plans*. Caitlin Alexander stepped in, seamlessly, to helm this project with grace, great ideas, and enthusiasm. Many thanks to publisher Libby McGuire and associate publisher Kim Hovey for their endless energy and spirited support. And to the gang at Ballantine who helped turn these pages of words into a book: assistant editor Rebecca Shapiro, cover designer Lynn Andreozzi, interior designer Mary Wirth, production editor Crystal Velasquez, and copy editor Michael D. Aisner. Thank you publicists Katie Rudkin and Lisa Barnes; and Quinn Rogers and Kristin Fassler from the marketing department—it's thanks to you that readers have found their way to these pages.

Thanks to Eliot Spitzer for inadvertently creating a scandal, which led to a million details about the call-girl business that I was able to garner from daily news stories. Insight and information also came from rereading the witty and wily Sidney Biddle Barrows's *Mayflower Madam*. Less controversial facts about the world's most dangerous professions and footwear came from *The General Book of Ignorance*. Many thanks to my friend, emergency room doctor Pamela Arsove, for information about heart attacks (and her great cakes). To Rosanne Kang for suggestions about the look of the book and for being Rosanne. To that haven, the Writers Room, where most of this book was written. My most beloved niece Lori Edelman's marriage to the wonderful Dejay Clayton inspired the Hawaiian wedding scene. Dr. Fredric Brandt is a real dermatologist and I count myself lucky to be his patient—as "Dr. B." in the book he finds himself in a fictional situation, but everything else I say about him is true.

My mother, Marian Edelman (who is nothing like Naomi, the mother of my protagonist), is nevertheless an inspiration. She, my honorary mom Julia Levy, and my "Aunt Marcia" Kirshner, are my biggest cheerleaders.

Friends, too numerous to name, know who they are. I am grateful for their love, support, and patience—thank you, all, for putting up with me.

About the Author

❧

LYNN SCHNURNBERGER is the bestselling author or co-author of five books, including *The Botox Diaries* and *Mine Are Spectacular!* She has written for *New York* magazine, *The New York Times, People, Parade,* and *Reader's Digest,* among others, and has made regular television appearances, most notably on *The Oprah Winfrey Show, Good Morning America,* and *Entertainment Tonight.* She is also the founder of Foster Pride, a nonprofit that provides art classes and mentoring to New York City foster children.

About the Type

This book was set in Horley Old Style, a typeface issued by the English type foundry Monotype in 1925. It is an old-style face, with such distinctive features as lightly cupped serifs and an oblique horizontal bar on the lowercase "e."